Colin Douglas was born in Glasgow in 1945, graduated in medicine from Edinburgh in 1970 and has since worked in a variety of posts, at home and abroad, on land and sea. His first novel *The Houseman's Tale* won the John Rowan Wilson Award for its contribution to 'wit, lucidity and style in the treatment of medical subjects'. He has written seven novels to date and has attracted an enthusiastic following. *The Houseman's Tale* has become a highly acclaimed and popular BBC-TV drama serial.

By the same author

The Houseman's Tale
The Greatest Breakthrough Since Lunchtime
Bleeders Come First
Wellies from the Queen
A Cure For Living
For Services to Medicine
Ethics Made Easy

COLIN DOUGLAS

Hazards of the Profession

GRAFTON BOOKS
A Division of the Collins Publishing Group

LONDON GLASGOW
TORONTO SYDNEY AUCKLAND

Grafton Books
A Division of the Collins Publishing Group
8 Grafton Street, London W1X 3LA

Published by Grafton Books 1988

First published in Great Britain by
Mainstream Publishing 1987

Copyright © Colin Douglas 1987

ISBN 0-586-20183-1

Printed and bound in Great Britain by
Collins, Glasgow

Set in Garamond

1

'Stop!'

Campbell stopped, not where he would have chosen to. His shoes, already sodden, let in another rush of cold water. He moved an inch or so out of the puddle to a little elevation in the uneven grass.

'I said stop! Don't bloody shuffle about. I'll tell you when to move!'

The shouting and the unusual sight of a lone figure in a white coat carefully pacing out one of the few remaining empty spaces in the hospital grounds in the tail end of a thunderstorm had drawn a number of spectators. A few stood in the glass-walled corridor to the left and right of Professor Sinclair at the open door, but not too near him. More were ranged at windows of wards and offices in the two three-storeyed pavilions flanking the space, and their numbers had grown over the ten minutes or so the whole silly business had been going on.

Campbell ignored them, and stood to an approximate attention facing the Pentland Hills, now beginning to emerge again as steel-grey curtains of rain thinned from the east. His white coat was soaked through, as were his shirt, his trousers, his socks and even his tie. His wallet was beginning to feel soggy. His watch was waterproof. He thought for a moment about his bleep and decided he didn't care whether it was or not. It might eventually be interesting to explain to some poor official how it had come to meet its watery fate.

'Right, lad.' The shouting voice had a shoulders-back, parade-ground ring quite appropriate to the odd little scene being enacted, but there was no accompanying hint of performance or irony: an observation that Campbell found somehow disquieting. 'Turn left,' roared Professor Sinclair over the steady hiss of the rain. 'Don't saunter and pay attention this time . . . Now!'

Campbell turned. There seemed to be more people watching than had been only moments before. A staff nurse at the window of a first-floor ward smiled and waved to him. He looked up at her and smiled back. The rain on his face seemed colder and heavier, and a chilly new stream coursed down between his shoulder blades.

'Fifteen, sixteen . . . Keep counting, Campbell! I don't want to be here all bloody morning . . . Twenty-one, twenty-two, twenty-three . . . And you don't either.'

Once more the east-west extent of the space came to fifty-three paces. Campbell stood in a place of relative shelter against the grey stone wall of the Intensive Care Unit while Professor Sinclair in the glass-walled corridor punched his pocket calculator, standing a little back from the open door so as not to get it wet. He straightened up again.

'Other way . . . Last time . . . Across a bit and keep to your line . . . Further . . . Further . . . No! Too far! Back . . . Back . . . Stop! OK . . . Last time and same pace as before . . . Now!'

Campbell squelched back across the grass, suddenly recalling when he had last felt like this. Once, with a hundred and twenty other officer cadets, he had marched three miles and stood for half an hour in a downpour in a rural cemetery in Western Norway to honour the graves of half a dozen casualties from a retreat marking the end of one of the most futile expeditions in the history of the British army. Afterwards, their tunics had taken two days to dry out, their kilts three or four, and by that time the whole thing had acquired such a transcendental pointlessness as to have become quite worth while.

The recollection was a cheering one. Campbell plodded

on. He had lost count but did not care. He decided it did not matter to him if the exercise went on for another half hour or longer. The thing had taken on a rich and free life of its own. He was as wet as it was possible to be and each repetition or new development told him a little more about his new head of department. He smiled as he reached the edge of the grass and stopped.

Professor Sinclair peered at him from the shelter of the doorway. 'Thirty-six?'

Campbell nodded.

'Good lad.'

There was a pause as Campbell awaited further instructions.

'Well, don't just stand out there in the rain, laddie.'

Campbell nodded again, crossed the gravel path and went up a few concrete steps to the porch, paused and turned to look out again. Slowly and silently behind her window, the staff nurse on the first floor was clapping. The rain eased to a few scattered drops. Blue sky had opened over the hills and the sun was beginning to break through gaps in the clouds to the south.

Professor Sinclair was still busy with his pocket calculator. Campbell stood politely dripping until he had finished. He grunted and smiled and snapped it shut. 'Good lad. Just over thirty thousand square feet on two floors if we get them, and I don't see why we shouldn't. Where do you live?'

'Marchmont.'

'Go home and get cleaned up. Back here by twelve fifteen, all right? We're going out to lunch.'

Campbell nodded. With new professors, all things were possible.

'Le Petit Perdreau,' he snapped, as though still ordering him about on the grass. 'Should be nice out there now it's clearing up. Twelve fifteen at my office.'

* * *

'You're looking very smart, David.'

'So are you.'

Andrea smiled. Normally she dressed well. Now she was dressed very well indeed, in a smart olive-drab silk two-piece lady-doctor number he hadn't seen before, a discreetly loud blouse and matching and impossibly glossy new brown leather shoes and handbag. Perhaps she had had more notice than Campbell of the lunch outing, or perhaps she had simply decided to overdo her usual women-in-medicine-don't-have-to-be-frumps thing in honour of the new professor.

It was twenty-five past twelve. Campbell had met the twelve fifteen deadline with some difficulty, driving round to Marchmont, first showering and then changing, for temporary lack of alternatives, into his interview suit, and driving back sitting on a couple of plastic carrier bags to avoid getting wet again, all in about twenty minutes.

Andrea glanced at her watch. 'Are you going to lunch with him?' Campbell nodded.

'He didn't say anything about inviting you.'

'I think he only decided to about half an hour ago.'

'He seems awfully nice.' Andrea looked up and down the corridor prior to getting any more fulsome. 'Terribly considerate. When I told him I was on call, doing my bit for the waiting med. reg. rota, he just rang Barry Swift and told him to come up and collect my bleep.'

'That was kind of him.'

'Yes. And Barry was quite happy. Keen to show willing, I suppose. And you know how he loves teaching.'

'Yes.' The current batch of senior medical students consisted of two nondescript but diligent youths, a tall blonde girl with blue eyes and a little brunette with glasses who laughed at all jokes, however feeble. An afternoon spent rushing around pestering the sick and the dying of the waiting day with a captive audience like that would suit Barry very well indeed.

8

'And it's only till five o'clock.'

'I know.'

'Of course. Then it's you.'

Campbell nodded. Andrea flashed a smile she might herself have thought dazzling. 'Yes. Friday nights are such a nuisance, but someone's got to do them. He seems full of ideas.'

'Barry?'

'No, Hamish.'

'Who?'

'The prof.'

'I thought he was James.'

'Yes, but he told me everybody calls him Hamish. Highland, I suppose.'

Campbell recalled the accent of the voice shouting through the rain. 'I think he's from the north-east.'

'Yes, a real highlander.'

The nuances of Scottish provincialism did not seem to interest Andrea, who, though an Edinburgh graduate, was from somewhere like Harrogate. Sinclair's accent, harsh and distinct, placed his origins as somewhere north of Aberdeen but still lowland, well clear of whining Gaeldom to the west. The Hamish thing was puzzling, but perhaps simply the legacy of a school classroom, at Cromarty Royal Academy or wherever, with too many Jameses already.

'He just hauled me off from coffee to his office and discussed ideas for twenty minutes then told me to meet him here to go to lunch. Pretty impressive for a first day in the job.'

'Ideas?'

'About ward organization. And teaching. And research. And reshaping neurology generally.'

'Really? Do they know?'

'Who?'

'The other neurologists. Who are going to be reshaped.'

9

'Don't be silly, David. He was just . . . discussing ideas. Very generally. I suppose that's why he asked . . . us both . . . to lunch today. But he's terribly persuasive, and bursting with good ideas, so the others'll probably just go along with him. And if they're honest, they'll probably admit they need a good shake-up. The whole thing was getting terribly sleepy under Aithie.'

'I rather liked him. His old-fashioned clinical lectures, and his Saturday cravats.'

'Neurology's changing, David. All that bedside charm because you couldn't do anything anyway is old hat.'

'I rather liked . . .'

'And Bobby Brown would have been a disaster for the department. Even you have to admit that.'

Campbell, who had never himself identified his medical fortune particularly closely with that of the late Dr Brown, had been made aware quite frequently over the past few months that other people thought differently. He had, while badly stuck for money to pay the rent, taken a job on the end of one of Bobby's less respectable grants and worked with him for a few months. For her own reasons perhaps, Andrea seemed to be interpreting this as whole-hearted commitment to a poor drunk academic fraud, now deceased.

'I suppose you know Hamish couldn't stand him.'

'No, but I'm not surprised.'

Andrea lowered her voice. 'Bobby didn't have a chance. You know, of the chair. I'd sort of suspected that myself, but Hamish confirmed it all this morning. So you probably shouldn't mention him, you know, in conversation. But don't worry. The most important thing about Hamish is that he's . . . terribly forward-looking . . .'

Andrea smiled again. She was smiling so much that Campbell was beginning to wonder if she had yet again fixed the duty rota to his disadvantage but was feeling guilty about it. The unit waited on Fridays, and waiting day call was shared between Barry, the senior registrar who officially made up the rota, Andrea, a registrar in neurology and Campbell, at present a locum lecturer with honorary registrar status because the job had come up and the rent had continued to need to be paid.

Campbell, who had had the overnight duty last Friday, had it again this Friday, and already had grave suspicions about what the next four-week rota was going to look like. Barry's enthusiasm, unstoppable during the standard thirty-hour medical week, was known to wane around five o'clock, and Andrea had been grumbling pointedly for a day or two about the amount of entertaining she had to do.

'It's been terribly quiet all morning,' she announced suddenly. 'It'll probably stay like that all night.'

'I suppose it might.'

'We've got twelve for dinner.' She smiled again and laughed. 'I suppose I'd really rather be up here sorting out a really worthwhile night's medicine. Avocado mousse, poached salmon Alastair caught himself and a raspberry fool thing that takes ages. Mostly lawyers, naturally. And you've no idea how much they drink, David. And it's got to be terribly *good* whisky.'

In Andrea's rather limited conversation, the trials of being an advocate's wife ran a valiant second to the trials of being a woman in medicine. The menus changed a little, but the whisky always had to be terribly good. Campbell closed his mind to pity and thought of the waiting night.

They were standing at the top of the stair in the Neurobiology Unit, now no longer known as such. With the eclipse and demise of Dr Brown following the withdrawal of the drug on which he had pinned his hopes, the suite of labs and offices donated by the drug company to facilitate and at the same time reward his researches had reverted to more general use.

There were already about the place sad hints of the fall

11

of empire. A smart notice board in glossy maroon had been replaced by a smaller one in hardboard tacked to a doorpost and stencilled simply 'Clinical Neurology' in letters that reminded Campbell of a prison movie. The chairs from the foyer downstairs had disappeared; an indoor plant, six feet high and irretrievably dried out, had not. The brave new world was signified by a half sheet of A4 reading 'Professor J. K. Sinclair' stuck to the door of the main upstairs office with a drawing pin.

As Campbell waited the purpose of his walk in the rain became clearer. If Sinclair had loathed Brown and all his works, then a new building was required and that was that. No matter that the available offices were as spacious and well appointed as any in the Institute. No matter that the proposed site for the new building was the last south-facing green space in the hospital grounds. No matter that money for such an unnecessary development might be hard to find. In the circumstances the incidental drenching of a locum lecturer was of infinitesimal consequence or none. All that mattered was that a forceful new man wanted to bury the past and start afresh.

'Did Hamish mention where we're going, David?'

'La Petit something. I don't know it.'

'Oh, super! Le Petit Perdreau.'

'Is it good?'

'Really marvellous.'

'Where is it?'

'Miles out. But I expect he's got a super car too. This should be fun, David.'

'Bloody terrible, the way this place has gone down. Look at that.' Professor Sinclair jabbed an accusing finger at a large plastic bag of uncollected rubbish. 'And that. A bloody disgrace.' A patch of doubtful plastering at about eye level on the wall bulged and cracked. 'And that.' A broken chair had found temporary use half obstructing the corridor and propping up a notice saying 'Cleaning in Progress', though there were no cleaners in sight. 'Typical. All wish and promise, and a floor you could plant tatties in.'

The floor of the corridor was not, by the general standards of the Institute, particularly dirty, but Campbell did not feel conversation would be helped along by his saying so. Instead he asked, 'Have you worked here before, Professor Sinclair?'

'Call me Hamish, lad. And the answer's yes. Some time ago, when they still cleaned it and painted it and kept it looking as if it might be safe to be ill in. You know its trouble? You know what's wrong with the place?'

A junior view was not seriously being invited. 'Complacency,' said Sinclair, scarcely pausing. 'The trouble with this place is it thinks it's God's gift to medicine, but anywhere else in the country it would hardly make it as a third-rate district general. They put up with a building that any half decent health authority would have knocked down twenty years ago, but they put up with it because it's the famous bloody Royal Charitable Institute for the Care of the Indigent Sick, Edinburgh, so it's a great hospital and that's it. No argument. And there's cracked paint, filthy floors and bloody rubbish everywhere. I notice it because I've been away. They don't because they haven't. As simple as that. Complacency.'

They passed the broken chair with a little pageant of deference which ended up with Sinclair making way for Andrea and Campbell standing back for both of them.

'They're talking again about a new Institute,' said Andrea brightly once they were walking side by side.

Sinclair let out a short cackle. 'They do that every ten years or so, for about nine years, then give it a rest and start again.'

When Campbell had been a senior medical student old Creech, the chief of his medical firm, had once returned gloomily from a three-hour meeting about plans to replace the Institute and remarked that he should have sent Campbell along instead, since he was the only one around likely to be still practising medicine by the time the thing was built. No progress had been made. Hurrying along beside the new professor, Campbell, for the first time in his career, began to wonder vaguely about his retirement date.

'I got the fright of my life when I went to London ten years ago. I'd been doing neurosurgery here. You know where it is, it's still there, a string of broom-cupboards tucked up behind the clock tower. Went to this place in London with a proper ward, a theatre built in the twentieth century, amazing basic changing facilities and no pigeon shit blowing in the windows. Couldn't believe it. For the first six months I didn't like operating there, in case I messed it up. And this lot here are still up there doing brain surgery through clouds of pigeon shit.'

Sinclair walked and talked quickly. He was a thickset man of slightly less than middle height, so broad across the chest and shoulders as to raise doubts about the wisdom of his standard Marks and Spencer suit. His colouring was swarthy, and in profile his features vaguely Levantine. Campbell recalled something he had once heard about the travelling people of the north-east, dark gipsies given to names like Amos and Obadiah and known locally as the Children of Israel, and wondered if his new head of department might owe something to that heritage. It was not, however, the sort of thing that came up in casual conversation and in any case most of them were called MacPhee.

But by far the most striking thing about the man was his impetus. Campbell had to walk uncomfortably fast, and Andrea, even in sensible flat shoes, could scarcely keep up. Though they were still fifty yards from the Institute's nearest car-park, keys were being rattled impatiently.

'We're all right for time,' said Sinclair. 'We'll easily make

14

'it up. Table's booked for one and it's only fifteen miles away. Get in, lad. Andrea, go round the other side.'

The car was a red Porsche, with sitting room for two dwarfs but no one of normal height in the back. Andrea settled comfortably in the front and smiled at Sinclair as he got in. 'Nice car.'

'Gets me around,' he grunted. 'Not the self-indulgence it looks. My time's precious and I don't waste it stuck in traffic. Bloody nippy, and they hold their value too.'

In thought-provoking discomfort Campbell considered that rationalization. 'Terrific,' said Andrea over the roar as the car started. They set off in a hail of wet gravel, left the car park with a gut-wrenching right turn and snarled in unnecessarily low gear up the hill to the gates of the Institute and the open road.

The last five miles out to Le Petit Perdreau were over a twisting, undulating coastal road that gave much scope for display of the Porsche's power and grip. Sinclair drove the way he walked and talked, at great speed and with minimal consideration for others. Any vehicle ahead was a challenge to overtake, and his standard overtaking manoeuvre involved lights, horn, a savage burst of acceleration and a sickening swerve to the left on completion. Campbell, cramped and askew in the back, first went off the idea of a heavy lunch and then realized he could scarcely bear to contemplate the return journey. When they finally jerked to a halt in the restaurant car park and he stumbled out, half an hour in the fresh air and a nice quiet bus ride home would have met all his needs.

'What'd do you think of that then?' Sinclair asked as they got out. Andrea smiled like a little girl being helped from a roller-coaster ride she felt she ought to have enjoyed and Campbell breathed deeply through his nose. Sinclair noticed neither. 'There you are. Twelve fifty-nine. And the others are bound to be late. Let's have a drink.'

The restaurant was small, expensive-looking and not

very busy. Sinclair marched in, barked his name at a lady hovering at the door and steered his juniors towards a table for six. The lady followed them, paused, then asked, 'Will that table be all right, Professor Sinclair?'

'Three to come. We'll have a drink while we're waiting. Andrea?'

Andrea asked for a dry sherry. Campbell, who was beginning to feel better, did likewise. Sinclair ordered a gin and tonic.

'Better tell you a bit about these folk,' he said before the waitress had turned to go. 'Pittendreichs. Nice people, and keen to do something about Parkinson's disease, as indeed we all are. The old boy, Jock Pittendreich, had a miserable time with it. Got to the untreatable stage before the treatment was any good, and died about six months ago. Businessman. Reached the point where he could still think but couldn't sign things. Depressed too, and reading between the lines probably constipated up to his ears. Might even have killed himself but we won't talk about that. Faithful retainer slipping him the pills, that kind of thing. Had a brother in medicine. Regius professor when I was a lad. Demented now, in nappies again, but that's beside the point. The family – a son and a daughter – are keen to do something about Parkinson's, and that's why we're here.'

'They live out here, don't they?' said Andrea, who was probably quite capable of collecting millionaires' addresses on the off-chance it might further her own or her husband's career.

'That's why we're here, lass. Bloody great ruin just over the hill. Made their money in shipping, whisky and battery hens ... but I'm not so much concerned with where it came from as where it's going. Thanks, sherries there. Yes.' He paused and glared at the waitress. 'More ice in that ... And a lot still needs to be done about Parkinson's, as well you know. So it's important they meet the kind of people whose work they'll be supporting.'

16

Campbell sipped his sherry and re-examined his simplistic notion that he was being rewarded for walking about, foolishly but uncomplainingly, in the rain.

'Don't worry, lad. They don't know enough about it to want to know the details. This is a social occasion, but they said they would probably bring their accountant. Ah. That's better. Thanks, lass. Cheers.'

Professor Sinclair sipped his drink, sat back in his chair and looked at his watch. 'We'll give the upper classes another ten minutes, then just order. How was this morning, Andrea?'

'Quite interesting. I was sorry to leave. Just getting stuck into a chap with a probable dissecting aneurysm, but I'm sure Barry's coping. Before that a probable pancreatitis and an old thing with funny turns who had to be admitted. The . . .'

'I don't want them, you know. I don't want a lot of social admissions cluttering up neurology teaching beds.' Andrea opened her mouth to speak but was not allowed to. 'Just remember what I said about teaching commitments.'

Andrea smiled and laughed. 'It's all right, Hamish. We were in luck. She'd broken her pelvis, so the orthopaedic registrar took her. Grumbled a bit, but took her.'

'He bloody better had. I just don't want . . . Oh. Here they are.' Sinclair rose to his feet smiling. The approaching Pittendreich party did lateness in style; gracious, unhurried, unapologetic. There was an obvious brother and sister, tall and aquiline with the general air of third-eleven royalty, and the presumed accountant, a cheerful, untidy man in a green suit and a Royal Scots tie.

Sinclair, on first-name terms already with the family members, did a swift, suave job on the introductions. Campbell, braced for lunch with a man who might not know how to use a knife and fork properly, was mildly astonished. The matter of who was going to sit where was also managed with unforeseen poise and, it had to be admitted, a certain shrewdness. Alec Pittendreich was put beside Andrea, who turned on him with a charm beyond the call of mere duty. Sinclair himself sat between Andrea and Rosemary Pittendreich, with the two dull men, Campbell and the accountant, in the remaining places, away from the main action.

The waitress returned. The Pittendreichs ordered Perrier water, the accountant a lager and Sinclair, whose glass was now empty, another gin and tonic. The menu appeared, chastely expensive and offering only minimal choice: avocado mousse, poached salmon and a small selection of sweets including something with raspberries. The Pittendreichs were scarcely interested. Andrea looked thoughtful and might have been avoiding Campbell's glance. Sinclair fidgeted until the waitress came back and was despatched for the wine list.

While Sinclair and Andrea worked on their respective Pittendreichs, Campbell made polite conversation with the accountant, asking him if he was based locally.

'God, no. Charlotte Square. Gordon, Grosset and Shiel. CAs. But it's nice to get out here once in a while, and on a day like this I quite enjoy the drive.' Campbell nodded without enthusiasm and the accountant went on to tell him about an idiot in a Porsche who had nearly killed him just this side of Aberlady. A bottle of superior white wine arrived. The mousse came and went.

Promptly with the salmon Rosemary Pittendreich turned to Campbell and asked him how long he had been in neurology. She was perhaps in her late thirties, and had the distracted, faintly wounded manner of one doing her social duty despite some inner sorrow. Soon she was talking about her late father. 'Perhaps Professor Sinclair mentioned that he died recently, of Parkinson's disease.'

'Yes, I'm sorry.'

'Obviously you know all about it, because you're a

doctor specializing in it. But we had no idea . . . what it was going to be like. Daddy had, a bit. We found out that he'd been reading all about it, and got ready, so to speak. We weren't.'

'Got ready?'

'That was what he was like. From the army and from business. He even diagnosed it himself. There'd been a scene, about closing something, actually, and his left hand started to shake. The first time he ignored it, but when it happened again and then again, usually when things were getting difficult, he sent out for some books, diagnosed himself, found out what happened to you and made up his mind to ignore it.'

She laughed damply and Campbell smiled. 'Typical of him. He called it "my foul fiend", and used to mutter "Defy the foul fiend!" when he was really angry with it.'

'How long did he . . .?'

'Ten years. Well, ten and a half. And he was terrific . . .' Her salmon was untouched and likely to remain so. 'He'd been brave in the war, and used to joke about that too, said he had to be because all his friends were, but he was really terrific with his . . . foul fiend . . . Patient and brave and sensible and even funny. That was really odd. He'd be stuck in bed and say the funniest things, and because of his disease he couldn't smile, so he was like the most amazing deadpan comic. If it was snowing he'd say, "Hmm, no tennis today." That sort of thing. He was really marvellous.'

'Who looked after him?'

'Mason. His servant.'

'Oh. I meant doctors.'

'Oh. Yes. Well, he eventually decided to see someone, and he's a terrific believer in the National Health Service, so Dr Webster came from the Southern and . . . agreed with him. Yes, it's Parkinson's . . . The treatment's not very good but we'll try one or two things. And he was

19

kind and sensible about how to live with it . . . Practical things like moving his bed downstairs, and resting a lot, and clothes that were easy. And daddy got more and more expert from reading things, and they'd have discussions about it, and agree nothing much helped. The dopa stuff came a bit late for us. Helped just a bit and made him feel sick.'

Across the table Andrea was doing her I'm-pretty-but-I'm-also-quite-bright routine for Sinclair and Alec Pittendreich, but perhaps laughing too loud to really carry it off. The accountant, evidently happy to eat quietly and well in the firm's time, was getting on with his lunch.

'I'm talking too much,' said Miss Pittendreich suddenly. 'What's happening in Parkinson's disease now?'

'Well, the dopa treatment seems to help a lot of people, especially the early cases. And there are new things coming in, combinations of dopa and something else to make it less . . . nauseating.'

'Good.' She picked up her fork. 'Is surgery going to get better?'

'For Parkinson's?'

'Yes. The thing they put in the bit of your brain that's wrong . . . Dr Webster didn't believe in it, but we wondered if it might get better.'

The procedure she was referring to, pallidotomy, described by Hadden as 'like sticking a red-hot poker into the back of your television set to make it work better' was on its way out, without detriment to anyone except the one or two local neurosurgeons who did private practice. The late Mr Pittendreich had missed nothing by avoiding it. Campbell explained that in suitable terms.

'So in future it'll be pills, but better pills.'

'I hope so.'

'It's a horrible disease.'

'Yes.'

Miss Pittendreich put down her fork. 'Daddy's very determined to do something about it.'

Campbell ate his salmon and wondered about her use of the present tense. Was she, like quite a few bereaved people, just blurring the present and the recent past, or did she harbour some of the odder convictions of spiritualism, including perhaps direct communication from her dead father on the subject of how to spend his money? It was all a little strange. If she had talked thus to Sinclair, might the square of damp grass back at the Institute soon disappear under a new laboratory of three, four or even ten storeys?

Perhaps it was not quite as simple as that. There was also the brother to be considered. He too was tall and thin, but quite definitely of this world rather than another: a well-cut, clear-eyed man of the kind seen around Charlotte Square without a briefcase; perhaps a young but high-flying banker who might easily bracket doctors with theatre workshops and string quartets and all the other miscellaneous scroungers after company charity. The accountant too could be presumed to lean towards such a view, but at least they had both turned up to lunch with Sinclair.

Or were they there simply to keep the dewy-eyed lady on Campbell's left under control? Campbell wondered about that and decided he was well out of his depth: he was there as an extra, a mute spear-carrier for his new boss, to eat lunch, be nice to people and leave talk of money to those who understood such things. And that was another puzzling aspect of the occasion: no one had yet mentioned money.

The waitress cleared the table and they ordered pudding, everyone except Andrea having the thing with raspberries. Conversation became briefly general, then Sinclair reasserted himself with a tale about the Pittendreichs' kinsman,

21

who had been the senior chief on the surgical side of the Institute when Sinclair was an undergraduate.

'Wonderful old chap, with a great touch for bringing silly discussion back to earth. I remember one Saturday morning meeting. Must have been a Murrayfield international day because it was a joint affair, with a lot of Glasgow surgeons, and a couple of them had been going on and on about their results for this and that. Fifteen per cent five year survivals, a great improvement on the results of the London lot who had reported thirteen per cent, but not as good as the Harvard results at sixteen per cent, that sort of thing. Sir Hector was in the chair, and he put up with a fair amount of this nonsense because they were visitors to Edinburgh, then sawed them off at the knees in his quiet, polite way with his closing remarks: "Thank you, gentlemen. You know, I sometimes think that surgery is a bit like playing the violin. The results are always a wee bit better if you're good at it. Good morning. Enjoy the match."'

The accountant laughed out loud but not as loud as Andrea. Alec Pittendreich smiled distantly. His sister smiled and blinked back more tears. Sinclair signalled for the bill and they were ushered into a chintzy little lounge for coffee. On the way Sinclair stayed close to Miss Pittendreich, his hand on her elbow as they moved through a doorway. From the back of the procession Campbell could see their heads together, Sinclair's nodding perhaps in sympathy. When they sat down again for coffee she was smiling.

The first person to mention money was Alec Pittendreich. Between sips of coffee, in the manner of someone issuing a deliberately vague dinner invitation, he said, 'Hamish, we've been wondering if a little funding might come in handy. Say half a million. A quarter for a little building and fifty thousand a year for five years to help things along. If you think it would do any good.'

Sinclair took a slow sip of coffee. 'We could probably do quite a lot with that, Alec. There's certainly a lot to be done.'

'Good.' He nodded towards the accountant. 'Balfour and I can sort out the details fairly quickly.' Sinclair remained impassive. Andrea was grinning inanely like someone about to start singing '*Happy Birthday*'. Miss Pittendreich reached into her handbag for a mauve paper handkerchief. The accountant whipped out a little note-book, scribbled something in it in pencil then popped it back into his inside pocket.

Alec Pittendreich had already moved forward in his chair, as though to indicate that he was prepared to waste money but not time on a profession which had done so little for the late chairman of the board. Sinclair noticed and was first to his feet. The waitress hurried across to return his American Express card and the party broke up. On the way out Miss Pittendreich, looking even more sorrowful than before, asked Campbell to thank Professor Sinclair on her behalf for lunch. Campbell, uncomfortably aware that no one had thanked anyone for the mighty sum just promised, nodded and said he would.

Outside once more, Sinclair walked so quickly back to his car that Campbell began to wonder if there was an architect somewhere to be browbeaten into producing draft plans for the Pittendreich Memorial Institute for Research into Parkinson's Disease, preferably by five o'clock. When they reached the Porsche Sinclair threw open the driver's door, folded the seat forward and said, 'Andrea'.

Andrea hesitated. Campbell moved to resume his Quasimodo existence in the back but was stopped by Sinclair. 'Go round the other side, lad. You were in there on the way out. I'm all for women in medicine, if they're prepared to be treated equally.' Andrea climbed in, folded up and settled down to sulk all the way back to Edinburgh. Sinclair fastened his safety belt, smiling to himself, and revved up for the journey home.

For several miles no one spoke, then Sinclair said something Campbell did not catch. He said it again. It sounded like 'Turandot'.

'Sir?'

'Don't bloody sir me. Turandot. In the door pocket. Just stuff it in there, lad.'

There were a dozen or so cassettes rattling around, none of them in labelled boxes. Campbell rummaged until he found something called *Puccini Highlights (3) – Turandot* and did as instructed. A tenor gave forth. Sinclair reached across to turn up the volume.

'Bloody good, eh?'

The Puccini seemed to be making Professor Sinclair drive faster. Campbell nodded hesitantly.

'He'll never miss it.' Over the music and the engine noise Sinclair was almost shouting again. 'And it'll make her feel a whole lot better about her poor old father. So everyone's better off. And there would have been absolutely no point in giving so much as a couple of test tubes to that bunch at the Southern, even if old Webster did go in and hold his shaky hand now and again. They've already got a lot more money than they have ideas . . . and a whole lot of lab space being used for nothing except making the technicians' coffee.'

'. . . nella tua fredda stanza . . . guardi le stelle . . .'

'They haven't done any decent animal work over there for about fifteen years. If old Webster so much as glimpsed a white mouse these days he'd probably scream and jump up on a chair.'

'. . . il nome mio . . . nessun sapra . . .'

'You know, that might be something we could use Brown's little hut for . . . Baboons. It's kind of central and they stink a bit but it's still a possibility. I'll have to look into the regulations when we get back.'

'Hamish . . .'

'. . .il mio bacio sciogliera il silennzio che ti fa mia!'

'Fifty thousand a year doesn't go far on baboons, but it's certainly worth looking into. And there's nothing like just setting up something and looking for money afterwards . . . And there might be things you could do about the smell.'

'Hamish . . . Would you mind . . .?'

Sinclair looked angrily round at his back-seat passenger. The Porsche swerved most of the way over the white line and back, then skidded to a halt just as Andrea began to retch. Campbell released his seatbelt, opened the door and leapt out. Andrea threw his seat forward and just cleared the sill with a powerful stream of assorted fine wines and food.

'Bloody hell,' said Sinclair, red with sudden rage. 'Get out, woman, and mind my bloody carpets while you're at it.' Campbell helped Andrea to her feet on the grass verge. 'Thanks, David,' she said faintly, wiping her mouth. 'Oh, no . . .' She lurched towards the nearest fence post and leaned on it, vomiting smaller amounts, pausing, then retching emptily between further attempts to wipe her mouth.

Sinclair had got out too and came round to join Campbell. They stood together looking out over the fields to the sea, as though they had stopped for the view, while Andrea continued unsteadily by her fence-post.

'Pregnant, is she?' Sinclair muttered. It seemed to Campbell that there was enough to explain Andrea's present state without postulating pregnancy, but Sinclair continued to glare at her as though it was possible to confirm his diagnosis from the appearance of the back of her neck. 'I'm all in favour of women in medicine, so long as they don't go around getting pregnant in the middle of registrar jobs.' He glanced at his watch. For a moment Campbell wondered if he were about to be told to stay with Andrea until

25

such time as they could get a lift or a taxi back to Edinburgh. 'We'll give her a couple of minutes. And it might be better if you got in the back now. Nothing personal, lad. It's for the seats and the carpets.'

'Great, Dave . . . Andrea feeling better now? No, it was no trouble. No trouble at all. In fact it's been what you might call a really worthwhile afternoon's medicine. Hasn't it, folks? We've had to think about the causes of polydipsia and polyuria in young men, and sort out our thoughts on upper gastro-intestinal bleeding, and we've seen a couple of coronaries, haven't we, Celia, and had to work out which kind give you rhythm problems and which don't. We've had a chap die on us but that's just part of what medicine's all about . . . Win some, lose some, take the rough with the smooth, don't take it personally and try to think of the relatives. Bereavement's very important to them and it's vital we get them off to a good start. So altogether a varied, useful and extremely general afternoon at the coalface, n'est-ce pas? And you'll be pleased to hear that our young friends are most keen to stay on, Dave, even though it's Friday. Very important for them to learn at an early stage that medicine's anything but a nine-to-five business, as well we know.'

Campbell nodded. Barry was sitting in the doctor's room in the male ward with all four senior students. The blackboard was covered with manic scrawls and diagrams concerning electrocardiographic signs of heart disease and the desk and much of the floor was strewn with looping yards of ECG tracings.

'And our young colleagues are highly informed on cardiological matters. Jenny here has membership level knowledge of the Wenckebach phenomenon and Bill's not far behind on Wolff-Parkinson-White.'

Campbell, who quite often got the two confused unless he sat down to think about it, had located Barry at quarter

26

to five anticipating a quick handover, not a performance like this. Even Bill, the keenest student, looked bored and embarrassed. To discourage further flights Campbell remained by the door and asked where the houseman was.

'Upstairs, giving Dennis a hand. That's where the action's been so far. Six female admissions, only one male. Would you like to go round, Dave?'

'Yes, please.'

Barry got up. 'A quick whistle round the patch? Check out the sickies and hear from our young colleagues about the waiting day cases they personally have clerked in? One of the other things we've been stressing this afternoon is presentation. How knowing the case is fine, but being able to present it really well is more than half the battle. And you'll see for yourself how they're coming on, Dave. Let's start down here. Who saw Ronald?'

Jenny, the Wenckebach expert, had seen Ronald some-body, a man of twenty-five who had been sent up to Casualty by his mother because he said he was always thirsty and seemed to be drinking more than usual. Perhaps she had been worried about diabetes, but no one else was. That most obvious of diagnoses had been ruled out by a few tests in Casualty and Ronald had therefore had the misfortune to have become an interesting patient while Barry Swift was the waiting medical registrar.

He had been admitted in mid-afternoon and Jenny had clerked him in. Her presentation was thorough to the point of tedium. Campbell listened impatiently to a long list of irrelevant diseases none of the patient's relatives had suffered from, and an even longer list of physical signs Jenny had not found when she had examined him. After ten minutes or so she rounded off with a differential diagnosis running to seven items, two of them rare, three of them almost unheard of.

When they went at last to Ronald's bedside and talked briefly to him he came across as a simple soul, not unwell

27

and certainly not clinically dehydrated; more just puzzled by what was happening to him. He was sitting up in bed in Institute pyjamas – frayed and pale, laundered as usual almost to destruction – reading a comic book. The jug of water on his locker was untouched.

'Interesting case, n'est-ce pas, Dave?' said Barry as they left to go upstairs. 'You don't see too many polydipsias in men under fifty, do you? Wouldn't be surprised if we ended up getting a BMJ case report out of it.' Campbell made a mental note to go back at ten or so and check just how much Ronald, now labelled, perhaps irreversibly, as suffering from pathological thirst, had actually got round to drinking.

Swift, Campbell and their little retinue left the male ward shortly before five o'clock. At the foot of the stairs Swift hesitated, then suddenly handed Campbell the red bleep signifying the office of waiting medical registrar. 'Dave, I don't want to cut into your time. Everything's fine upstairs among the ladies. Both the housemen are up there and they'll tell you all about the problems, not that there are any. I've got a . . .' He posed on one foot, leaning forward with his right arm curving upwards, like winged Mercury in flight. A passing porter gazed open-mouthed and the students glanced uneasily at each other. Swift winked conspiratorially at Campbell, mouthed the words. 'big . . . darts . . . match' then skipped away along the corridor, shouting over his shoulder, 'Bye, Dave . . . have a great night's medicine.'

Since three out of the four students were looking at their watches, Campbell suggested that they take a break and that if any of them wished to join him later he would make a point of being across in Casualty at about seven o'clock. They brightened up and went off. Campbell climbed the stairs to the female ward, alone with his responsibilities.

In the duty room Dennis, the houseman for the female ward, was sitting at the desk scribbling in some notes.

Around him was a clutter of case-notes, coffee mugs, blood tubes, lab forms and unfiled letters and reports: the normal detritus of a waiting day but present, as was usual in Dennis's office, in extraordinary profusion and disarray. He looked up. 'Anyone else?'

'Not so far. How are things?'

'All right. Any students about?'

'I've just sent them off to eat.'

'Oh . . . I've got a couple of cases that need clerking.'

'Well . . .'

'When are they coming back?'

'I really don't know. Maybe round seven.' Most housemen clerked in the majority of their patients, delegating a few to students if it was busy or if the students were especially keen. Dennis, who appeared to think that all students needed as much experience as it was possible to give them, clerked seldom and badly.

'How many new patients?'

'Not sure. Didn't Barry take you round? Seven maybe. Nobody terribly ill.'

'What about the bleeder?'

'All right, I think.'

'Cross-matched?'

'Barry probably mentioned that to the student.'

'Let's go round, Dennis.'

Dennis made a face. Campbell moved to the other side of the desk and looked over his shoulder. At the end of rather a nicely done admission note signed by Jenny, who had obviously had a busy afternoon, there was a barely legible scribble, 'History and examination as above. D. Nelson.'

'Who's that?'

Dennis closed the case notes and looked at the name on the front. 'Mrs Vaughan.'

'What's wrong with her?'

Dennis looked round at Campbell as though he had

asked him the square root of a large prime number. There was a pause while he rifled through the folder. 'Oh . . . She's the bleeder.'

'Fine. Let's go and see her.'

Dennis made a face again. 'Dave . . . Wullie and I had arranged that I would go and eat first . . . Would it be all right to?'

'No.' Dennis, whom Barry referred to as 'our problem boy' had been in trouble before, with Barry, with Andrea and with Campbell. He was an Edinburgh graduate of almost a year's standing. He had come from his previous six-month job in the Institute's urology unit with no particular adverse comment attached, though that might not be too significant, as it was known that urologists were busy surgeons with little time to take detailed interest in the lower levels of medical management.

His failings were intermittent but sometimes alarming. He seemed to regard his medical duties as burdensome if not pointless. He was exasperatingly vague, though not often as bad as he was on this occasion. He had to be told things and then told them again, which was worrying for registrars covering his ward. To Campbell's knowledge he had never actually killed anyone, but perhaps the most worrying thing about him was that it didn't appear that he would be particularly upset if he did.

'Right, Dennis. Get the notes on the new people who've been clerked in. We can check with the staff nurse who else is still to be done.'

The houseman got up and rooted among the debris strewn over his desk and the trolley that stored the case notes. 'Won't be a minute. I'm pretty sure most of them have been done. There's the bleeder, a stroke that's doing badly but no one seems worried about, a belly the surgeons are pretty sure isn't surgical, and a funny neurological thing Barry said Celia should clerk.'

'Celia?'

'The student. The blonde.'

'And what's the neurological problem?'

Dennis shrugged. 'Barry mentioned a neuritis.'

'Optic?'

'Could be.'

'That's four.'

'Then a coronary that intensive care didn't want, and . . . another one.'

As Campbell leafed through the student effort on the lady who had vomited blood, with its methodical, neat if somewhat long-winded account of things, it occurred to him that life might actually be a bit simpler and safer for a number of people if Dennis just went off to eat and somehow didn't manage to find his way back to the ward; assuming of course Jenny and perhaps one of the keen young men turned up at seven o'clock. 'What's this? What's wrong with her back?'

Dennis looked blank.

'Come on, Dennis. Backache, high lumbar, eighteen months and gradually getting worse. In the student's notes . . .'

'Oh. That.'

'So you haven't actually seen her . . .'

'I was going to go over as soon as I'd eaten.'

Campbell thought for a moment about how his new head of department might deal with a situation like that, and found himself astonished at his own moderation. 'Then you shouldn't have written what you've just signed.'

Dennis took the notes back from Campbell and checked the name on the cover. 'Sorry, Dave . . . Wrong notes . . . I've just been looking at the stroke . . . Mrs Boyle. The student got most of the points.'

'How is she?'

'Flat. Big left hemi.'

'How was she before?'

'No history available. She's virtually unconscious.'

31

Campbell remained suspicious. The mixed-up notes story just didn't hang together, unless the man was even more chaotic than everyone thought. And he himself had been a houseman sufficiently recently to know that if you were going to bluff about a patient you should choose one who couldn't talk and therefore wouldn't contradict you on a ward round. 'What about the chest pain?'

'The what?'

'The coronary that intensive care didn't want.'

'Oh . . . her. She didn't actually have chest pain. Just a funny turn with palpitations, apparently. But not much of a history there either. Japanese tourist. Doesn't speak a word of English.'

Nice one, thought Campbell as they went into the ward. All looked set for quite a worrying waiting night.

'Six,' said the staff nurse, 'leaving us five empty beds, or seven if we put a couple up the middle.'

'Can we go round quickly, staff. Just the six new ones, starting with anyone you're worried about.'

'Nobody's terribly ill. Mrs Boyle was the worst . . . Over here.'

Campbell and the staff nurse, with the houseman trailing behind perhaps to make the point that he had intended to go off for a break, headed a little way down the ward and stopped at a bed labelled Mrs J. Boyle. The patient was an obese, grey-haired female, lying on her right side and breathing noisily. A small plastic airway had been inserted into her mouth. Each time she exhaled her left cheek puffed out quite a lot.

'Dennis?'

'Huh?'

'Mrs Boyle . . . The lady you've just seen.'

'Um. Stroke. Left-sided weakness.'

Campbell waited in vain for further details. The staff nurse rolled her eyes upwards and shook her head. Dennis managed a bovine smile. 'There's not really much else to tell you about her.'

'Conscious level?'

'Oh . . . that . . . Pretty flat, really.'

Campbell took a closer look. 'She's actually lightened a lot,' said the staff nurse through clenched teeth. Dennis smiled again.

'Mrs Boyle?' Campbell leaned over, catching a whiff of foetid breath. 'Mrs Boyle?'

The patient's eyelids flickered then opened, the right more than the left. She made an indistinct gurgling sound, spat out her green plastic airway, looked round then suddenly focused on Campbell. 'What's all this?'

'Hello, Mrs Boyle.'

'What are you doing in my house?'

Campbell glanced back. The staff nurse smiled an I-told-you-so-smile. Dennis wore an embarrassed grin.

'You're in hospital, Mrs Boyle. The Institute. You were taken ill . . .'

'Right enough. Don't feel too well.' Her speech was slurred like a stage drunk's.

'Put out your tongue, please.' It deviated to the left. 'And just lift up your arms.' Her right arm moved normally, her left hardly at all. 'Do you feel any weakness?'

'Nothing wrong with my arms. Here, what is all this?'

'Mrs Boyle, it looks as if you might have had a little stroke.'

'I've got a cat at home to look after . . . What is all this?'

'Mrs Boyle, Dr Nelson here is going to come back shortly and ask you some more questions. Your left side's a bit weak but it should start to get better soon.'

'Here, son . . .'

'Dr Nelson's going to come back shortly, Mrs Boyle. Staff?'

'Mrs Vaughan's next.'

'Is she the bleeder?'

'Supposed to be. No more vomiting, doesn't even feel sick and her readings are steady. She's much more bothered about her back.'

'Really?'

'And that's why she's been chewing aspirins and making her self sick up blood.'

'Thanks, staff.'

Mrs Vaughan was a woman in her early forties, lying flat in bed with just one pillow and looking uncomfortable rather than ill. Campbell asked her about the vomiting and learned that no very impressive amounts of blood had resulted ('just streaks, really') and that the amounts of aspirin involved had been quite substantial.

'It's the only thing that works, really.' She moved in bed to talk, wincing as she did so. 'I've tried Distalgesic and Fortral and they make me feel funny but not comfortable. Fortral especially. So I've been taking aspirin, four or five at a time, every three or four hours. My ears have been buzzing, but I don't mind, because aspirin really does help the pain.'

'What?'

'And at night . . .' She hesitated. 'It sounds awful but the best way to get anything like even half a night's sleep is to take four or five aspirin and a pretty stiff gin and tonic.'

Mrs Vaughan giggled and winced again. 'And I suppose that's not very good for the lining of your stomach.'

'No . . . And how much blood actually came up?'

'Hardly any, really, but it gave me a bit of a fright and I rang my own GP and he said it was serious and I should just go up to Casualty. So here I am.'

'D'you feel sick now?'

'No . . . Just sore.'

'Not thirsty?'

'No.'

'Any pain around here?'

Campbell indicated the general area of the upper abdomen. The staff nurse looked sharply at him and whipped the screens round the bed.

'No.'

'Can I take a quick look?'

There was nothing of note to see or feel or hear: no lump or other swelling, no area of tenderness to suggest an ulcer, no excess of bowel sounds to suggest a really big bleed. A glance at the charts was reassuring too. Pulse and blood pressure were beyond reproach. Campbell was inclined now to agree with the staff nurse and the patient: the bleeding was neither significant nor mysterious. There was a ritual of observation and cross-matching for possible transfusion to be gone through, but in cases like this it was only a ritual. The real problem was the back pain.

Dennis was looking out of the window and in any case had not examined the patient. If the lady had had a sore back for eighteen months it would still be sore in the morning and a more orderly assessment could be done then, but a few minutes now might at least allow a provisional diagnosis.

'And your back's very sore?'

'Very, very sore.'

'Worse with moving about?'

'Yes.'

'Goes away in between?'

'There all the time . . . And it's hard to explain but it's been getting worse, sort of gradually and in fits and starts, for months and months and months.'

'When did you first notice it?'

'About eighteen months ago.'

'What were you doing when it came on?'

'Hurrying up the steps at Waverley Station with a great big suitcase because I thought I was going to miss a train.'

'And you've had it ever since?'

'Yes.'

'Been to see anybody?'

'Yes. Lots of people. My own doctor, who said it was a wee disc, and it would settle down, then when it didn't he sent me for X-rays that didn't show anything, and then he thought I was depressed and those pills made me feel funny too, and I went privately to a man in Moray Place, a sort of osteopath that was highly recommended, does golfers and my husband's friends when they wreck themselves at squash . . . Oooh.'

Again she had laughed and moved a little in bed and had been stopped short by the pain, not in the overdone, Tom-and-Jerry way Campbell had seen in men in Casualty looking for a certificate to free them from the burdens of employment for a month or so, but with a kind of quiet desperation.

'What happened with him?'

'He had lovely manners and nice warm hands and it helped.'

'Really?'

'For about fifteen minutes. For thirty guineas, if you please.'

'Hmm . . . Can you sit up?'

'If I take it really slowly.'

Once more the staff nurse had whipped the screen round. Mrs Vaughan edged upwards with caution, in obvious discomfort.

'Sore anywhere when I press?'

'About there . . . No, higher . . . Not any particular spot.'

Another hallmark of the unconvincing back was the customer's tendency to identify a minute area of exquisite tenderness whose exact location might be forgotten if he or she was distracted for a moment or two.

'Any particular movements make it worse?'

'Twisting, and bending forward.'

'And does it tend to get worse through the day?'

'No . . . Well, maybe recently . . . But it's really, really awful at night . . . that's why I'm into the mother's ruin.'

'And the sorest bit? There?'

'No. Lower . . . But it's not any very exact spot.'

'Hmm. I see.'

Campbell recalled one of Professor Aithie's remarks about making a neurological diagnosis: that if you're going to get it at all you're going to get it on the history. ('Examine them too, by all means. With most of them you won't find anything, but it gives you time to think . . . which would otherwise be spent standing at the foot of the bed scratching your head.')

The soothing routine of straight leg raising and the traditional scraping of the sole of the foot while observing the reflex movement of the great toe resulted in neither abnormal clinical sign nor diagnostic inspiration. Not a hysterical back, and probably not a routine back: that was about as far as Campbell could go. And it was all a little more complicated because Mrs Vaughan had come in with the label of upper gastro-intestinal bleed.

'We'll give you something for the pain. Not aspirin . . . And start a few tests to find out a bit more about your back.'

'Thanks,' said Mrs Vaughan, settling back and wincing again.

Fortunately for Campbell and his Japanese patient, the Mission to Seamen had made available to the Institute a card with a wide of selection of useful phrases in English and Japanese. Passing swiftly over 'It hurts to make water' and 'I have a discharge from my penis', they went through pain in chest, feelings of dizziness, pains in stomach, head pains and feelings of sickness, with nothing too alarming to show for their efforts. Heart and chest sounded normal. Pulse, blood pressure, temperature, electrocardiograph and routine chest X-ray were all entirely reassuring, but the card did not help in passing on such information. Campbell said 'OK' a lot, and the lady nodded and smiled and mimed going to sleep. Campbell nodded too and followed the staff nurse to the next waiting day patient.

'Dennis?'

Once more the houseman looked vaguely puzzled and perhaps irritated that anyone would expect him to know about the waiting day admissions. He stood impatiently, evidently unaware of Campbell's implied censure and the rays of hatred and contempt now fizzing from the staff nurse, holding the case-folders of the three or four patients he had managed to get other people to clerk on his behalf.

Part of the trouble was that, however badly he func-tioned, Dennis still looked and sometimes sounded like a doctor. He was tall and, in a clean-cut officer-class way, quite handsome, with an accent to match: a subdued variant of received pronunciation, perhaps the legacy of a minor public school. Old Aithie, who must have appointed him to the post as one of his last gestures in medicine, was known to be quite keen on that sort of thing, and if Dennis, as was quite possible, was a doctor's son as well, his presence in a sought-after teaching hospital housejob was sufficiently explained.

'Miss Prosser,' said the staff nurse. 'Optic neuritis.' To say what was wrong with the patient she had come closer to Campbell and lowered her voice.

'I've been really busy,' Dennis said. 'And Barry really wanted Celia to clerk her in.'

The girl was twentyish, thin and slightly glamorous in a filmy nightdress. Her story was a sad and common one in neurology. The sight in one eye had become blurred gradually over the course of a day. Now she could not read even the largest print with the affected eye, and could scarcely count the fingers that Campbell held up to test her vision.

Even if she had no other neurological symptoms, she had a one in three chance of going on to develop multiple sclerosis; if she had had anything else in the past, even transiently, such as dizziness, slurring of speech or patchy alteration of sensation, then she had it already: a progressive but unpredictable illness, sometimes killing within months, sometimes teasingly remittent over decades.

With a disease like that there were always problems about when and how much to tell the patient. Some neurologists took the cheerful line to the point of absurdity, talking blithely about a little bit of inflammation of the nerves, nothing more, shouldn't bother you much, until the patient was a paraplegic wreck. Others came clean right away and spared the patient the touble of looking things up in the public library. Either way problems could arise.

When he tested the girl's sight Campbell sat on the bed and said 'Ever had anything like this before, Miss Prosser? Blurred eyesight, or feeling unsteady, or pins and needles that stayed longer than usual? Anything like that?'

She paused as though aware that her answer might be of some consequence for her future. 'No . . . Nothing like that.'

'Good.'

'But one funny thing happened, once. Just for a few days. I handed my wee brother a plate and he dropped it.'

'Has he had trouble like this?'

'No. It was his tea from the oven, and the plate was really hot . . . But it didn't feel hot to me, and afterwards I got blisters on my fingers, just like normal. But . . . it hadn't seemed hot at the time. So for a while I tested things with my left hand before I picked them up with my right, know what I mean? Then everything just went back to normal.'

'Yes . . . When was this?'

'Oh . . . two or three weeks ago?'

That was more bad news, because incidents as close together as that made it more likely she had multiple sclerosis in one of its more agressive variants. The cheerful,

39

healthy, slightly anxious girl in the filmy pink nightdress might look very different in as little as a year.

'So what have I got, Dr Campbell?'

'Not sure. I think we need some tests.'

'That's what Dr Swift said. Just a few tests, probably nothing serious. He's really nice.'

Campbell got up and nodded in the direction of Dennis. 'Dr Nelson's going to come back and examine you in a bit more detail soon.' The staff nurse pursed her lips and prepared to move. Dennis was looking out of the window.

The belly that the surgeons didn't think was surgical turned out to be a woman in her seventies who had had pain for several days, or perhaps a couple of weeks, starting up under her right ribs, or maybe round a bit in the small of her back, maybe made worse by coughing or breathing deeply but maybe not. It was all a bit vague. Campbell asked her her age and she said she was about forty, maybe.

When he pressed her hard up under her right ribs she said 'Dinnae, son,' and when he sat her up and tapped her gently over the right kidney she said, 'Here, dinnae dae that.' Both the surgeon who thought she wasn't surgical and Wullie, the downstairs houseman who had clerked her in, had been uncertain whether she had an infected gall bladder or an infected right kidney, but since the treatment was the same it really didn't much matter, and Wullie had put her on the treatment already.

'Her temp's down, and she's drinking nicely and we still haven't got a urine specimen,' said the staff nurse.

They moved on. 'She's fine,' said the staff nurse as they stopped by the bed of a woman clearly dying from a massive stroke. 'Having all care, and the relatives are fully informed. They've just gone out for a smoke and we're moving her into the side room when we get a minute.'

'Have you seen her, Dennis?'

'I think Wullie might have ... Not sure. Or maybe Barry wanted one of the students to see her.'

'Perhaps you should start with her. Now. And then see the girl with MS. If you give me the notes I'll go over the rest and scribble something, then we can go down and eat.'

Dennis handed over the notes and seemed at last to capitulate on the early break issue. The staff nurse enjoyed that quietly. The houseman drew the screens round the stroke lady now unconscious and noisily wheezing her last. At least he wouldn't have to spend time taking the history and asking her a lot of questions. Campbell and the staff nurse withdrew together.

'Problems?' Campbell enquired as they passed out of earshot.

'He's an idiot. Doesn't know and doesn't care.'

'Getting worse?'

'His usual, for a waiting night.'

'Oh.'

'And he doesn't come when we bleep him. Not that he's much use if he does, but he doesn't. At least not for ages.'

'I think Wullie's on from about eleven.'

'Good.'

'Thanks, staff. And if you're really worried about anything, get Wullie, or me.'

'We always do.'

Campbell went back and had another look at the lady with the left-sided stroke, who couldn't find her left thumb with her eyes shut and seemed to be ignoring her left side. The sore back, after a further five minutes questioning and examination, remained mysterious. The old lady with right-sided abdominal pain, who had forgotten seeing Campbell only minutes before, was, apart from her pain, remarkably well. The Japanese lady was asleep.

In the doctor's room he wrote out a half page summary of each of these cases and, in case she died before Dennis had written anything about her, something on the moribund stroke lady too. Since there was no record of anyone cross-matching the lady who had bled a bit he left a note on the houseman's desk telling him to check up on that, then rang the doctors' residency and asked the butler to book him in for dinner.

He looked at his watch. He had been on duty for an hour and his red bleep had remained silent. Realizing with a fair flicker of guilt that he had not checked it when he had taken charge of it from Barry, he whipped it out and pressed the test button. It sounded loud and clear. No one had been summoning him frantically for the last half hour to heal the sick in Casualty or try to raise the dead in the orthopaedic operating theatre. Sometimes all the waiting medical registrar had to do was wait.

For reasons that no one could remember, far less understand, the bedroom allocated to the waiting medical registrar was an attic above the top surgical corridor, four flights of stairs and perhaps a quarter of a mile of corridor away from where he was most likely to be needed. Since nothing seemed to be happening for the moment Campbell went down to his office in the erstwhile Neurobiology Unit and collected the briefcase with his tooth-brush, current paperback and change of shirt, socks and underpants, then strolled up towards his temporary lodging.

Outside, the light was fading. Through the corridors of the Institute an early evening calm prevailed. There were no visitors about. Porters steered meal trolleys back from wards to kitchen and a few cleaners chatted peaceably amid the grime. Campbell ascended the second-best staircase, from the residency to the main surgical corridor, past subscription lists painted in gold on black, transferred from a previous building in the middle of the last century and recording the benevolence of a century before that.

David Hume and one Commissary Smollett had contributed, as had dozens of soldiers, colonials, lawyers, divines and Edinburgh widows with no other claim on the attentions of posterity. What would become of their small immortality when the Institute was at last replaced? Or was it simply, Campbell wondered, that their shades had conspired triumphantly, decade by decade, to frustrate oblivion as successive plans were discussed and discarded?

The last stair up to the medical registrar's garret was narrow and wooden and painted in the gingerbread and custard of a bygone institutional age. Definitely a fire risk, thought Campbell as it creaked under his tread, but only in the servants' quarters.

His bedroom was little better: an irregular wood-panelled space under the eaves with a bed, a telephone and a solitary and uncomfortable chair. A tiny window looked out over the consultants' car park and the main entrance to the hospital, with its statue of George III in chaplet and toga, arm raised in salutation to a BMW, a couple of Volvo estates and a commercial orthopod's Bentley.

Campbell sat down on the bed and began to worry again about his bleep. It was simply unnatural that it had not bothered him in just over an hour. He picked up the telephone and rang the exchange to ask them to call to check it.

'Dr Campbell? Oh. It's you now. Nobody tells us anything. No, it's been very quiet this past wee while . . . Oh . . . Hang on . . . Yes. I've got him here. Putting you through now, doctor.'

'Hello?'

'Waiting medical registrar?'

'Yes. Dr Campbell.'

'Good. I've got an old lady here you sent home this afternoon. A woman of eighty-three who's really not right . . . I sent her up, you know, not coping at home, probable stroke, that sort of thing, and you sent her home from Casualty this afternoon. The relatives aren't too pleased and I thought . . .'

The call was broken off by the shrill noise of a payphone running out. Campbell waited. The call was restored.

'Sorry about that, Dr Campbell. I'm phoning from a call

43

box in the middle of East Saltoun. Yes . . . The family were pretty upset. The ambulance men left the old thing leaning on the railings outside her cottage. And nobody let me know you were sending her home. So I wonder if I could maybe send her in again. She's really not right . . .'

'I'm sorry, Dr . . .'

'Matthews. . . . The Mid Saltoun practice . . . It's all right . . . I know these things happen. But I'd be grateful if you'd take another look at her . . . I'll just send her in with a wee note. Mrs Williamina J. Irvine . . . Nice old woman, normally. About eighty-three, I think. Thank you, Dr Campbell.'

'Thank you, Dr Matthews.'

Order was restored, and East Saltoun was sufficiently far away for Campbell to have time to get down to the residency for something to eat before his evening's work began.

'Hello, Dr Campbell, sir. Nice tae see ye again.'

Billy, the residency butler, had retired into the NHS office after half a lifetime of soldierly sin as mess corporal in one of the lesser cavalry regiments. Campbell, revisiting the residency as waiting medical registrar a few years after his twelve-month stretch as a houseman at the Institute, realized that in Billy's eyes he had made it from subaltern to perhaps junior captain, and responded with due civility. Billy was keeping well but housemen were not what they had been.

'Awfy quiet, this lot, sir. The half o' them's married and hardly use the place, and there's a lot mair women gettin' jobs here, so it's no like it was. A lot mair women . . . And some o' them dinnae pay their share o' the papers.'

In Billy's world there was no accounting for the ways of women, and standards had been falling steadily since the foolish abandonment of the lance as a weapon of war some years before his birth. 'I'm afraid the bouef bourgignon's

44

a' gone, sir. There's a corned beef hash I wouldnae recommend, so maybe the kedgeree?'

'Thanks, Billy.'

The dining room was almost empty. Dennis and Wullie sat at the far end of the table. Campbell joined them. Dennis was talking about his plans for the future, but paused to acknowledge his immediate superior's arrival. 'The bourgignon's all right, Dave ... but this pudding might be worth avoiding. So maybe a year loafing round Europe and the Middle East with a camera, just seeing what turns up, because it's no good being totally obsessed with medicine, as though nothing else existed, and I've been at it for nearly six years now without a break. I've always liked the idea of the Lebanon, and if you don't mind going a bit native you can live very cheaply indeed.'

'There you are, sir. I didnae give you too much cabbage.'

'Thanks, Billy.'

'Hm. You should have taken the bourgignon, Dave. And then maybe a year's full-time photography course, if I still like it. London. There's nowhere else. What about you, Wullie.'

'Oh, I was thinking I might just try and earn a living. General practice, probably. Or maybe ballet-dancing.'

'Really, Wullie?' said Dennis, in a gosh-aren't-the-natives-interesting voice.

'No. Just kidding.'

Wullie was older than the average houseman, because he had been a lab technician who had done a biochemistry degree then gone on to support himself through medical school by means of a large and highly organized milk round. He was knowledgeable and hard-working and remarkably good with all sorts and conditions of patients. When Campbell had commented on that last virtue Wullie had been embarrassed, but had gruffly admitted that in the milk business you probably learned quite a lot about people. Though he had never got round to it, Campbell had wondered for some time afterwards about writing to the Dean of the medical school with a radical suggestion for the undergraduate curriculum.

'Or maybe Israel, but it's been overdone. I mean, everybody's photographed Israel. Masada and all that is vieux jeux these days.'

'Right enough,' said Wullie. 'Anybody else on their way in, Dave?'

'An old lady from East Lothian, nothing very specific from the sound of her. GP rang her in ten minutes ago.'

'God, not another female. That must be about a dozen. And you're still stuck at one, Wullie?'

'Don't worry, Dennis, I'll catch up eventually. On a Friday the men all wait till the pubs shut. It's a known fact.'

The kedgeree was cold and the cabbage unspeakable. The unrecommended pudding was the sole remaining choice. Campbell ate without pleasure as Dennis fantasized and Wullie quietly teased him. Some things about the residency had indeed changed. Half a dozen more recent photographs of successive six-month mess groups had nudged Campbell's vintage round the wall and a little nearer the door. One, he noted with some disapproval, had ventured into colour and another had posed in decorative disorder like an Edwardian cycling club, with the class idiot, now an SHO in cardiology, draped languorously along the knees of the front row. Perhaps Billy was right, and all change was for the worse.

They had coffee in the lounge, then Dennis went upstairs to his room, inviting Campbell to bleep him if he needed him, rather as though he and not Campbell were the registrar. Wullie and Campbell made their way back to the wards.

As they passed the main X-ray department Wullie asked, 'What's your new boss like?'

He had not said 'our new boss'. Sinclair was simply the

new head of a university department, and though Campbell's appointment was an academic one, Wullie's was purely NHS. In practice, and because of his remarkably direct approach, Sinclair would probably count for quite a lot around the wards, though if Dr Temple and Dr Walters, the NHS consultants, chose to do so they could exercise a certain amount of negative power over things like the timing of ward rounds and long-established rights to the coat hooks of their choice. 'Interesting chap. Pretty forceful. From the north, Dingwall or somewhere like that, but he's spent the last ten years in London.'

'What are his research interests?'

Money and power, thought Campbell. 'Parkinson's disease,' he said.

'I would never even have heard about any of this if her neighbour hadn't seen her outside, standing where the ambulance men had left her, and phoned me at work. I went out as quick as I could and they'd got her inside and put her to bed but I still don't know why you sent her home in the first place, because she's obviously not a well woman. I rang Dr Matthews from the phone box and he came straight away, still in his gardening things, and such a gentleman, and he said her condition might have deteriorated since she'd been seen at the Institute. Of course it has, I said, the poor old woman was left standing on wet grass, leaning on the fence and not able to walk a step without somebody holding her up. And it's my mother we're talking about . . .'

'I'm sorry,' said Campbell. 'Dr Matthews rang me at six o'clock, just after I'd come on duty, and we agreed she should come in. I'm sorry she's had such trouble . . . I'm just going to have a look at her now, so perhaps if you could wait . . .'

Dr Matthews' letter was brief and not especially helpful. 'Dear doctor, re Mrs Williamina J. Irvine, Aet 83, 2

Cornbank Terrace, E. Saltoun. You will recall this pleasant old lady whom you kindly saw in Casualty this afternoon. Since her return home she has deteriorated further, with weakness, malaise and a low fever. O/E Dehydration, sl. right sided weakness, nil else of note. P. 90 Reg. BP 130/ 80. Thank you for admitting her. She is on no medications. Yrs M. F. Matthews.'

Behind the screens the Casualty staff nurse was shaking down her thermometer. 'No temp now. Readings all right, but definitely not well.'

'Whit, dear?' said the patient, a pale old lady with bright eyes, receding hair and a silver-grey moustache.

'Thanks, staff . . . Mrs Irvine?'

'Yes, son.'

'Mrs Irvine, I'm Dr Campbell. Sorry you've had all this trouble. How are you feeling now?'

The old lady smiled and coughed. 'Terrible.'

'Pain, or sickness, or just weakness?'

'Them a', son.'

'Where's the pain?'

'My body mainly, and my heid.'

'When did it come on?'

'Och, maybe yesterday. But worse the day. Definitely worse the day.'

'Where is it worst?'

'Oh, son, I'm a' sair.'

'And your head?'

'It's no' bad just now.'

'And what about the sickness?'

'No sae bad noo I'm oot o' that ambulance.'

'I'm sorry.'

She was pale but probably not anaemic. The right side of her mouth drooped a little but when he asked her to show him her teeth it evened up again. A quick run over chest and abdomen yielded no clues. It could be anything from flu to polymyalgia rheumatica. The safe, sensible

48

thing to do with an old lady like this who lived alone, even one who hadn't been thrown out of hospital already that day and then sent back in, was to start a few basic tests, get her into the ward and think about things again in the morning.

'Would you mind coming into hospital?'

'Son, I'm past caring.'

'We'll get you up to the ward shortly. I'll tell your daughter.'

'Thanks, son.'

The daughter remained suspicious. Campbell could see why. If the Institute had had the unwisdom to send her mother home that afternoon when she wasn't fit for it, what guarantee was there that better judgement would prevail when she was admitted? What might happen or not happen to her in a busy medical ward, far from the protecting eye of a watchful neighbour? 'We still might complain,' she said, looking at Campbell as though trying to memorize his appearance in case of a future identification parade. 'And I should warn you that we've got a very good MP out there.'

Campbell found an unoccupied phone and bleeped Dennis, at the same time filling in a form so that the old woman could be X-rayed in Casualty before she went up to the ward. While he was waiting a clerkess brought him some notes from the encounter with Barry in the afternoon. Nursing records showed that her pulse had risen and her blood pressure fallen a little over the past four hours. Barry had been unimpressed. 'Elderly female in no apparent distress. 2/7 malaise. No specific features in history. Readings unremarkable. Clinical examination normal for age. Diagnosis viral illness. Discharged home to care of GP.'

Dennis was taking so long to answer his bleep that Campbell began to look round for some paper in order to get on with his half-page summary on Mrs Irvine. There was none in sight. He thought about the case whose admission he was arranging, and why Barry had handled it differently in the afternoon. A firm nudge from a polite and senior GP was only part of the explanation. Perhaps the old woman had been in better general condition earlier, and the nursing observations tended to support that. It was also somehow less uncomfortable to commit doubtful discharges in daylight. Once the sun had set the balance of judgement shifted towards greater caution. On the other hand, of course, there were to be considered Professor Sinclair's briskly worded remarks on what he called social admissions.

'Dr Campbell?' A short fat girl in a white coat advanced on him. 'I've been looking all over for you.'

Campbell's brain failed to engage. 'Jenny Brown,' said the girl. 'I'm one of the senior students.'

'Sorry, Jenny.'

'Is anything happening? Have I missed anything? Anyone to clerk in?'

Dennis was taking a very long time to answer his bleep. 'There's just been the one admission. Still in Casualty. An old lady who's just not well. Really not sure about her. Would you mind taking her X-ray form round to the radiographer? Speed things up a bit.'

Jenny took the form eagerly and hurried off. Dennis continued not to answer his bleep. Eventually Campbell gave up and dialled the ward. The staff nurse hadn't seen the houseman since before six. Campbell told her about Mrs Irvine.

'Any special observations?'

'Just the usual . . . Daughter's a bit upset.'

'We'll be nice to her.'

'Thanks, staff.'

Jenny came back smiling, perhaps even looking for more forms to carry about. 'Can I clerk her in, Dr Campbell?'

'Why not? She'll be up in the ward in ten minutes or so.'

'How's the lady who was vomiting blood?'

'All right. No more blood. Complaining more about her back.'

'Yes,' said Jenny. 'I nipped into the library to look up backs. Could it be a disc, even after all that time?'

'Don't think so.'

'What about ankylosing spondylitis? I know it's usually men, but maybe . . .'

'Just doesn't sound like it. And she'd be more rigid.'

'Good. It's a horrible disease . . . And what about the man downstairs with polydipsia?'

'I haven't really been over him,' said Campbell, uncomfortably aware of sounding like Dennis.

'There's lots of interesting things he could have.'

'Yes,' said Campbell. 'That's probably why Barry admitted him.'

She started to laugh and then stopped. 'Really, Dr Campbell?'

Mrs Irvine's chest X-ray appeared in a few minutes and did not help much. Her ECG, done on the spot by one of the Casualty staff nurses, was also normal. She went up to the ward followed by Jenny, who was going to clerk her in and who carried the X-ray and the ECG under her arm with an air of unusual purpose and fulfilment, as though they would change her life.

Campbell hung around Casualty because that was where, on a Friday evening, you expected to be needed next. At eight he was asked to see a thin, grubby man of around forty who had been sent in from a lodging house 'to get his cough seen to'. He was wasted and hollow-eyed, with a huge area on the left of his chest where the normal signs of air entry had been replaced by a sinister dullness. There were lumps in his neck, and odd little shotty lumps across the skin of his abdomen.

Campbell asked if he had any other skin trouble.

'Just my legs.'

'Can I look?'

'If you want.'

The man rolled up his trousers. Both legs were wrapped in greyish-brown bandage that had once been white. He unwrapped them, remarking 'Nae germs is going to get at me', and uncovered several hand-sized patches of greenish yellow ulceration. Campbell looked closely, all but gagging on the stench. The edges of the ulcers were firm and irregular, and around them were more of the little skin nodules.

The chest X-ray was a formality. The man had a massive tumour in his left lung. It had spread to skin and he was falling apart.

'Are you in pain?'

'No . . . More of an itch. And maybe a dull pain when I've been coughing a lot.'

'Are you a smoker?'

The man paused and laughed. 'I know what you're going to say, doc. I should give it up . . . Well, you're the medical man. I've made my decision.' He smiled proudly and leant forward to wrap his legs again. A staff nurse swooped on his bandages and snatched them away. He looked bemused.

'How would you feel about coming in to the ward?'

'You're the medical man.'

'I'd advise it.'

'Fair enough.'

The nurses on the male ward bathed the man and dressed his ulcers. Wullie clerked him in and he died at half past ten. By that time another four patients, three male and one female, had been admitted. Campbell sat again in the doctors' room of the female ward, now even untidier than before. Once more he was bleeping Dennis. 'Wait a minute,' said the operator. 'I'll try his room . . . He's not the easiest man to find.'

Campbell waited. Wullie came in, followed by the

upstairs night auxiliary with tea and toast. Following her was Jenny, bright and eager and looking generally as if the worst thing that could happen to her would be that someone might suggest it was time she went home. The auxiliary left and Jenny, infinitely capable of finding useful things to do, took charge of the teapot.

'How many?'

'Make it four,' said Wullie. 'He generally turns up for his tea.'

It was a waiting night convention of the unit that the housemen and registrar met in the late evening to take stock of things over tea and then go round both wards together. In the absence of Dennis, Wullie began to report on the state of things downstairs. 'Your polydipsia's no more a polydipsia than I am myself. Barry's got him so scared he's hardly touched his jug, and his urine output's nothing to write home about either . . . Getting on with his comic, though. Page five when I last saw him. And your fitter's settling down on intravenous Valium. Just the odd twitch. Nothing you could really call a proper fit in the last hour. And that's it. And six empty beds again because of the wee chap . . .'

'We'd better get a post mortem. Who's the next of kin?'

'A daughter he thought was in Canada.'

'Oh well. We'll just have to ring up the fiscal and . . .'

'Hello, everybody.' Dennis had come in as though expecting a big welcome. He reached for the fourth cup of tea and the remaining toast and sat down. 'Have you begun without me?'

'How are things up here, Dennis?'

'Good, going on wonderful.'

'Mrs Vaughan?'

'Settling on panadol, as far as I know.'

'Bleeding?'

'Nothing so far. The nurses haven't said anything.'

'Cross-matched?'

'Did you want her cross-matched, Dave?'

'I left you a note.'

'Really? Probably here somewhere . . .' He gestured airily around his chaotic office and smiled. Wullie scribbled something on a card he kept in the right-hand pocket of his white coat.

'And the lady from East Lothian? Mrs Irvine.'

'Settled,' said Dennis firmly.

In Campbell's view 'settled' was a word used by the dimmer sort of nurse, usually to indicate that the condition of the patient being enquired about was unknown to her. 'Lab results back?'

'Haematology OK, I think. Clinical chemistry should probably ring back pretty soon.'

'Urinalysis?'

'Um . . . Normal . . . It's all in the notes.'

'The woman with Crohn's and asthma? Mrs . . .'

'Barron,' said Jenny, who had clerked her in. 'A bit better on her steroids.'

On these and other patients, Dennis was vague or evasive or both. As they got up to go round Campbell reflected for the fourth or fifth time that evening that the only thing in Dennis's favour from the point of view of the waiting medical registrar was that he would go to bed at eleven and remain there, except in the event of multiple dire emergencies, until the next morning, and that Wullie, with his sound scientific background and his milkman's common sense, would be in immediate charge of both wards and any further admissions to them overnight.

After the round Jenny, with a little prompting, went home and Campbell went back to Casualty, where there were a couple of youngish coronaries who needed only a firm diagnosis, something for the pain and a bed in the Intensive Care Unit, where they then became someone else's problem. At about quarter past eleven there was nothing else to do, and he headed upstairs to the garret bedroom. His bleep went off just as he had got undressed. He dialled the exchange and waited.

'Hello?' said a male voice from far down a cracked line. 'Waiting medical registrar?'

'Yes . . . Dr Campbell speaking.'

'Dr McVittie, Tansey Street, here. I've just seen an old chap of about ninety . . . one of my colleague's patients, actually. In a pretty bad way with chest pain and breathlessness. Can I send him in?'

'Certainly. Do you have . . .?'

'MacAffleck . . . Jimmy MacAffleck. A classical paroxysmal nocturnal dyspnoea, I think you'll find, doctor. I've tried the usual things. He's a little better, but he's on his own . . . you know how it is . . . Thank you so much, doctor. I'll just send him up to Casualty. Good night to you. Good night.'

Campbell rang Casualty so that the admission just arranged would be expected to be there, then, since a straightforward case of paroxysmal nocturnal dyspnoea should be well within the competence of a houseman like Wullie, decided there was no particular point in waiting up himself. He bleeped Wullie, who answered within a minute and was quite happy to take the case on.

'Nae bother,' he said. 'Anybody else on their way in?'

'Not that I know of, Wullie. How are things over there?'

'OK. Most of them are the same or a wee bit better. Except maybe the wifie from East Saltoun . . . Mrs Irvine. She's looking more like a stroke now. Bit of right-sided weakness.'

'Hm. That's what the GP sent her in as.'

'And a wee headache. Nothing much.'

'Lateralised?'

'Mainly left. Probably her stroke. I'll keep an eye on her.'

'Thanks, Wullie.'

'Cheers.'

Campbell reached for his paperback but had barely found his place when a Casualty SHO rang asking him to see 'a drunk who might not be just drunk'. He dressed and went down the creaking staircase, then along the corridor past the surgical ward where he had served his time as a houseman, and down another couple of flights of stairs to Casualty.

The drunk was lying on a trolley in the tiled recess which Hadden referred to as the vomitorium, and he was very drunk. The trouble with drunks, as Campbell had found out in his own spell in Casualty, was that the healthy ones quite often claimed some mortal illness as a cause of their unseemly condition, and the ones who really had something quite serious wrong with them were likely, in a state of alcoholic euphoria, to deny it.

The man was called Crofton Strong, and was smiling at the ceiling when Campbell leant over to talk to him. Taking a history was not easy. He admitted his name, but only reluctantly. He wanted Campbell to guess his age. Though smelling powerfully of fresh and stale whisky, he confessed only to the occasional shandy. When Campbell pressed him on his drinking habits he demanded to see his lawyer then closed his eyes and refused to answer any further questions.

With the help of a Casualty staff nurse Campbell examined his chest and belly and did the rather limited neurological things that circumstances permitted. Mr Strong's pupils were equal, and reacted to light. Reflexes, if caught between efforts at resistance, appeared normal, apart from a possibly abnormal plantar response: the left toe quivering undecidedly as Campbell scratched the sole.

'He was a lot worse when they called you,' said the staff nurse. 'Out cold, fast pulse and a definite upgoing toe. A blood alcohol's on its way, and we've checked a sugar. Normal. And he was quite chatty a few minutes ago, and not complaining of anything.'

'No story of head injury?'

'No.'

Campbell checked the man's scalp for bleeding or other evidence of trauma. 'They've done all that,' said the staff nurse.

'ECG?'

'There.'

Campbell went across to the desk to look. The ECG seemed to show nothing other than a rather rapid heart rate. As Campbell studied it in detail a retching sound made him turn back to look at Mr Strong, who was now leaning over the side rail of the trolley and vomiting large quantities of blood.

They moved his trolley off the puddle, checked his pulse and blood pressure, then, because he was still demanding to see his lawyer, spent ten minutes or so persuading him he was in a hospital rather than a police station. He was at best partially convinced, and gave a blood sample only after Campbell had solemnly assured him that it was for cross-matching and that no criminal charges would result.

By half past one he was in the waiting male ward under Wullie's care, sedated with chlorpromazine but still eyeing his blood transfusion with drowsy suspicion. His wife, who had been telephoned after the nurses had turned out his pockets to get an address, sat at his bedside anxious but perhaps also working on what she might say to him when they were eventually left alone together. At two fifteen Campbell got back to bed.

'Dave . . . Sorry to bother you . . . Wullie here. I'm up on the female ward. Mrs Irvine.'

'Yes?'

'Her headache got worse, and she just wasn't well, so I wondered if she might have meningitis, or maybe a subarachnoid.'

'I'll come down. Sounds as if we should get a needle into her back.'

'I just went ahead and did a lumbar puncture half an hour ago. And the lab's just rung me to say that the sugar in her CSF is over twelve hundred.'

'*What?*'

'Over twelve hundred. The chap sounded quite surprised himself.'

'Bloody hell. A missed diabetic. But her urinalysis . . .'

'Well, that's a problem.'

'Dennis said it was normal.'

'I checked it. It's loaded with sugar.'

'What about her electrolytes?'

'Not as bad as you'd think. Not acidotic.'

A few distant bells rang. Old lady, non-specific illness, very high blood sugar, not acidotic. 'Bloody hell. Hyperosmolar something. Not very common. They need a lot of IV fluids, and there's something funny about the insulin dose. I'll come right down. What time is it?'

'Half past three.'

'Thanks, Wullie.'

Campbell dressed and hurried down towards the ward, through empty and echoing corridors and stairways, reassembling his scattered knowledge of something that he was now fairly sure was called aketotic hyperosmolar diabetic coma. Fluid replacement was unusually difficult and dangerous. There were usually problems with potassium. The dose of insulin was in some way odd, and even if you knew what you were doing the mortality was around fifty per cent.

Halfway down the curved, sloping corridor joining the medical and surgical blocks another thought struck him. Ideally, the management of aketotic hyperosmolar diabetic coma did not, even in its early stages, include sending the patient home and leaving her standing on wet grass propped up against her garden fence until spotted by a concerned neighbour. The shrill voice of her daughter and the gentler but no less reproachful tones of the GP rang once more in his ears. And there was something about an MP.

As Campbell turned the corner into the main medical corridor he ran into the person who, if he had thought about it, made a wish and believed in fairies, he would have desperately hoped to run into: the registrar from the Institute's specialist diabetic unit.

'Hello, David.'

Polite conversation, perhaps about fifteen seconds' worth, seemed indicated.

'Hello. What are you doing in here at dead of night?'

'Oh, I've just been sorting out a silly old judge with a boil on his bum. The surgeons were a bit worried about his sugar, but I'm not. What about you?'

'I'm the waiting med. reg. The houseman's just rung me because he'd done an LP on an old woman from the waiting night and the sugar's twelve hundred.'

Mhairi's eyes widened. 'Aketonic?'

'From the sound of things. But probably not the best way to pick it up.'

The diabetic registrar laughed, not unkindly. 'It happens once in a while. They can look like meningitis.' There was a pause then Mhairi said, 'I'd be happy to cast an eye . . .'

Campbell, pleased to be spared the minor indignity of having to ask for help from a colleague who was not only a year junior to him, but a woman as well, said 'Yes, please,' and they went up to the female ward together.

'They can be quite tricky, even when you see them fairly regularly,' said Mhairi. 'And most people don't.'

'I watched Ronnie Bertram sort one out when I was a student.'

'The main problem is rehydrating them. If you treat them like an ordinary diabetic coma they do very badly. Hypotonic fluids give them cerebral oedema, brain death and nasty stuff like that. And the slightest whiff of insulin can knock their sugars right down.'

Campbell, quite grateful for a tactfully delivered tutorial, realized that if he had gone straight in without reading it up or taking advice he would probably have got the second bit right but the first bit disastrously wrong.

Wullie was sitting in the doctor's room with the case notes and the recent results on Mrs Irvine. He did not appear to be surprised that Campbell had, within the last five minutes, acquired a second opinion, and seemed to know Mhairi already. 'You'd be pleased to hear she hasn't got meningitis or a subarachnoid, Dave, but I thought it was worth mentioning her sugar was a wee bit high. I've put a drip up, with normal saline going through slowly just to keep it open until we decide what to give her.'

'Thanks, Wullie.'

Mhairi leafed through the notes. 'Her urea's not too high . . . That should help. And from the sound of things she was pretty good before all this. Oh. Barry sent her home . . . Naughty Barry. And we probably ought to do an ordinary blood sugar as well.'

'It's off,' said Wullie.

'Dull, isn't it, but it's what we usually do. Where is she?'

They went down the dimly lit ward to the bed right next to the nursing station which was normally reserved for critically ill patients. Mrs Irvine, waxy pale under a dimmed Anglepoise, lay inert and, at first glance, scarcely breathing. Mhairi felt her pulse and lifted a fold of her skin. 'Hello, Mrs Irvine.'

'Unresponsive since two o'clock,' said the third-year nurse in charge.

'Hmm,' said Mhairi as the skin folded slowly settled. 'Dry as a bone. But you've still got to be very careful. Any localising neurological signs, Wullie?'

'She looked a bit like getting a right hemi just before she went off.'

'They sometimes get that and then get better when you sort them out.'

'I hope so,' said Wullie. Campbell thought of the daughter.

They looked at the pulse and blood pressure readings from the last eight hours. Mrs Irvine's respiration returned to normal, then she sighed heavily a few times and it faded again: a clinical sign first described by Drs Cheyne and Stokes, and not an encouraging one. Wullie picked up the drug chart and the fluid balance chart and they went back to the doctor's room.

'Sometimes there's a cause, like a bronchopneumonia.'

'Her chest sounds fine, and the X-ray's clear.'

'Or a UTI.'

'A specimen's gone off.'

'And sometimes it just happens ... Let's say five of soluble now and five in an hour and check her blood sugar again ...', Mhairi glanced at her watch, '... around half past five, and it might be right down, so just take it from there. And for fluids, just half a litre an hour, and keep a really close eye on her potassium. She might need some and she might even need a lot. But an ampoule in the first bottle won't do her any harm. And isotonic fluids. Ringer lactate would do. And an awful lot of them still die ... Sorry.'

Wullie did the necessary on the drug and fluid balance charts. Mhairi got up. Campbell escorted her to the door and thanked her. 'No problem' she said. 'A bit more interesting than his lordship's bottom. Let me know how she gets on, David.'

'I will. Thanks.'

Campbell went back down the ward to the nursing station thinking about how the case had come to be so mismanaged. If Mrs Irvine had produced a specimen of urine on her first visit to Casualty Barry would have had all this in hand by the middle of the afternoon. If Dennis had not lied about an admission specimen of urine he couldn't be bothered to check up on they would probably have been on to it at around eight o'clock. If the patient had had an ordinary diabetic coma they would have probably picked it up in Casualty just on the smell of her breath. But she had the difficult one and had been unlucky, and it was now almost four in the morning and the odds on winning had lengthened considerably.

Wullie was explaining new developments in the case to the girl in charge, who was sufficiently junior for Campbell to worry how she might relate events in the morning handover. ('The doctors thought she might be diabetic so they did a lumbar puncture and it turned out she was.') Mrs Irvine's pulse had gone up a bit, her blood pressure down since the last set of observations. She lay in her pool of yellowish light, serenely ill, perhaps already moribund.

Houseman and registrar went on round the darkened ward, stopping beside the old lady with pyelonephritis or cholecystitis, whose temperature had come down, and at the sideroom where the lady with the bad stroke was still dying, but more quietly now, with a couple of relatives dozing in chairs at her bedside.

'Dr Kirkton didn't waste any time getting here,' said Wullie as they left the ward.

'Pure luck. She'd been called in for something else. Ran into her on my way down. Quite helpful, really. How do you know her, Wullie.'

'Sat next to her at a unit night out in my surgical job.'

'Was she at the Southern last year?'

'No. Her husband was registrar there, in the GI unit. She was just at the dinner, same as my wife. Nice lass.'

Mhairi's husband, an ambitious but not over-intelligent surgeon, was an Edinburgh graduate in Campbell's year. No one had ever thought of him as nice. Perhaps Mhairi, in all respects a clever and evidently sensible girl, had taken him on as a sort of challenge, like the management of a troublesome case of hyperosmolar aketonic diabetic coma.

'How's downstairs?'

'Your bleeding drunk's stabilized now. Nothing coming up his tube. On his fourth unit and still needing his chlorpromazine. It's people like him that really put you off your pint. And the old chap, MacAffleck, with the breathlessness . . . he was just about cured when we got here.'

'Yes. Sorry about that, but he's on his own at home.'

'Oh, it's fine by me. But you know how it is when they're sitting there looking great in the morning, and everyone thinks you're daft for bringing them in.'

Again Sinclair's remarks over lunch the previous day on the subject of 'social admissions cluttering up neurology teaching beds' sprang to mind. 'Yes . . . well, we can try and sort him out with a home help and maybe a district nurse on Monday.'

'Fine. I'll see to it.'

They went quickly round the male ward then Campbell left Wullie at the residency and climbed once more to the bedroom under the eaves, where he kicked off his shoes and lay on the bed reading his paperback because sleep seemed far off and the old lady from East Saltoun would need to be reviewed with her latest lab results in not much more than an hour.

When the results came through they were quite cheering. The blood sugar, formerly astronomical, had fallen on to the merely grossly elevated and the potassium, if not exactly normal, was at least easily compatible with life. There was good news too from the nurse who had been specialling Mrs Irvine: her patient had regained consciousness shortly after five and asked for a wee cup of tea if it wouldn't be a bother to anybody.

Her pulse and blood pressure had both drifted unsteadily back towards normal over the last two hours. When Campbell asked her how she was feeling she murmured drowsily that she was tired but her headache was better, and asked him what time it was and whether her daughter knew she was in hospital again. When he had answered her she squeezed his hand and closed her eyes again. The power in her right hand now seemed normal.

They wrote her up for a little more insulin and the same fluids as before then retired to the doctors' room for more tea and toast. As Wullie was catching up with progress notes Campbell was called once more to Casualty, where another coronary required to be despatched to Intensive Care. When he got back to the female ward around daybreak Mrs Irvine was sitting up, fully conscious and apologizing for all the trouble she had caused, and the lady in the sideroom had died.

'It's actually turned out much *better* than Le Petit Perdreau's. Really, David.' Andrea was sitting on the desk in Wullie's office on the male ward. Andrea was wearing a stunning ensemble that was just right for the subtly informal ambience of Saturday morning in hospital: broadstriped primrose and white cotton dungarees with a chunky saffron silk blouse and white cravat picking up themes from a generously cut and essentially functional hospital white coat. 'Or maybe I just think that because Alistair actually caught our salmon himself. But really super. If you're going to be scientific about it I suppose it's really all in the bouillon, and being terribly laid-back about just letting it sit. I mean, if you boil it, you might as well just open a tin.'

'I quite like it out of a tin.' said Wullie. 'Especially for sandwiches.'

'Oh, for sandwiches, definitely. But for half a dozen lawyers and their wives, Wullie . . .'

'Right enough, Andrea.' Wullie had been up all night. Campbell, who had had about an hour's sleep, wearily admired his forbearance and once more wondered if his slightly rural style was actually a complex jest at the expense of selected colleagues. 'You sometimes get these wee bones in it,' Wullie added pensively. 'And I suppose a lot of them have false teeth.'

Andrea looked puzzled and fell silent. Wullie continued to file his lab results. 'Mrs Irvine's last sugar was only a hundred and fifty, Dave. Coming down nicely . . . And she was asking for her breakfast. Looks like she's going to make it.'

'Morning, folks . . . Been putting the diabetologists out of business then, Dave?' Barry, with a grand gesture from the door, ushered in a stocky figure in a white coat. 'I think you've all met Professor Sinclair . . . Yes . . . Jenny? Perhaps not. Jenny is one of our keenest students, Hamish. Jenny, this is Professor Sinclair. And of course Wullie . . . Hamish, Dr MacFadden is the houseman down here.'

Wullie smiled up from his filing. Sinclair scowled down, glanced round with some irritation at Barry and then addressed Campbell. 'Well, lad?'

'Sir?'

'You were waiting medical registrar, weren't you?'

Campbell nodded.

'Take me round, lad. Take me round. We haven't got all day.'

Sinclair had already turned towards the door again. A loose procession formed up behind him, with Andrea and Barry jostling for proximity to their new chief, Campbell and Wullie content to follow and Jenny, still bemused and vaguely excited by the rituals of acute medicine, smiling along behind.

'New cases only,' Sinclair grunted over his shoulder. 'Where are they, Campbell?' By the time the little group was approaching the bed of the man who might be interesting to investigate for polydipsia, the staff nurse in charge had joined them. 'Well? Who's this?'

Barry coughed. 'A very interesting case, Hamish. And I

know Jenny here would be only too happy to present the facts for you.'

From a quick glance round it did not appear to Campbell that Jenny would be in the least happy to present the facts, or that Sinclair would be willing to listen. He was glaring at Barry rather as he had glared at the waitress who had brought him a gin and tonic with insufficient ice. 'Campbell?'

'Ronald Docherty . . . Twenty-nine . . .'

'I don't want his bloody biography, lad. Just tell me what's wrong with him.'

'History suggestive of polydipsia. Nothing to confirm it over twenty hours' observation. Investigations normal so far.'

'Home today. No follow up. What next?'

It could not be said that Sinclair's unusual bedside manner had upset the patient, who appeared unaware even that the brief discussion had concerned him and who would in any case be delighted at its outcome. The nurse approvingly jotted something in pencil on the corner of her apron. Jenny still seemed relieved at not being asked to perform. If anyone had suffered it was Barry, the clinical polymath and impresario, whose smile had faded badly. They moved on.

When they stopped opposite the man who had come in almost cured of cardiac failure, Sinclair did not even speak. Campbell, who felt he was getting the hang of things, said, 'LVF. Good response to therapy,' he grunted as they got under way. The staff nurse looked surprised and Wullie opened his mouth to speak. Sinclair glared at him. 'No, laddie. He's pink and he's breathing and I take it he's got a home to go to. Out today. Next?'

The alcoholic with the upper GI bleed did not interest Sinclair. He listened and scowled, and said, 'Sort him out and get him out, Campbell. Just don't take all week. Next?'

'That's it for downstairs, um, Hamish.'

66

'Where's the neurology, lad?'

'One or two patients upstairs . . . sir.'

They strode at speed out of the ward, with Barry nodding and smiling at Jenny as though to indicate that brilliance in clinical medicine might show itself in many ways other than his own, then followed Sinclair upstairs.

'Apart from the pain, then . . . what else?'

'The pain was bad enough, Dr . . . Professor . . .'

'But there must have been other things. Numbness? Pins and needles? Hot patches on your legs?'

'Well, funnily enough . . . I thought it was a bit of sciatica . . .'

'Never mind what you thought. What did you feel?'

'A numb patch . . .'

'Where?'

'My left leg . . . at the back . . .'

'All the time coming or going?'

'Coming and going.'

'If you'd been sitting down for a while?'

Mrs Vaughan looked surprised. 'Yes . . .' she said. 'Come to think of it. If I'd been sitting down.'

'And warm patches? Other leg?'

'Yes,' said Mrs Vaughan, even more surprised.

'And what would happen . . .' Sinclair sat heavily on Mrs Vaughan's bed. She moved, wincing. 'What would happen . . . say if you had to jump down two or three feet and land on your heels?'

Mrs Vaughan winced again, evidently just at the thought.

'So where would that hurt you?'

'Well, in my back?'

'Down your legs? Or funny feeling with the jolt?'

'Yes . . . Now you mention it . . . Tingling . . .'

'And if you coughed, or sneezed?'

Mrs Vaughan made a face.

'Do it. Cough.'

She gave forth a genteel little bleat.

'No, woman.' Sinclair was impatient, even annoyed. 'A big loud cough that'll hurt.'

Mrs Vaughan coughed as instructed, and gasped as though stabbed.

'Good,' said Sinclair. 'Now where did that hurt?'

'Sort of down here . . .' She gestured with her left hand under her breast. Sinclair stood abruptly and rounded on his junior staff in general, and Campbell in particular. 'What's she got, doctor? I'll tell you what she's got. She's got spinal cord compression. She's within millimetres of paraplegia. She's got something on a mid-thoracic right dorsal root squashing the hell out of her spinal cord. With an eighteen-month story the chances are it's benign, it's operable, but it needs doing right away.' He raised his voice further. 'And what the hell have you done about it? You've been about as much use to her as a convention of bloody chiropractors. *And* she'll have signs. Watch me.'

He tore the bedclothes back, baring her legs and much else, and grasped both thighs firmly half way up with his thumbs inward. Mrs Vaughan moved uncomfortably. 'No push up . . . Lift up your knees . . . That's it.' He turned to Campbell and spat. 'Wasting on the right . . . Come back and try that when we've finished.'

Mrs Vaughan had begun to move slowly and painfully to adjust her nightie. Sinclair threw the bedclothes back before she had achieved much. 'Little tumour pressing on your spinal cord. Needs an X-ray on Monday and an operation, probably on Tuesday. You'll do well. Got it just in time.' As he turned to go she broke down in painful, stifled sobs, and a staff nurse, glaring over her shoulder at the retreating neurologist, strove to comfort her.

The Japanese lady was dismissed summarily in very loud English. The old woman with either cholecystitis or pye-lonephritis was now cured of whichever of the two it had been. Sinclair was not interested in details. 'I warned you about social admissions, Campbell. No point in sneaking them in as if I won't notice, because I will. You've done nothing for that woman that the GP couldn't have done at home with a handful of ampicillin and don't try and tell me different.'

'Whit's he sayin', son?' said the patient, clutching Campbell's arm. Campbell nodded and smiled and patted her hand. Sinclair had moved on already. 'Out today. No excuses,' he ordered the staff nurse. 'Who's next?'

The lady with the left-sided stroke was pulled around a bit but not addressed directly. On the move again, Sinclair said, 'I don't want them, you know . . . That's not neurology . . . And if I take them, what the hell are the geriatricians going to be left to do? Get them in to see her, Campbell, and get her out. Monday at the latest.'

Miss Prosser at least had the benefit of an audience. Sinclair sat on her bed for all of a minute, confirming the history and the diagnoses with remarkable directness. 'Multiple sclerosis, that's what you've got. No cure, of course. And yours is pretty rapid . . . Paralysis, I'm afraid. Incontinence, probably, but you're not very likely to go permanently blind, which is something. And you're not pregnant, or engaged, or anything like that, are you? Good, because there's no point. Keep in touch . . . you'll be sent an outpatient appointment. Six months.'

Mrs Irvine, whose tricky and unusual diabetes had taken half the night to sort out, was of no neurological interest. 'There's a diabetic unit, isn't there? Ring them up, Campbell. They're experts and you're not . . . and we don't want her blocking a neurology bed.' As they moved on Barry looked momentarily thoughtful.

'Is that it, Campbell?' Sinclair asked, finding himself once more at the door of the female ward. 'Is that them all?' Campbell nodded. 'Who was the fair chap with the teeth?'

'Sir?'

'Tall chap, blond, didn't say anything. Just grinned.'

'Dennis Nelson, sir. Houseman on the female ward.'

Sinclair considered that information. 'He's trouble. Probably mad.'

'Sir.'

Sinclair nodded a dismissal. Campbell thanked his chief, who declined an invitation to stay for coffee and left, walking faster than ever. '*Brilliant*,' said Barry, before he was out of earshot. 'She just *has* to have a dorsal root Schwannoma. Classical clinical neurology. I think we're all going to learn a lot from our Hamish.'

While the rest were having coffee Campbell bleeped Mhairi to pass on the specialist referral ordered by Sinclair. 'No problem,' she said. 'As it happens we've got a bed. Just send her over. Glad she's doing well.'

'Thanks for your help last night. And thanks for taking her.'

There was a pause, then Mhairi said, 'How's your new professor?'

Campbell thought about that. 'It's probably too early to say.'

'They've just been talking about him over coffee along here. The chief, Tom Leslie, knows him from way back. Says he's clever but mad. And not just eccentric, really mad. Stark raving bonkers, as he puts it, in his old-fashioned way. Made him sound quite interesting.'

'Could be . . . Thanks, Mhairi.'

'See you, David.'

2

'Hello, David. May I join you.'

Campbell nodded. Mhairi unloaded her tray, and while she was taking it off to the stack in the corner he poured a glass of water for her.

'Thanks, David.' She sat down and slid her white coat from her shoulders to the back of her chair. 'How are you? Oh. Did you get my summary about the old woman with aketotic diabetes?'

Campbell hesitated. Mhairi smiled. 'Everything takes so long . . . Discharge summaries down in Sleepy Hollow get typed about eight weeks after the patients go home, so you probably got it, but just didn't recognize her because it was so long ago.'

'Sorry.'

'I'm sure I sent you one. Anyway, she did fine . . . Nice, bright old woman once her sugar came down. Didn't need insulin. Went home on diet and the pills, and her daughter wrote us a very polite thank-you letter.'

Though it had been perhaps two months since the incident, mention of the daughter brought it back in disturbing detail. 'Good,' said Campbell. 'When I saw her she was talking about questions in the House.'

'She was fine. Chocolates for the nurses – the lot. How's Andrea?'

'You know she's . . .'

'Yes. That's what I meant.'

'Well . . . better, I suppose. Or maybe just talking about it less. Still spends half the morning in sister's room sipping diet soda water . . . and quite a lot of the afternoon buying little things for the nursery, we think.'

Mhairi smiled. 'I had lunch with her the other day. Just in here. Quite amusing. "Honestly Mhairi . . ."' Andrea's accent and wide-eyed emphasis were quite nicely done. '"Honestly, Mhairi, if you think being a woman in medicine's bad, try being a *pregnant* women in medicine . . .". But she was quite enthusiastic about the mad chap.'

'Sinclair?'

'"*Hamish.*"'

'Same chap . . . They seem to get on.'

'And you?'

'Hmm. Perhaps I'm not enthusiastic enough.'

'But you're supposed to be his lecturer.'

'Not quite. His locum lecturer.'

'Is there a proper lecturer job coming up?'

'No. Not unless Bobby Watson decides to stay on in the States. So back on the dole in November, probably.'

Mhairi looked genuinely concerned. 'Really, David? But something's bound to turn up.'

'It's too far away to worry about. How's Richard?'

She paused, then said, 'Surgery's much worse than medicine . . . Far fewer jobs and fiercer competition. And they've all been at each other's throats at least since they were housemen.'

'How's he liking the Southern?'

'Well . . .' She glanced across the dining room and brightened. 'Look. A friend of yours. The jolly green giant.'

Hadden, a large man carrying a large lunch, had seen them and was advancing from the cash register. 'The what?'

'The jolly green giant. Because that's what he looked like in theatre kit. You know him, don't you?'

Campbell nodded. Hadden, now a lecturer and senior registrar in orthopaedics, had worked in the general surgical unit where Campbell had been a houseman. They had worked together again in Casualty, and still kept in touch, sporadically and usually over a drink.

'God save us from silly buggers who think they can fly,' said Hadden, putting down his soup and roll, spaghetti bolognaise with peas, and apple pie. 'Been in theatre since five o'clock this morning with a lad on LSD who launched himself from George IV Bridge down the side of Bauermeister's bookshop. You can imagine the flight plan. Passing general fiction, poetry, academic and technical, bargain basement, so far so good, then . . . splat! Cobblestones. So seven hours jobbing carpentry, nailing, wiring, pinning, nipping and tucking. And he wasn't very big to start with . . . Sorry, Mhairi . . . Save your gentle diabetic presence. It's been one of those mornings. How are you, lad? And of course every time something like that happens and clogs up theatre time you get a queue of old ladies with broken hips forming and stretching twice round the female ward. How are things?'

'Dull,' said Campbell. Mhairi smiled.

Hadden propped his tray against a table leg, put a lot of pepper on his soup, tasted it, then added salt. Conversation became general. Hadden and Mhairi seemed to know each other quite well, but only after a few minutes did Campbell realize why: Mhairi too had worked in Ravelston Orr's unit, as a house surgeon shortly after Campbell had gone off on prolonged sick leave, at a time when Hadden had still been the senior house officer there.

'Yes,' said Hadden. 'Where are they now? Gavin eventually got a consultant job, after twenty-one or thereabouts interviews, believed to be a Scottish if not a UK record. And he's still a miserable sod. And Ravelston Orr's only got a year to go, so he's beginning to write those little whither now something-or-other journal articles normally associated with early dementia. And his cutting, when he does it, takes longer than ever.'

'I rather liked him,' said Mhairi. 'Terribly nineteen thirtyish about lady doctors. "My dear, sometime soon we shall do a *little* hernia together. If you're sure you'd like to."'

Campbell laughed, then remembered his old chief's rather more robust approach with male house officers. On one occasion Ravelston Orr had thrown him out of theatre for not knowing enough about some obscure arteries in the thigh. On another he had sacked Campbell and his fellow houseman, though as it turned out only for about ten minutes. Men in medicine had problems too.

Campbell had slowed down over his main course as if to allow Mhairi to catch up. Hadden, despite doing much of the talking, had overtaken both. 'That new chap in neurology . . .' He set aside a well-cleaned spaghetti plate and reached for his apple pie. 'How's he shaping up?'

Over the last two months there had been many similar enquiries. 'Interesting,' said Campbell, as usual. Hadden snorted. Mhairi looked from one to the other as though anticipating lively indiscretion.

'When I was over at the Southern doing my six months compulsory brain surgery for bone setters . . .' Hadden ran a finger over his scalp and made a buzzing noise to indicate sawing open a skull, '. . . he came up from London to talk. Obviously a protégé of Marcus Mackail, his blue-eyed boy, in fact. Old Marcus got up and introduced him. Local lad, gone to the smoke and made good. Man to watch. And so many bloody degrees. MD, FRCS, PhD and MRCP in four consecutive years . . . a clear case of multiple diplomatosis. And a very odd lecture. The usual cruelty to animals, minimal clinical applicability, how to get on in medicine stuff, but all Sinclair this and Sinclair that. The Sinclair probe. The Sinclair co-ordinates. At the end of it I half expected old Marcus, instead of giving the usual vote of thanks, to raise his arm and shout Heil Sinclair. The rest received the lecture, as they say, with polite interest. I thought he was a psychopath and probably manic to boot.

So a natural for a much-sought-after Edinburgh chair, I suppose. We wish him well in his new appointment.'

Mhairi was gratified. Campbell asked about the odd mixture of degrees, the higher qualifications in both medicine and surgery. 'It's not unknown. There are a couple of others about. It usually happens to mad, bright people who can't make up their minds. From the sound of things, he was one of Mackail's clever boys, going places in neurosurgery, went to London as an SR and got sidetracked into neurophysiology, then returned gradually to a semblance of reality via academic clinical neurology, rising all the way. Here today. Tomorrow the world. What research is he doing?'

'He's still mainly setting things up. A new building's on its way, but he's got some baboons somewhere to be going on with.'

'What's he doing to them?'

'Something on Parkinson's disease.'

'If his talk was about anything, it was about that. How to give your baboon Parkinson's disease. Yesss . . . Probably one of the three crucial issues facing medicine today.'

Campbell thought of the lunch out in East Lothian, and the half million pound grant that had resulted. 'He seems to be able to raise money.'

'Never a problem for your really intelligent psychopath. Just a question of choosing. Fringe banking, asset stripping, pyramid selling or medical research. The money's there, and the punters can't wait to part with it. And think of all those poor little rich people who die of Parkinson's.' Hadden finished his apple pie with a few determined scoops. 'Ah, well. Back to the production line. Half a dozen hips and is there honey still for tea? I'm thinking of training some baboons. Perhaps separate teams for left and right hips, so as not to confuse them. Cheers, folks.'

With Hadden gone, lunch went quiet. When they had finished Mhairi said 'Are you having coffee, David?' and they walked through the dining room towards the coffee lounge. They had just joined the queue when Mhairi's bleep went off. She made a face. 'I'd better skip coffee . . . I'm waiting med. reg. today, so I suppose I was lucky to get lunch. See you around, David.'

Campbell had coffee alone, taking it outside to a memorial bench overlooking a dank and trodden lawn. He sat in cool spring sunshine for five minutes, then went back through the stale and smoky lounge and upstairs to look in on the wards before the afternoon outpatient clinic.

'Just like you say in your notes, Dave. He's got a few signs . . . a possibly upgoing toe, and bit of fuzziness on two-point testing in his hands.'

'Did you find a spleen?'

Dennis hesitated. 'Maybe minimal enlargement. A difficult one, Dave.'

Campbell had examined the patient and suspected Dennis had not. 'Really? So what did you think was wrong with him?'

'Well, he's got pernicious anaemia, hasn't he? And you get spleen enlargement in that. I mean not enormous spleens, but some enlargement.'

Halfway through their six-month appointments the housemen had changed wards, so that Wullie now looked after the women and Dennis the men. Wullie continued to do most of the work. Dennis, after a warning or two from Barry, had improved enough to avoid dismissal but not sufficiently to inspire confidence. In Campbell's eyes he had just gained half a point for knowing about the spleen in pernicious anaemia, lost three because that wasn't what was wrong with the patient, and another six, almost certainly, for not having examined him.

'I don't think it's quite as simple as that, Dennis. He's B12 deficient, but almost certainly not from proper PA. Did you ask him about his diet?' If Dennis had read the notes carefully, he would know the man was a gross eccentric, a truly outlandish diet freak, without having to go to the trouble of asking him about it. He seemed to have done neither.

'Well . . . he's a fairly ordinary chap. Well nourished but a bit pale. Eats the usual things, so far as he told me.'

'Let's go and have a quick word with him, Dennis.'

They went into the ward, past the hostile glance of a staff nurse not quite senior enough to enforce the absent ward sister's views on 'the poor patient's quiet time' normally observed after lunch. The man in question, a maths teacher who looked like a minor disciple painted by El Greco, lay reading a magazine about something called naturopathy.

'Hello, Mr MacNaughton. I'm sorry to keep bothering you. Would you mind explaining again about your diet? It'll help us sort out your anaemia.'

The patient laid down his magazine, and started out more as one attempting to save two souls from perdition than as one co-operating in clinical history-taking. 'Quite simply, I'm a very strict vegan,' he said, 'and happy to explain it. "Thou shalt not kill." Everyone knows that, but very few of us seriously try to totally avoid the mass and cruel slaughter of of fellow creatures . . . and when you think about it, the earth can provide for us in a way that none need ever kill again.'

'And what about eggs, dairy products, that kind of thing?'

The maths teacher smiled patiently through his wispy beard, as though setting out to explain tangents yet again to a dim fourteen-year-old. 'As I told you in the clinic, doctor . . . for the animals involved, the life we give them is simply living death. Caged, cut, burned, stuffed and terrified for most of their lives, whether for milk, eggs or slaughter to be eaten it hardly matters. And all we need can be found in nature without killing or . . .'

'Well . . . almost all. And how long have you managed to live like this, Mr MacNaughton?'

'It'll be eight years, this summer solstice.'

'I see . . . As you know, you're a bit anaemic now . . . and one or two other things have been affected. You should be feeling better soon, though. Thank you, Mr MacNaughton.'

The man smiled again, showing strikingly pale gums, and went back to his magazine.

'Not a difficult dietary history to get,' said Campbell as they retreated down the ward.

Dennis was unabashed. 'That's really quite interesting, Dave. He may have a point. And that's before you start to think about carcinogens. Anyway, I'll sort him out this afternoon. Thanks.'

'Good, Dennis. I'll be down in outpatients if you're worried about anything.'

The GP's letter was unpromising. '. . . clearly senile, and suffering from both falls and confusion accordingly, but since the relatives insist on a second opinion I would be grateful . . .' Apart from the patient's name, address, age and blood pressure, that was all. Unusually for a seventy-five-year-old with a central Edinburgh address, Mrs Robson seemed never to have attended the Institute before: the case folder, unexpectedly slim and fresh, contained only the note from the GP and half a dozen blank sheets. Campbell went to the door of the consulting room, looked along the corridor for the nurse, said 'Mrs Robson, please' and returned to his desk.

There was a pause of some minutes, then an old, stooped lady came in, steered and supported at the elbow by a nurse who would clearly rather have been dealing with someone a little more agile on their feet. 'There you are, dear . . . Sorry, doctor . . . Yes . . . Just sit down there. Mrs . . . Mrs Robertson. Not be a minute, Dr Campbell.' They inched across the room. Campbell recalled that he had once, in Casualty, heard two ambulancemen referring to an elderly patient they had just brought in as 'a right old dinnae-shove-me'.

Mrs Robson sat down on the hard and narrow chair provided and folded her hands together in her lap. She looked across at Campbell with an expression of blank gloom. 'Terrible constipation,' she said slowly, in a small high voice. The nurse shook her head and left.

'How long, Mrs Robson?'

'Months and months, son.'

'Anything else?'

'That's the main thing. Terrible constipation.' Her tone was strangely expressionless. She had moved her hands a little, and the left one, especially its thumb and forefinger, trembled briefly until held again by the right. That helped a lot.

'Mrs Robson ... are you ever troubled by shaking? Your hands, perhaps?'

'No' much, son ... It's this constipation.'

'Have you ever fallen?'

'What can you expect at my age, son? The doctor said ...'

'When you fall, do you fall forwards or backwards, or to one side?'

'Forwards, son. But I don't think it's anything to do with this constipation.'

'What about walking, Mrs Robson? Have you slowed up a bit lately? I saw you walking just now ...'

'Maybe ... Yes, now you mention it ... Yes.'

'I'm sure we can help you quite a bit, Mrs Robson.' Campbell relaxed and ran through a series of routine questions, reflecting that patients always seemed a lot nicer once you knew what was wrong with them. When he had finished taking the story he buzzed for the nurse and did a quick clinical examination that amply confirmed the diagnosis. She would do very well on the pills. Even her constipation would get better.

He was writing out the prescription when Fiona, the unit's NHS secretary, put her head round the door. 'David . . . I'm sorry. I should have given this to you earlier . . . My fault. And he really means it.'

Sensing something that the nurse and Mrs Robson might have no special need to know about, Campbell got up and went out into the corridor with Fiona. 'Sorry, David, but it really is the edict of the week. You were all supposed to get one on Monday, but I missed you at coffee. That's it.'

Fiona handed Campbell a brief memo on Department of Clinical Neurology notepaper, from Sinclair and addressed to the unit's junior medical staff. 'It has come to my notice that new patients with Parkinson's disease are being seen at outpatients and treated without being properly assessed. All such patients will now be admitted for full evaluation before starting on standard therapy.

Campbell shrugged. Fiona touched his arm and said, 'I'm really sorry, David. But I was worried you might have got into trouble over Mrs Robson. I . . . happened to see her coming in.'

'Hm. Yes. Good. And you've got the diagnosis . . . More than the GP did.'

'I know. I read his letter.'

Campbell went back into the consulting room and sat down beside his patient. 'Mrs Robson . . . How would you feel about coming into the ward for a few days? It would give us a chance to get this constipation of yours sorted out . . . and we could maybe get you walking a bit better.'

The old lady sat gloomily for a moment then said, 'Maybe, son. But I'd really have to talk to my daughter.'

'That's fine. Would it help if I phoned her?'

It would. Mrs Robson commenced a slow and thorough search of her handbag, eventually locating a piece of grubby card with some telephone numbers on it. Campbell jotted down the one for 'Jean's work', and said he would explain it all to the daughter and try to fix up an admission to the ward for the following day. The old lady shuffled out, leaning once more against the nurse.

Campbell scribbled briefly in the notes, dictated a letter to the GP and then went along to the reception desk to use Fiona's telephone, there being none in the sort of consulting room allotted to locum lecturers. It transpired that there were several Jeans at the telephone number, that of a largish shop, but one was soon found whose mother was Mrs Robson.

'She's not senile, doctor. She does the wee crossword in the paper . . . and all she talks about is her bowels but it's her walking we're worried about. And our own doctor at home. I'm thinking of reporting him. Says it's her age. My granny lived to be twenty years older than my mum is now, and she could still walk and had twice the sense of that man that's calling my mum senile.'

'I'm sorry, Mrs . . . Mrs . . .'

'Lambie.'

'Mrs Lambie, I think your mother can be helped. We want to bring her into hospital. Tomorrow if that would be all right. I think we can probably do quite a lot for her. We can talk about the details when you're in seeing her. Ward six . . . The Institute.'

'And who are you?'

'I'm Dr Campbell. But her consultant will be Professor Sinclair.'

'Oh? A professor indeed. That'll teach him. Thank you, Dr Campbell. Thank you very much.'

There were four more new patients and twelve follow-ups. At ten to five Campbell, since he was second on call overnight, went over to the wards again to catch up with the problems. In the doctors' room on the male ward Barry was taking off his white coat. 'Nothing too difficult, Dave. All quiet on the front, the back and round the sides. No. I tell a lie. One chap's gone off a bit. Guy in his late forties, anaemia, got a bit of angina after a sternal marrow, then had a reaction to his GTN.'

Campbell thought about that. Though Barry made it sound as if it happened all the time, it was rather an odd story. 'I don't think there's anything to worry about. Chap with a haemoglobin of about seven. In for transfusion and investigation. At his age with an anaemia like that it's surprising he didn't have angina already, but after his sternal marrow he had a bit of chest pain and breathlessness.'

Angina was chest pain, and a sternal marrow involved having someone stick a thickish needle in your breastbone. 'It's not just pain from the biopsy needle, is it?'

Barry shook his head.

'ECG changes?'

'Dennis is just doing one now. At least I told him to . . . Anyway, we gave him some GTN and it didn't suit him. Went quite pale and flat, the way people sometimes do with it, especially if they've never had it before.'

'Mr MacNaughton?'

'Who?'

'This patient . . . Teacher with a beard?'

'Could be . . . You're right, Dave. We should go and take a look. You just never know with Dennis. Still our problem boy, after all the time I've spent on him. And I mean to say, this chap needs an ECG.'

Halfway down the ward on the left there were screens round a bed. Barry looked inside and turned back towards Campbell, nodding vigorously and smiling. They joined Dennis and the patient behind the screens. Dennis was indeed doing an electrocardiograph, using the ward's own portable machine, but at first glance it appeared to Campbell he was doing it on a corpse.

Mr MacNaughton lay back with his mouth open and his eyes half shut. Having been pale at lunchtime, he was now simply white. For several seconds he appeared to be making no attempt to breathe, then a tiny surge in his chest and neck indicated that he was still alive. Dennis looked up from the controls of his machine. He was grinning.

Like Campbell, Barry had realized that something was far wrong. He reached for Mr MacNaughton's wrist with one hand and the emerging ECG with the other. 'Probably an MI, Dave . . . I mean, with a haemoglobin like that, he wouldn't have to have much in the way of coronary artery disease to go straight from angina to a proper coronary . . . Let's see . . . Rate around a hundred and ten . . . Bit of ischaemia . . .'

The site of the sternal marrow biopsy, in the middle of the man's chest, was marked by an irregular stain of a magenta antiseptic and two crossed strips of white elastoplast. Campbell leaned over. 'Mr MacNaughton? Mr MacNaughton?' The half-closed eyelids fluttered and the lips, clumsy and the colour of fresh putty, moved only momentarily and soundlessly.

'Let's get a drip up, Dave, and move him down to ICU.'

'Coronary?'

'Could be . . . Yes. Probably. Not a neurological problem, anyway. Is there a staff nurse around?'

Campbell turned to go and get one and organize things for an emergency IV infusion and a transfer to ICU. He found himself face to face with Professor Sinclair. 'Campbell,' he barked. 'Where have you been all afternoon? I'm off to Zürich and . . .' He paused and looked over Campbell's shoulder. 'What the hell's going on here? Swift? What the bloody hell are you all up to? Let me see . . .'

Sinclair pushed Campbell aside and leapt to the head of the bed. He seized Mr MacNaughton's left earlobe and tweaked it very firmly. There was hardly any response. He pulled a stethoscope from the pocket of Campbell's white coat, listened briefly to the man's heart then rolled him violently to the right. 'Hold him, damn you, laddie,' he growled at Dennis.

There evolved, in the limited space behind the pink flowery screens, a gauche pastiche of one of the more necrophiliac tableaux of Mediterranean religious art. Like the dead Christ, the maths teacher – naked to the waist, gaunt, bearded and melodramatically colourless – was stretched immobile between supporting figures, arms wide and head drooping, for timeless seconds while Sinclair glowered angrily around.

'Nurse!' he bellowed. 'Nurse!' A staff nurse appeared. 'Get me the IV trolley and the biggest cannula you've got.' The girl rushed off and he stooped over the pale figure on the bed again, listening briefly to the lung bases, then percussing, loudly and expertly, with the middle finger of his right hand hammering against the knuckles of his outstretched left, systematically over the back of the man's chest.

'I bloody thought so,' he said, straightening up. The IV trolley, propelled by the small but highly efficient staff nurse, rattled up and Sinclair seized from it a large bore cannula. He snapped off its sterile packaging, plugged to it a twenty-ml syringe and then turned towards the dying man on the bed. 'Hold against me, laddie . . . Now!'

He stabbed the cannula upwards into the chest about six inches below the right armpit and withdrew the plunger. Dark blood filled the syringe. 'There you are. See? Chest full of blood . . . Campbell, ring thoracic theatre and tell them to set up an emergency thoracotomy. Ten minutes. And get their registrar down here at the double. Swift, get a line up and running as fast as it'll go . . . Plasma, anything . . . And you, laddie . . .' He glared at Dennis. 'Just get out of the way.'

Campbell tried to contact the duty cardiothoracic registrar first, since he did not feel that the unsupported request of a junior neurologist would impress the theatre staff. The registrar answered his bleep straight away.

'Dr Campbell, clinical neurology, here. Got a man of forty-one with a chest full of blood after a sternal marrow that . . . went wrong.'

'Fine,' said the probably Antipodean surgeon. 'Start draining it, get some blood into him and send him up. I'll tell theatre. Where is he?'

'Ward six. Mr MacNaughton. Thanks very much.'

'Don't mention it. Cheers, mate.'

Campbell, who had frequently had far more trouble getting surgical help for things as straightforward as an acute appendix, was taken aback. He put the phone down and returned to the screened bed. In the few minutes he had been gone some useful things had happened. Barry had a bottle of plasma expander streaming into a vein in Mr MacNaughton's left arm. Sinclair had improvised a chest drain by joining a length of IV line to his cannula and running it to a catheter bag on the floor, which now contained between one and two litres of blood. Dennis had gone away.

The dying Christ had begun to pick up a bit. He was still spectrally pale, but shifting a lot more air, breathing regularly if not deeply and beginning to look now as if he might probably go on doing so. The foot of the bed had been raised in a traditional gesture towards improved cerebral circulation, and a nurse was filling in readings on a pulse and BP chart. Order had been restored.

'They want him straight across to theatre . . . With some blood if possible.'

'That's organized,' said Barry. 'What's his pulse doing, love?'

'Settling,' said the nurse.

'Grand.'

'Keep an eye on this drain, Campbell,' said Sinclair, perhaps irritated by idle chatter. '. . . and don't waste time if theatre's ready. I've got a plane to catch in half an hour. See you on Friday.'

Sinclair swept out as suddenly as he had arrived. A few minutes later six units of universal-donor blood, reserved for the direst emergencies, came up from the transfusion service. Even though it was now well past five o'clock Barry seemed quite happy to remain in charge, pumping the first two units of blood in and rattling away the while about the hazards of routine investigations, Sinclair's dramatic contribution to the case and the renewed need to be hard, but not too hard, on Dennis, 'a bright lad whose mind isn't always one hundred per cent on his work . . . And only a few months into his medical career, of course, so lots of time there to improve . . . Fine, love . . . Now just tell us what his systolic pressure is doing . . . Wonderful. And his pulse again? Great. Super.'

The polythene catheter bag on the floor was beginning to bulge. The staff nurse, now fully entered into the spirit of the occasion, detached it, nipping the end of the tube to prevent air bubbling up into the man's chest, and fixed an empty bag in its place as if dealing with something much more humdrum. Mr MacNaughton's colouring slowly returned to its pallid normal.

By the time the fourth unit of blood was going in his readings were steady and he was judged fit for transfer to the cardiothoracic unit for definitive surgical management. Barry glanced at his watch and suggested that Campbell, since he was on call overnight, might want to accompany him. Porters and a trolley were summoned, the various tubes and containers arranged for the journey and the patient, who had come into the ward a few hours before with anaemia and neurological signs for leisurely investigation, left again at the brisk pace of a surgical emergency still not far from death. Campbell and the staff nurse, one on each side of the trolley, walked and trotted respectively up the long winding corridor towards the lift to the cardiothoracic unit.

The thoracic registrar, waiting in the anaesthetic area outside the operating theatre, took him over without ceremony, running through the story, checking the physical signs and readings, and dismissing his escort so casually ('Thanks, mate. We'll let you know.') before going off to scrub that on the way downstairs it occurred to Campbell that perhaps things like this happened all the time in hospital circles in Australia.

Why had it happened that afternoon in a respectable Edinburgh teaching hospital? Of course if the man were now to die, a lot of people would devote a lot of effort to finding out. If, as seemed more likely, he lived, the law would keep its distance and a traditional cloak of professional discretion would protect the public from disquieting and discreditable gossip. Campbell, perhaps because he had been qualified only a few years, wondered about the propriety of that, and was also sufficiently close to the whole ghastly business to worry about it in some detail.

A houseman had taken it upon himself to carry out an investigation not directly requested by his immediate superior. That investigation, safe in experienced hands, involved boring through the outer layer of bone and sucking marrow from the cavity beneath. Experienced people who did not strike marrow first time got out quickly and tried elsewhere. Inexperienced and unsupervised people might conceivably go deeper instead, get through the inner layer of bone and find themselves rummaging around with a large needle in the huge blood vessels entering and leaving the heart, with the disastrous effects just demonstrated.

Housemen had to learn investigative procedures, but men did not have to die for the cause. If Dennis had done a couple of marrows under supervision and a couple more on his own no one would have objected to his doing this

87

one, though ordinary caution would have led him to check with someone that a marrow needed to be done. Had Barry, in Campbell's absence, told Dennis to get on with it himself checking on his experience and what was already known about the cause of Mr MacNaughton's anaemia?

The fact was that no marrow biopsy had been necessary. The patient, with his curiously fanatical respect for animal life, had for years denied himself the benefits of vitamin B12. He had a dietary anaemia, though an unusual one, with a remarkably clear dietary history. He had needed transfusion – electively, not in the mad scramble just witnessed – and a series of painless pink injections that would boost his B12 levels yet still, since B12 nowadays was made in nice clean laboratories rather than squeezed as previously from the livers of our dumb friends, respect his dietary principles.

Instead Dennis, perhaps simply as part of an effort to pull his socks up and generally try harder, had nearly killed him. Barry, who at least knew when someone was ill, had come near to letting him die by default, by not going to see him earlier. Sinclair, in a matter of five minutes or so en route to the airport, had saved him by a formidable diagnostic coup and a piece of near-psychopathic direct action that only a former surgeon might attempt. For perhaps the twentieth time, Campbell revised his views on his new head of department.

The staff nurse had been thinking about things too. 'Seems quite a clever chap, the new professor.' Campbell nodded. She turned towards him as they walked. 'But that houseman of yours . . .'

'Dennis?'

'He needs locking up.'

'We've bleeped Wullie but it might be better if you saw them.'

'Who?'

'The MacNaughton relatives. I didn't say too much. They're down by his bed.'

'Thanks.'

The third-year student nurse who had been left in charge during the staff nurse's absence pointed down the ward to where a middle-aged woman and three teenagers stood silently by an empty bed.

'What have you told them?'

'That he's been moved temporarily to another ward. Is that all right?'

'As far as it goes. Thanks. Is there somewhere I can take them?'

'You could use sister's room.'

Mrs MacNaughton was plump and prematurely grey and wore a thick, grubby surgical collar which, with her lean, rather hooked nose, made her look like a budgie. Her children, boys of around thirteen and seventeen and a girl somewhere in between, were lean and dark in their father's image. 'Where is he? Where have you taken him?' she asked while Campbell was still ten or twelve feet away.

'Mrs MacNaughton?'

'Yes,' she said with visible impatience.

'Your husband is up in one of the surgical units. I was with him just a few minutes ago. He's getting a bit better.'

'From what? Better from what? Something's happened . . .'

The children, previously bored rather than anxious, paid more attention. The girl narrowed her eyes.

'He's getting better,' said Campbell firmly. 'Would you like to come this way?'

He led them to sister's room and they sat down, the two boys sharing a chair as though quite accustomed to doing so. Mrs MacNaughton sat on the forward edge of the only armchair, rigid and intent. 'Just tell me what's happened to him. Is he . . .?'

Campbell waited.

'. . . dead?' The daughter gasped and sobbed.

'No. As I said, he was improving when I saw him a few minutes ago. But he had to be transferred urgently to a surgical unit because of . . . internal bleeding.'

'You know I thought so . . . I was forever telling him that vegan nonsense would get him into trouble. Thins your blood, doesn't it?'

'Well, sort of. But what happened was that . . .'

'So you bleed . . . And you need an operation . . . So he'll be all right?'

'I hope so. He was . . . quite seriously ill for a few minutes. Needed a transfusion and then an operation.'

'I hope he'll see sense about eating now. He should, shouldn't he, doctor. I keep telling him.'

Campbell nodded then said. 'Well. Sort of. He could have supplements, if he really wants to go on.'

'No. It's a warning . . . Right?' She looked round her little brood. 'Good . . . It's been a strain, you know.' She fingered the grubby surgical collar which seemed to deprive her of a neck. 'I have a touch of spondylosis myself, doctor. I'm sure it's the strain.'

Campbell nodded sympathetically. The children grew restive. It was all rather unfair. A preventable disaster, a near-death by negligence, had been blamed on its victim and now he was going to have to eat his mince like everyone else. Campbell felt that justice was not being done, yet was reluctant to complicate his next few minutes unnecessarily by answering questions that had not been asked. And how did you tell a woman that her husband had just narrowly escaped death at the hands of someone who should not even have got into medical school?

Mrs MacNaughton had risen to her feet. The children followed. She smiled as though several problems had been solved and her neck was better. 'So where do we go now? To see him. Where is he?'

It took time to open a chest full of blood and find a leak

and fix it. With luck Mr MacNaughton would be out of theatre in an hour or two. After a thoracotomy breathing was so painful that most people were flattened with opiates for anything up to thirty-six hours. He would spend a few days in a ward indistinguishable from an intensive care unit, with tubes in most places and a monitor flicking beside him suspecting his every heartbeat. His family seemed to expect he would be sitting up in bed smiling and ready for a lecture on the folly of his dietary ways.

'Well . . . he'll still be having his operation. And he was actually quite ill for a while.' This time all the eyes narrowed. 'He . . . He started to bleed while he was having an investigation for his anaemia. He'll be in ward ten . . . fairly soon.'

'I don't like the sound of this one bit, Dr . . . Dr . . .'

'Campbell. I'm sure that there'll be much more to tell you after his operation's over, Mrs MacNaughton. I could ring the ward and see when he's expected there.'

'Ward ten?'

'Yes.'

'We'll just go up.' She collected her brood with a glance. 'First we'll find out how he is . . . Then we'll try to find out how he got to be that way. Thank you, Dr Campbell.'

As they left the ward the girl clutched at her mother's hand and began to sob.

Later that evening Wullie phoned Campbell at home. 'Sorry to bother you, Dave, but I thought you'd like to know. The cardiothoracic registrar, the Australian bloke, just phoned to tell me that Mr MacNaughton's died.'

'What happened?'

'They opened him up, and found what they expected, a wee rip in one of the great vessels. The pulmonary artery, I think he said. Repaired it, drained the chest of a whole lot of blood, closed him up but had to re-open him because the bleeding wouldn't stop. Terrible clotting problems, apparently. He said he was on some funny diet that really fucks your blood up, was how he put it ... I never saw the chap myself, so I don't know.'

'He was on a funny diet.'

'Wife? Kids?'

'Yes. And three kids.'

'A sternal marrow, the Australian bloke said.'

'Yes.'

'Did he know it had gone wrong.'

'Did who know?'

'Dennis, Dave. Or whoever did it. Well, Dennis.'

Campbell recalled the circumstances of Dennis's departure. 'Well, he probably does ... Sinclair sent him away, but only after it was pretty obvious what was happening.'

'Maybe not to Dennis.'

Another of Wullie's admirable characteristics was his uncomplaining politeness towards and about a co-houseman who had caused him immense trouble. The last remark was the nearest he had come, in Campbell's experience, to a lapse from it.

'That's obviously part of the problem.'

There was a pause, then Wullie said, 'I'm surprised he did a marrow at all.'

'Why, Wullie?'

'Because he was saying the other day he'd never done one.'

'Really?'

'Or even seen one done since third year.'

'Bloody hell ... Thanks, Wullie.' Campbell put the phone down. Sinclair's language was catching.

'She's settled,' said the nurse. 'And definitely less constipated.'

'Good. Good afternoon, Mrs Robson. How are you feeling?'

'A lot better, son.' Like most people just beginning

treatment for Parkinson's disease, she looked better too. One of the more subtle effects of the condition was a gradual loss of facial expression, so that the patients looked glum or stupid or both. Often after only one or two tablets they looked brighter and more alert, and since the tablets worked only for Parkinson's disease, this was additional confirmation of the diagnosis.

'That's good. You should go on getting better for a week or two, as we get your dose of the tablets right. And you'll have to stay on them, you know. Now, can we see you walking?'

She rose slowly in her chair, pushing herself upwards and forwards. A physiotherapist working with the next patient down the ward leaned over and said, 'Better. We did all the pre-treatment assessment this morning, and she's speeded up.'

She was still very slow, but physiotherapists claimed special skills in assessing locomotor disabilities so Campbell didn't argue. Their views, and those of the occupational therapists who came along and annoyed the new Parky patients by getting them to cut up pink plastic sausages and timing them as they did so, constituted the assessment on which Professor Sinclair was so keen. They would repeat it as her dose was increased, until eventually it was decided she was free to go home and walk about on her own and tackle real sausages if she fancied them.

She shuffled a few steps, perhaps less slowly than in the clinic the previous day. 'Very good, Mrs Robson.'

'I'm sure it was just the constipation, son. Can I go home now?'

'We'd rather you gave it a few more days, Mrs Robson. To get your tablets right.'

'I'll have to speak to my daughter.'

'I expect she'll be in later on. Good afternoon, Mrs Robson.'

Wullie was smiling. 'I like the Parkies,' he said as they

93

moved on. 'They're about the only people we get in here that we can do anything for.'

The next patient was a woman with motor neurone disease still in its early stages: an excellent example of the unhelpable majority. Her illness had begun with minor weakness and clumsiness in one hand, followed by uncontrollable flickering of the little muscles at the base of the thumb. Deep in her spinal cord nerve cells were dying and would continue to do so until she was too weak to breathe or cough, at which point, anything from one to five years from now, she would develop a pneumonia that no one would treat. She was thiry-six, well informed and very frightened.

She had been admitted for tests that were partly a formality and partly a professional enthusiasm. Since he had arrived, four or five cases of motor neurone disease had been brought in for a series of lumbar punctures at three-week intervals, the resulting cerebrospinal fluid being analysed for everything in it that was measurable in the Institute's NHS laboratories. The words 'collaborative MND study' were variously muttered and barked on Sinclair's ward rounds, but Campbell had never seen any protocol for the study or any standard documentation for the individual patients concerned.

Mrs Burns lay flat on her back, as patients who had just undergone lumbar puncture were advised to. Campbell asked her how she felt. She looked up at him. 'Either you're getting better at it or I'm getting tougher. Definitely not as bad as the last time, thank you, doctor.'

'I'm sorry.'

'It's all right. Just hurry up and find a cure. And can I go home straight after breakfast this time?'

Campbell nodded.

'See you in three weeks, Dr Campbell.'

Before they had reached the next Sinclair patient a

student nurse came up, winked at Wullie and said, 'It's the police for you, Dr Campbell.'

Campbell had expected a call from the police, but had not expected it so soon. The cardiothoracic unit would have routinely informed the procurator-fiscal's office of Mr MacNaughton's death, since it had occurred as a result of an investigation that had gone wrong. Someone in that office would have started a file whose first contents would have been the substance of the phone call: where the patient had died and when; what had happened that might have contributed; under whose care the patient had been at various points. Now the police were coming round in search of first hand information.

There was a sergeant and a constable, both in uniform and between them making sister's room look very small indeed.

'Dr Campbell? I'm Sergeant Lowther and this is Constable MacAndrew ... We're making some preliminary inquiries into the death of the late Mr MacNaughton.'

The constable, a pale man in his twenties with a moustache that still had a long way to go, flicked a notebook from one pocket and a pencil from another.

'Christian name?' said the sergeant.

Campbell hesitated. 'Sorry. But I could find out from the ward admissions book.'

The constable looked puzzled. '*Your* christian name,' said the sergeant. 'And your age and your address, please. And I think that we should all sit down. These things sometimes take longer than you expect.'

In this instance it took about fifteen minutes, though to Campbell at the time it seemed more like fifty. The sergeant did not think quickly, and the constable wrote very slowly indeed and needed quite a lot of help with the spelling of technical terms. At their own pace, they went through everything about Mr MacNaughton's brief stay in the ward of which Campbell had direct knowledge, and seemed particularly interested in who had ordered the sternal marrow.

To Campbell's mild embarrassment, he had to admit that he did not know, so questioning then proceeded in a way that made him feel that he should have been in charge and wasn't. Eventually they wanted to know who was ultimately responsible for the case. That was explained, and their last question concerned the spelling of 'Zürich'. Campbell obliged, wondering for a moment about the umlaut but deciding to omit it because of vague anxieties about seeming too clever, or seeming to waste police time.

As they emerged from sister's room Sergeant Lowther thanked Campbell for his help and asked how they could contact Dr Nelson. Campbell directed them to the male ward downstairs and explained how the nurses would bleep Dennis if he happened not to be around. The interrogation-centre atmosphere was suddenly dissipated.

'I'm sure all this will be cleared up quite quickly, Dr Campbell,' said the sergeant. 'These things happen oftener than you think. We might have to get back to you in a week or two, but that'll just be a formality. So we'll be on our way . . .' He reached a hand out to Campbell. 'Thanks for your time . . . I know you chaps are busy . . . Neurology, is it now? You've come a long way from Casualty.'

'Oh . . . Yes. Sorry . . . I didn't recognize you. The van. With drugs or something.'

'Something like that. And I was a plain-clothes detective then . . . In my police tweed jacket.'

Sergeant Lowther and a colleague had once called on Campbell at his flat, at a very inconvenient time, in pursuit of the truth about a consignment of oriental goods in a van whose driver Campbell had extracted after a crash.

'Interesting case,' said the sergeant. 'We never got it sorted out.'

Constable MacAndrew also wanted to shake hands. His hand was cool and damp and his grip possibly masonic.

Campbell reciprocated because it kept people happy and never seemed to do much harm. The constable smiled and said. 'Be seeing you, Dr Campbell,' whereupon the sergeant looked at him as if he were talking too much, and the pair went off downstairs in search of Dennis.

'Coffee, Dave?'

'Thanks, Wullie.'

'You look like you could do with one. Nothing else on the round. That woman who was probably depressed is definitely depressed, and the maybe maybe normal pressure hydrocephalus can't have her pneumo-encephalogram until next week, so we might as well send her home.'

'Fine.'

'And I've doubled Mrs Hardy's heroin. She's not got long, and she's not very comfortable.'

'Thanks, Wullie.'

'Everybody else is fine. How was the fuzz?'

'Oh, doing the job. Not trying to be nasty. Quite reassuring, really, to know they check up.'

'If you're in the clear . . .'

'Yes . . . Is Dennis about?'

'They after him now?'

'They want to talk to him.'

'Sat beside him at lunch. He's probably downstairs.'

'How was he?'

'Kind of hard to believe. Said something about the post-mortem. It would probably show an abnormally thin sternum. He'd hardly used any pressure, he said. But they're bound to talk to the wee nurse who was there when he did it. I had a word with her last night just before she went off. Upset by the whole thing, understandably, especially when word came across that the man hadnae made it. And she was basically saying he hadn't a clue what he was about, and she wished she'd got somebody senior –

97

Andrea or Barry or you – before he'd got himself into trouble. But you know how he is.'

Yet again, the trouble was that Dennis looked and sounded like a doctor. A first-year staff nurse, no more established in her own trade than Dennis was in his, would have had to be very brave and very sure of herself to halt a procedure undertaken by a provisionally registered medical practitioner on the grounds that it wasn't being done properly.

'I told her she couldn't have done anything. He would have ignored her. He's a funny bloke. He's said to me a couple of times . . .' Wullie paused.

'What?'

'Well, he's kind of funny about the nurses. Thinks they're against him.'

Campbell recalled this conversation with the same staff nurse on the way back from thoracic theatre. 'Difficult.'

'So when this wee girl shops him it'll just bear out his theory. That's how he thinks. And I get it all from them when I'm on call. They're having trouble, they really are.'

'What sort of thing?'

'It's not really my place to say, Dave . . .' Campbell put down his coffee and waited. 'But I suppose . . . all this carry on with Mr MacNaughton makes it a bit more serious. Well . . . He takes ages to answer his bleep. He says things to patients and to relatives that aren't true. He says he's done things he hasn't done. Honest, Dave, if he'd been one of my milk boys I'd have given him the big boot. Just tae protect my customers.'

There were no major surprises in that. In retrospect, the astonishing thing was that no one had done anything about Dennis earlier, that he had been allowed to drift more than halfway towards full registration with nothing more against his record than a couple of mild reproofs from Campbell, a serious talk with Barry and the occasional outburst from

Sinclair, the last being inflicted on more or less everyone anyway, like the rain falling on the just and the unjust.

'Probably not as easy with doctors,' said Wullie after a pause. 'And in a place like this probably the worst thing that could happen to a bloke like him would be somebody having a quiet word with him and telling him to think seriously about a career in general practice.'

Campbell thought about that. Aithie, Sinclair's predecessor, would almost certainly have dealt with the problem in those terms. Sinclair himself might be capable of more vigorous action. Perhaps meeting the police when he came back from Zürich would prompt him to it.

Next day there were no policemen about, but their visit, and the case which had occasioned it, seemed to have affected most of the staff of the unit and perhaps some of the patients too. Simply going round the wards as usual, Campbell was aware of reserve, caution and even gloom. People who normally chatted and joked just got on with their jobs, perhaps checking things more often, and quiet conversations took place in which versions of events were exchanged or elaborated as those most concerned confided in those less concerned, and information about what had happened and speculation about what was going to happen spread outwards.

There was much sympathy for the staff nurse, and very little for Dennis, but for someone at the centre of an unpleasant enquiry he seemed remarkably untroubled, going about his duties with customary vagueness and lack of concern, as inaccessible as usual to the various reactions of irritation and exasperation he provoked. When Campbell asked about meeting the police, more just to let him talk about it if he wanted to than to find out what had happened, he seemed surprised. 'Yes ... That. They just wanted the facts, so I told them. Thin sternum. Blunt needle. And the nurses really don't make it easy. Sad, of course, about the chap, but on the surgical side people were dying all the time, even after routine things like gall-bladders. Bad luck, I suppose. For him and for me.'

'Had you done a lot of them before, Dennis?'

Dennis looked at Campbell as though he had asked a very stupid question. 'I was on a haematology unit as a senior student. Six or seven, I suppose.' He smiled, showing unusually good teeth. 'Bad luck. Nothing more to it than that. I can't see why people are so upset . . . I mean, there have been three other deaths on the unit this week. Two of them younger than that chap.'

To Campbell it did not seem so simple. 'But if they're looking for someone to blame,' said Dennis, 'they could do worse than start in cardiothoracic theatre. If we got him there alive they should have been able to sort out a minor laceration in a blood vessel.'

'Hm. I don't know. He was pretty ill. But there was another thing I was wondering about, Dennis . . . I don't remember us discussing whether or not we were going to do a marrow.'

'You were down in outpatients . . . I just cleared it with Barry. "Chap with a haemoglobin of seven . . . OK to do a marrow?" "Go right ahead," he said. And he's an SR.'

Had Dennis said as much to the officers of the Lothian force? And had those officers also interviewed Barry, with resulting versions that did not fit together (in a way that Wullie's report on Dennis's marrow experience failed to coincide with that now offered)? It was all getting rather complicated, and probably best left to the mills-of-God processes of Lowther's brain and MacAndrew's notebook: no intuitive short-cuts, just get it all down from a series of individual interviews and see how it looked and come back and try again, and if necessary again after that; so that eventually even Dennis would notice that this was serious.

Outwith the unit the incident had conjured up the

reaction usual to rumoured medical disaster. Bones, Campbell's flatmate, now working in the Institute's urology unit, had heard of it within hours, with some puzzling accretions. 'A Jehovah's witness, poor chap, so he couldn't have blood even with his haemoglobin in his boots and five pints swilling around in his chest. That's the story that's going round. So naturally he did badly, with a bloody great hole in his heart, even though some mad neurologist opened his chest on the ward. And the houseboy who did it is a nutter. That right, Campbell? People are going to ask me. They know I share a flat with a man from the guilty unit.'

Mhairi was better informed and more sympathetic. Campbell happened to meet her in the medical corridor not long after his curiously dissonant talk with Dennis. She had had another lunch with Andrea, and was not given to exaggeration in the manner of Bones. She said something sensible about people being morbidly interested in other people's disasters, but mainly out of relief that it hadn't happened to them, at least this time. For some reason Campbell told her he had not ordered the investigation that had gone so badly wrong, and was assured in turn that Andrea's version had included this detail.

A couple of days later, when Campbell was again second on call, Dennis rang him at home because a woman of forty who had come in with headaches had developed something that sounded like a stroke. Calls from Dennis were unusual: despite various experiences that would have educated lesser men, he seemed to regard asking for advice as evidence of weakness or ignorance. Problems therefore tended to surface the next morning, sometimes by then irretrievable, at which point he would maintain either (a) that the nurses had not informed him of any adverse developments, or (b) that the patient's condition must have deteriorated sharply in the last half hour. Campbell drove round to the Institute wondering if Dennis had begun to improve at last.

On detailed review the woman appeared to have something called hemiplegic migraine, alarming but not as bad as a stroke, although a few cases later turned out to have dangerous abnormalities of the blood vessels around the brain. Campbell wrote her up for some Cafergot and explained to the patient and her husband what he thought was going on, and how she would probably need some special investigations later.

In the doctors' room he found the notes near the top of a heap on the desk. Dennis had written a brief summary after a long and fairly competent admission note by a senior student. It read 'Sore head a while. Both sides or one side not sure. No sickness or bowels. Can't help right hand getting worse. Discuss with D. Campbell.'

Dennis, whom Campbell had bleeped in vain as soon as he had arrived on the ward, was still not around. Campbell sat amid the chaos of his office and wrote a longer and more organized account of the case, ending with his immediate treatment and planned investigations, all of which could wait till tomorrow. Dennis was not getting better, he was getting worse. Although his telephone call had at least been coherent, his note was beyond belief: a garbled scrawl that would have raised eyebrows in a first-aid class for traffic wardens, if such a thing existed.

Campbell was still looking at it when Dennis came in quietly behind him. 'Dave . . . That was quick. Thanks. I'm really not sure . . .' He sat down and seemed to have forgotten what he was going to say. Instead of the infuriating glassy grin there was an expression of subdued bewilderment, as though he could not remember why he'd asked Campbell to come in, or had at least forgotten the name of the patient concerned.

Had he been drinking? He was sitting too far away for the smell of it to be picked up with any confidence, and in any case no one had ever suggested that the trouble with Dennis was anything as simple as alcohol. But he had been under new pressure over the past four days, and might just have had two or three cans of beer in the residency, where they were all too freely available.

'So what's wrong with her?' he said. 'Should we be getting the brain surgeons in?'

'Don't think so, Dennis. Looks like a hemiplegic migraine. Some ergotamine should help. We'll see.'

'Thanks, Dave. Sorry to drag you in. Especially if it was something I should have sorted out myself.'

'No trouble. It's pretty uncommon, and it still might be something else, but she should be OK if we keep a close eye on her. I've written something in the notes.'

'You're a decent chap.' Dennis looked at Campbell as though their conversation required particular concentration and attention to detail.

'I think I'll hang around for a while,' said Campbell. 'See if that stuff does her any good. Is there some coffee about?'

Once again Dennis reacted as though faced with a major intellectual challenge. 'Sorry, Dave,' he said eventually. 'I wouldn't know.'

Campbell got up. 'Maybe the nurses . . .'

'No . . . I'll have a look.' Dennis went over to his desk and opened the bottom right-hand drawer. Inside was an unbelievable jumble of paper and ward disposables such as blood tubes, needles and syringes. Worryingly, much of the paper seemed to consist of lab reports, screwed up and discarded rather than filed in the patients' case folders. Campbell looked over the houseman's shoulder, wondering what little mysteries of the last few weeks might be solved by a detailed look through the drawer.

'All right, Dave . . . In here somewhere. No need to bother the nurses. Cups, hot water, in the kitchen. Milk too, if you want it. Never touch the stuff myself.'

Campbell went out to the ward kitchen and came back

with two cups of boiling water, the one for himself with a splash of milk in it. Dennis tipped instant coffee straight from the jar, giving Campbell the equivalent of three or four spoonfuls, and stirred it in with the butt of a ball-point pen. 'Thanks,' said Campbell. Both sat back. There was a pause. Dennis took a nervous sip at his coffee.

'Anything else happening?' Campbell asked.

Again Dennis seemed puzzled. 'What do you mean?'

'Well, anything else I should see while I'm in anyway? Downstairs OK?'

'Oh. Yes. As far as I know.'

'Anything back on the polyneuropathy?'

'The what?'

'The chap who came in on Tuesday . . . Even basic stuff, like his ESR.'

'I'd need to check, Dave.'

'Sure . . . I was just curious. He seemed stable enough.'

Dennis was hunched uncertainly over his coffee cup, 'I don't know,' he said. 'I don't know.'

'The . . . marrow business?'

'That's part of it. An important part, but only part of it.'

Campbell took another mouthful of fiercely concentrated coffee. 'You're still going to take a year off?'

'Yes.'

'Because medicine's getting you down?'

'And this place . . .'

'But not long to go now. Three months?'

'Something like that. It's really getting me down. And it's getting me worse.'

'Really?'

'Him, mainly . . .'

'Sinclair?'

'He's going a long way out of his way to screw me up.'

'About the . . . recent business?' Had Sinclair decided, perhaps on the way to the airport, that something must be

104

done, and then started, perhaps by telephone to the medical superintendant from Heathrow or Gatwick, to do it?

Dennis looked up and grinned. 'Are you in it too, Dave?'

'I haven't seen him since Monday.'

'He hasn't been in touch?'

'No. He's not back till tomorrow, as far as I know.'

'He's been getting on to me.'

'From Zürich?'

Dennis looked puzzled then said 'He didn't say . . . But really getting on my case. Called me a murderer. Said he'd fix me if it was the last thing he did. No messing.'

Campbell was taken aback. 'Fix you?' Even for Sinclair, that seemed to demonstrate lack of finesse.

'Contacts,' said Dennis. 'And he must have good contacts.'

A long time ago Hadden had remarked to Campbell, on the subject of young men making their way in medicine, that 'if you take one step out of line they've got you by the testimonials'. It was as true for Dennis as it was for anyone, except possibly more so, but unusual for Sinclair to be so frank about it in direct conversation with his intended victim. 'When was this?'

'He didn't say. Just that even if it was the last thing he did . . .'

'No. When did he say it?'

'Oh. That. A couple of hours ago. I suppose. I mean, I didn't write it down.'

If it had been as recently as that Sinclair might well be back in Edinburgh. 'Did he say anything about seeing you tomorrow, or about the police stuff? You don't know if they've been to see him at home?'

'Dave, you know him. You don't have a conversation with him. You listen. And what he was mainly telling me was that he was out to get me. Tell me straight, Dave . . . Have you been talking to him?'

'I told you. I haven't seen him or heard from him for three days.'

'Then he must have been talking to the nurses . . . That's it. The bastard . . .'

Campbell put down his coffee. 'Are you all right, Dennis?'

'Would you be? With that bastard after you? I know what he wants.'

'What?'

'My resignation.' There was another long silence, then Dennis said, 'He's not going to get it.' He brightened. 'Thanks, Dave. Sorry to go on and on. It helps to talk about stuff like that, but I'd be grateful if . . .'

'Sure.'

'D'you want to go downstairs and look at that chap's results?'

'Fine.'

The laboratories had produced nothing of value in explaining the polyneuropathy. By the time Campbell and Dennis had checked everything that had been reported, seen the patient and gone upstairs again, the lady with hemiplegic migraine had begun to improve a little. Campbell drove home around eleven, worrying a bit about Sinclair and quite a lot about Dennis.

Perhaps Hadden was right, and Sinclair was both psychopathic and hypomanic; the former disorder explaining his abrupt indifference to the feelings of others, the latter his energy and strange confidence for sudden and drastic action. Hadden, Campbell recalled, had also diagnosed intelligence, and it could certainly be argued that the quickest and neatest solution to the Dennis problem would be simply to force his resignation; but the means adopted, a telephone call – no witnesses, nothing on paper – threatening vague but drastic action, were probably a little extreme even in the darkly feudal world of Edinburgh medicine.

The problem remained. Dennis was definitely getting worse. He was no longer merely unreliable: a houseman who did little but not much harm. He had now, by his inexperience, his lack of judgement and his failure to seek help when he needed it, killed someone. Mr Mac-Naughton's death had been entirely preventable. In another ward, with another houseman, it would simply not have happened, and in his bovine way Dennis seemed to have realized that. That knowledge in turn was making him worse, to the point that he was now barely capable of articulate thought.

As Campbell waited at the traffic lights at the corner of the park, a quite separate and horrific possibility occurred to him: Dennis wasn't thinking straight because he couldn't, and he couldn't because he was a paranoid schizophrenic. Sinclair had not telephoned Dennis. Dennis was having auditory hallucinations. Campbell tried to recall specific details of their conversation. Occasional phrases had had oddities of language ('It's getting me worse.') or idea ('are you in it too?') that would fit the diagnosis all too well, and Dennis had avoided a series of direct questions about something Campbell had assumed was a telephone conversation but which on second thoughts might not have been.

It was sad and horrible. The voice of Sinclair, accusing Dennis of murder, was not an unconventional approach to unit discipline by a maverick professor, but one of somebody's nine cardinal symptoms of schizophrenia, as it now affected a very unfortunate houseman. The earlier indifference and incompetence were explained, even the death of Mr MacNaughton became a bit more understandable and the outlook for Dennis, a ghastly and degrading disintegration of personality and intellect, just didn't bear thinking about.

Behind Campbell, headlights flashed and a couple of horns sounded. They were real and the traffic lights were now green. He hurried his car into gear, stalled, restarted and got away only as the lights went back to red again. The horns behind sounded long and angrily. As Campbell drove on he decided to have a word with Sinclair as soon as possible when he got back from Zürich.

On the upper floor of the former Neurobiology Unit there had been more changes. The door leading from the corridor into Sinclair's office had been blocked off. Further along the corridor a door was now labelled 'Mrs G. Greenlees: Secretary to Professor J. K. Sinclair'. Campbell knocked and waited. There was no reply. He opened the door and went in.

The room was a large one, furnished with only a desk, a chair, several filing cabinets and some pot plants. Under the windows there was a long laboratory bench, bare except for the usual clusters of three-pin sockets and gas taps. A curious musty smell hung in the air. At the far end of the room a door led back into Sinclair's office. Again Campbell knocked and waited.

Once more there was no reply, but since Sinclair was due to start a ward round in a quarter of an hour and usually looked in on his office before doing so, Campbell decided to hang about in the outer office.

He was, he now realized, in the former laboratory of his late chief, Dr Brown. Oddly, despite having worked for him for six months, Campbell had never previously entered it. For whatever reasons, Bobby Brown had gone to some trouble to preserve the privacy of his little administrative and scientific headquarters on the upper floor, where he had spent many of his mornings and most of his afternoons working on what he had called his 'mashed brains'. Somehow, despite a great deal of optimistic talk, no scientific papers had emerged for publication, and after Brown's suicide the lab had been cleared without ceremony. It hadn't taken long to sort out, according to Fiona, because all that Bobby had ever done there was sleep.

Campbell walked from one end of the room to the other, looking out on to the little lawn, in the middle of the Institute's jumble of buildings, where people took their coffee after lunch when it was sunny. The long worktop, throughout its length, was dusty but otherwise completely clean and unmarked. Perhaps the mashed brains had indeed been utterly fictional.

The strange musty smell persisted: a curious admixture of staleness and harsh cleanliness, like old kippers and Persil. The longer Campbell waited the more oppressive it grew, and after about five minutes he leaned across the bench and opened one of the windows. Cool fresh air swept in and the sad ghost of Bobby Brown and his pathetic and fraudulent career seemed to wither and fade amid the rustle of the trees outside.

On the desk was a scattering of correspondence. Without any particularly guilt-inducing effort at snooping Campbell spotted a couple of letters about a conference in September, a circular from the Dean inviting suggestions for economies that could be effected without detriment to academic standards and a long, single-spaced diatribe in halting English, on the notepaper of a hospital somewhere in Belgium, which seemed to be complaining about plagiarism.

He was still a bit too near the desk when a middle-aged lady bustled in, stood glaring at him for a moment then stumped across and slammed the window shut. She turned and bore down on Campbell, eventually stopping far closer than he had expected. She was stout and garishly dressed, with a low forehead from which sprang a threatening vertical array of stiff orange curls. The musty smell had become a lot stronger.

'What do you want here?' she snapped. 'Is it about those baboons again?'

'No,' said Campbell. 'I thought I might have a word with . . .'

'Haven't I told you before the professor doesn't want to be bothered about baboons when he's busy with his clinical commitments.'

'That's what it's about,' said Campbell mildly. 'I'm Dr Campbell, from the ward, and I wondered if . . .'

'Oooh?' said the middle-aged woman, pursing her lips, the upper of which was decorated with an unlikely Cupid's bow in glossy pillarbox red. 'Dr Campbell, are you?'

'Yes, and I wondered if . . .'

'He's terribly busy, you know, Dr Campbell. A terribly busy man, but if you wanted a word with him I could always see what I could do. Tomorrow? No . . . Saturday, isn't it?' She grinned and giggled. 'Silly Gladys . . . So how about Monday? I'm sure I could fit you in some time on Monday. How about first thing? Half past eight? An early starter is Dr Sinclair . . . I mean Professor Sinclair. Silly Gladys again. I really must get used to it. Professor Sinclair is a very busy man, you know. So eight thirty? Or maybe around six on Monday evening. Works late, does the professor, on Mondays. Either of these times suit you, Dr Campbell?' The Cupid's bow thinned to a wide upward-curving line and a large set of false teeth, daubed here and there with scarlet lipstick, shone out in a pantomime grin.

'I tried his office a minute ago,' said Campbell, indicating the door behind the desk. 'Professor Sinclair wasn't there, so I thought I'd just wait, to catch him before the ward round.'

'Tried his office, did you indeed?' The pantomime grin had faded suddenly. 'And you want to see him, eh? I don't know about that, Dr Campbell, I really don't . . . We've got a fearful lot to do, the professor and I, before there's any suggestion of anybody seeing anybody. Can I suggest that you come back . . . Five thirty, perhaps, or even six?'

The woman still stood menacingly close. Campbell

110

abandoned his previous suspicions as to the origins of the smell, and offered up posthumous apologies to Dr Brown. Mrs Greenlees stared impatiently at him, clicking her false teeth. 'I'll wait,' said Campbell.

There was a short, angry silence then the clicking resumed. Campbell stood his ground against that and the anger and the stare and the smell. He had heard a little about Sinclair's secretary, mainly from Fiona, but had discounted it on the grounds that Fiona had probably wanted the job herself. Mrs Greenlees had been brought up from London, along with one or two laboratory staff, in Sinclair's wake. 'Bad manners and worse typing,' had been Fiona's terse verdict. Campbell now found himself reflecting on her comparative restraint.

'Then perhaps you'd better wait outside,' said Mrs Greenlees. 'There's a great deal of very confidential correspondence for the Professor comes through this office . . . And you could have perfectly well left it until this afternoon and telephoned properly, requesting an appointment to see the professor. Oh . . . Good morning, professor.'

Sinclair, in a fawn tweed coat and carrying a bulging briefcase bedecked with airline baggage tags, swept through the outer office. 'Morning, Gladys. Come in, lad. Two coffees, Gladys, quickly. Thanks. Come in, lad. Sit down. How are things?' Sinclair closed the inner door and kept talking as he removed his overcoat and hung it up. He opened the briefcase and extracted a bundle of files and threw them down on the desk, then fished through his pockets, eventually locating a small dictaphone. He flipped out a cassette and tossed it on to the top of the heap of files.

'Bloody hard, dictating properly on a plane. If you speak up everybody listens, and if you don't it all gets lost in the noise of the bloody thing. Ever been to Zürich, Campbell? If you went you'd notice one thing and probably one thing only. It's clean . . . Don't know how they do it but they do. Just wish they'd come over here and give lessons to our lot.'

'Have you just got back, Professor Sinclair?'

'Hamish. Yes. Stepped off a plane . . .' he glanced at his watch. '. . . seventeen minutes ago. And there was a lucky connection at Heathrow.' He opened the door again and shouted, 'Gladys!'

'Yes, professor?'

'Two coffees.'

'Coming, professor.'

'Don't take all morning . . . Yes, Zürich. Good meeting, Campbell. Very good meeting indeed. Whatever you do something goes wrong, but in this case it was only the Portuguese. Four of them turned up to vote against me. I had been expecting two, voting for.'

'Really?'

'But in the end it probably didn't matter. The thing got stopped anyway because there were a few spare votes kicking around, mainly Scandinavian. They don't want to affiliate because they hate the Russians even more than we do . . .' He paused and turned the bundle of files over, replacing the tape of top of it. 'Nearer, I suppose.'

Campbell was puzzled and must have looked it. Sinclair sighed as though he had been deliberately obtuse. 'If the European Association affiliated to the International Federation we'd get swamped by the commies and our friends from the third world, Campbell, that's what would happen.' Campell continued to be puzzled. 'Worth avoiding,' said Sinclair. 'So that's why I was in Zürich. And the key to the whole thing was the Hispanic vote. Obviously they're going to hang in with the likes of us, pretending they're whiter than white, to keep out the black doctors and the Eastern hordes. But the thick Paddy who's in the Chair until September's all in favour of the brotherhood of man regardless, so it was quite tricky over the first couple of sessions.'

Sinclair grinned like a man with a silly secret. 'But a good dinner in a half-decent Swiss restaurant is a great persuader, and by Thursday the whole thing was looking much more straightforward. I even came back as far as Heathrow with old Dermot, swearing blind that it was a terrible thing, to be sure, just the same as he thought, because I'm going to need all the help I can get from him in October . . . How are the wards?'

'Not bad,' said Campbell. 'But there are one or two problems that might . . .'

'Fine. We'll get them sorted out. I often think, in the middle of all these silly wrangles about what the Finns might or might not think about waking up in bed with a couple of thousand black communist neurologists, that I'm bloody lucky to have my clinical work to come back to. How's that polyneuropathy doing? Anything specific turned up?'

'Not so far, Hamish, but he's stabilized. Even getting a bit of return of . . .'

'And have you found me any more Parkies?'

'One. An old . . .'

'Good. We'll see him in a couple of minutes. Gladys!' This time he did not open the door, but merely bellowed.

'Coming,' sang a voice on two falling notes that hinted once more at pantomime. The door opened and Mrs Greenlees fussed in with two mugs. 'Now,' she said. 'Does Dr Campbell take sugar?'

Campbell shook his head. She handed him his mug with a smile rich with the promise of vengeance to come. 'And yours, professor. There we are. All right?' The smell of Persil and old kippers hung heavily in the air of the smaller room as she retreated.

'And there was another quite useful development in Zürich.' Sinclair took a sip of his coffee and put it to one side. 'I've found a co-ordinator for the collaborative motor-neurone disease study. A Dr Delatorre. Over here

113

on a kind of fellowship thing in London that hasn't worked out. Been rattling around between Queen Square and the Hammerstein, not getting much out of it and not very happy. Keen to move and we could certainly use her up here. Starts at the end of next week or the beginning of the week after. Yes. I'll have to think about her accommodation. Gladys!'

'Yes, professor?' The door opened and Mrs Greenlees peered in, evidently displeased to see Campbell still seated, having coffee and engaged in conversation with Sinclair despite having by-passed the proper channels.

'Accommodation, Gladys. A flat or something. Just a couple of bedrooms for six months starting this week. New Town if you can and money's not a problem. Ring round the agencies, let me know this afternoon and we'll get a letter off to Dr Delatorre.'

'I'll do my best, professor.' The pantomime head disappeared again, but the door was left open. Despite that Campbell had decided to broach the topic he had come to discuss with Sinclair.

'Hamish . . .'

'Couldn't have come at a better time. For a number of reasons, but mainly because there's a lot of interest in the study itself now. Quite a few of the people at the Zürich meeting are going to be sending material in . . .'

'So Dr Delatorre will . . .'

'Co-ordinate the whole thing. Get the data together, remind people about follow-ups, maybe travel a bit, probably with me initially but later on her own, I suppose, as the thing takes off. And languages aren't a problem, fortunately. Altogether a very bright young neurologist.'

'From?'

'Spain. Madrid. Instituto di Neurologia. Her uncle's the director.'

'Oh.' Sinclair's earlier remark about the importance of

the Spanish vote in the politics of international neurology had acquired new meaning.

'Very bright girl,' said Sinclair, getting up, taking off his jacket, throwing it into a chair and reaching for his white coat. Neither he nor Campbell had had more than a few mouthfuls of coffee.

As he was buttoning up his coat Campbell tried again. 'Hamish . . . The houseman on the male ward . . .'

'The mad chap?'

'Yes. Dennis. I had a word with him the other day and . . .'

'Don't worry.' Sinclair was already half way across the outer office. 'Ward round, Gladys,' he called over his shoulder as they reached the door, 'then a baboon at twelve.'

On the way downstairs, Campbell said, 'Dennis is actually in quite a lot of trouble, Hamish . . .'

'Yes?'

'A couple of days after that marrow went wrong.'

'Didn't the cardiothoracic surgeons sort the chap out? Once you're into the chest it's as simple as repairing a puncture on your bike.'

'He actually had a bit more trouble, Hamish. Sounded like disseminated intravascular coagulation. He, um, died later that night.'

'Hm,' said Sinclair. 'The chest surgeons haven't improved either. Their problem, I suppose. If we got him over there alive they should have done the rest. Fiscal been in touch?'

'Yes. And the police. They came round on . . .'

'Basically the chest surgeons' problem, but I suppose they'll swear it's ours. And they could be right, up to a point. Our investigation and it went wrong. But these things happen.'

Campbell was surprised at how closely Sinclair's view of Mr MacNaughton's demise corresponded with that held by Dennis, but still hoped, in the last twenty yards or so before the ward, to raise with his chief the possibility that one of the housemen was probably suffering from one of the worst psychiatric illnesses in the book.

'I had a word with Dennis a couple of days ago, sir. He seems to have some very strange ideas . . .'

They were almost at the entrance to the ward. Sinclair stopped and put his hand on Campbell's shoulder. 'Laddie, you don't have to worry about a thing. He's going. In fact he's probably on his way already . . . I made a couple of phone calls from Zürich and I'm pretty sure I've fixed him. Now let's see what's in the ward.'

In the doctors' room downstairs Wullie was waiting with Barry, Andrea – now visibly pregnant but wearing a quite unnecessarily voluminous Laura Ashley dress – and a handful of students. As the customary little procession formed behind Sinclair and the trolley of case notes, Campbell fell in beside Wullie and muttered from the corner of his mouth, like a prisoner in the exercise yard, 'Where's Dennis?'

'Off sick, apparently.' murmured Wullie like another hardened convict. Sinclair, already shepherding the students around the first of his patients, had not heard anything, and either had not noticed the absence of the customary houseman from the round of the male ward or, having gone to some trouble to engineer it, was simply taking it for granted.

At the bedside of the first patient, the man with the polyneuropathy, Sinclair spent fifteen minutes pestering and bullying the students about the various diagnostic possibilities opened up by that unusual and difficult problem. In the course of the performance ('Come on, lass, you're four-fifths of the way through the medical course, and this man's paying taxes to support you . . . What do you think he's thinking now? Well, sir? I agree. She's

116

bloody terrible . . .') one of the girls cried and one of the men went quite pale, either from fear or anger.

Campbell, who had so far failed to establish any reason for the patient's symptoms, which were in any case improving, thought it unfair that students should be made to feel miserable about their inability to do any better, but did not feel their plight would be helped by his saying so. Eventually the ward round moved on to a couple of new MS patients and a man with an advanced brain tumour, who was to be despatched as quickly as posible to the care of the local hospice. At half past eleven they reached the last male patient.

'Campbell? Campbell . . . Where's the new chap with Parkinson's?'

'Sir?'

'You told me less than half an hour ago that you'd brought in a man with Parkinson's for proper assessment, at long last. Where is he?'

'Oh. No, sir. The new Parkinson's patient is upstairs . . . a lady.'

'Campbell, you clearly said . . .' Campbell had said nothing about the sex of the new Parkinson's patient, and knew he hadn't, but Sinclair, having clearly misunderstood and formed a firm conviction on the basis of his misunderstanding, would not be moved. 'What do you mean, Campbell? Don't you know? Or can't you tell?'

There was a dutiful snicker from a couple of students. Sinclair grinned fiercely. 'Makes me wonder whether you ever look at these patients you're supposed to be responsible for, or whether you're just leaving the whole thing to the housemen.' He bared his teeth again, perhaps anticipating another cheap laugh. There was none. 'And what did I tell you about strokes? Look at this.'

The patient, a man in his early sixties with a right hemiparesis, who could understand what was going on but could not speak, turned pink. 'Get a geriatrician to come and see him. That wee Glaswegian with the beard. And I don't care what he says . . . I want this chap out of here within the week. Right?'

'Right, sir.'

'And the new Parkinson's patient's a woman? You're quite sure about that?'

'Yessir.'

'Let's have a look at her.'

As usual, Sinclair bounded upstairs far faster than a casual glance at his short, stocky figure would have suggested was possible. The students trailed, puffing far behind, and Andrea, no doubt making some point about the plight of pregnant women in medicine, billowed up in her own stately time, like a kite ascending on a gentle breeze. In due course the little procession re-formed upon the trolley of case notes from the upstairs doctors' room and proceeded to the bedside of the first female patient, who happened to be Mrs Robson.

'Is this her, Campbell?'

'Mrs Robson, sir. Parkinson's disease.'

'I can see that for myself, laddie. How old is she?'

'Seventy-three, Hamish.'

'That's a bit old.' His eyes narrowed and he looked at Campbell as though suspecting he was lying again. 'You sure?'

'Yessir.'

'Well . . . we can still assess her. Properly, I mean. Then try her on triple therapy.'

Campbell experienced immediate disquiet. Mrs Robson had already started on treatment which had helped her a lot, but in no sense was it triple. Had Sinclair issued another memo which, like the one Fiona had passed to him in the clinic, he had for some reason not immediately seen? And what was proper assessment? Getting up out of a chair, walking about a bit and cutting up plasticine sausages? Or was it something more? Campbell glanced across at Barry, who had suddenly decided to look out of the window.

'Well?' Sinclair's face had darkened to a purplish red and his jowls were bulging over his collar. He stooped to where the drug chart hung on a grey clipboard at the end of the bed, lifted it up and read it. 'What? What's this? What the hell are you playing at, Campbell? Well?'

'Sir?'

'You signed it. Look!' He threw the clipboard at Campbell, who was sufficiently alert both to avoid injury and to catch it before it clattered to the floor. 'Your signature? Right?'

'Yessir. I put her on Parotrim and . . . she's actually doing quite well. But if you'd like her on something else . . .'

Mrs Robson, who had over the past few days become something of a fan of Campbell's, was watching the little drama at the foot of her bed with interest and concern. The young doctor who had sorted out her constipation and even made her walk a bit better was in some sort of trouble with another doctor. She craned forward and cocked her head to one side in order to hear.

'You're bloody idle, Campbell. You're a dead loss from the clinical academic point of view and now you won't even do as you're bloody told. I'm not asking you to think. No point. I'm not even asking you to make simple decisions, because I don't trust you. All I ask is that you do as I bloody well tell you. Right?'

The louder Sinclair shouted the more the students had edged back, so that now the group around the foot of the bed had spread out quite considerably. Andrea stood still but had closed her eyes. Barry had continued to find much of interest outside the window. Campbell took out his pen and held it over the drug chart, awaiting further instructions. In the silence Mrs Robson made a loud tut-tutting noise.

Sinclair ignored it. His facial colour receded a little and his manner subsided from outrage to more-in-sorrow-than-in-anger. 'What we are trying to do, Campbell, if you'll bear with us, or at least try not to get in the way, is to drag the management of Parkinson's disease into the second half of the twentieth century. First, we're going to make sure we know what we're treating, and second we're going to standardize treatment on a rational basis. For diagnosis we're not going to rely on a collection of nineteenth-century clinical tricks that have been handed down like the folklore they almost certainly are. Not bloody likely. We're going to get something we can look at under a microscope so that we know what we're up against, just the same as we do with tubercle or sarcoid or just about any cancer you care to mention. Make sense to you, Campbell? You've no objections to the advance of reason in neurological diagnosis, have you?'

Campbell nodded politely and waited, pen poised, for the bit about treatment. 'So when I say assessing them, Campbell, I mean assessing them properly, by biopsy. That's what I've just spent the last seven years working on, and it's made the diagnosis of Parkinson's intellectually respectable for the first time in the history of the disease. All right by you? Good. So she'll go across to the Southern for stereotactic biopsy next week, Campbell. And meanwhile you'd better take her off treatment because frankly you don't know what you're treating. You're just fiddling around with something you don't understand. Got it?'

'Sir.' Campbell drew a line through his previous prescription. Mrs Robson looked puzzled but did not venture to speak, presumably because no one had spoken to her.

No one did, and the group moved on, with Sinclair looking round for Barry, who had sidled up to him like a dog expecting a biscuit. 'Sort it out, Swift. Quickly. Stereotactic biopsy next week and triple therapy as soon as she gets back from the Southern.' In a position of disgrace back among the students Campbell noted that at least he could find out from Barry, when an opportunity arose, about Sinclair's new look for the management of Parkinson's disease.

'I'm fine now, thanks Dave. It was just a bit of a headache. Sorry to miss the ward round this morning. Was there anything important?'

'Nothing much. We're trying to get Mr Johnson over to St Cicely's for the home straight, and the younger of the two MS bods is discharging himself against medical advice.'

'What about the polyneuropathy?'

'No answer, and getting better.'

Dennis smiled. 'Patients have no idea how to behave. How was Sinclair?'

'A bit noisy. Worse than usual. He's just had some new ideas about Parkinson's disease that we were all supposed to know about.'

'Yes. Barry mentioned that. He seems quite keen on the whole thing.'

'Sinclair?'

'No. Barry. Well, Barry as well. We're supposed to tell Barry about the new Parkies, and he keeps an eye on everything. Didn't he mention it to you, Dave?'

'No.' It was easy to see how Barry, given the responsibility of co-ordinating one of Sinclair's pet projects, might use the opportunity to play unit politics. Had Campbell known a little more about recent developments, he would have looked less silly on the ward round, and Barry less clever.

'Gosh. He didn't tell you?'

'Not yet.'

'They're funny here. I thought I was lucky to get a professorial house job at the Institute, but I wish now I'd gone to Kirkcaldy or Bavelaw or somewhere like that, where they just get on with the work. People here seem to spend most of their time getting at each other, or doing each other down. Like Barry, not telling you about the stereotactic assessments.'

'When did they start?'

'I don't think they actually have yet, but they're going to soon.'

'Yes. Mrs Robson's going over to the Southern next week. Dennis, has Prof Sinclair been in touch with you again?'

Dennis smiled again. 'No. He seems to have eased off. But of course I missed his round this morning.'

'And you're going to . . . stay the distance?'

'Right. Serve out my sentence here, get on the register, and then take a year out doing what *I* want to do.'

'Sounds fine. But if there's anything you're worried about, Dennis, you can always have a word with me, or Barry, or Andrea.'

'You mean if I think someone needs a marrow?'

'Well, clinical things you're worried about . . . or just anything . . .'

'Thanks, Dave.'

Later that afternoon Campbell went across to the medical library to do a bit of reading round the subject of stereotactic assessment of Parkinson's disease. A rummage in the Index Medicus produced the titles and publication details of half a dozen recent papers, all with one Sinclair, J. K., as the principal author, but none in familiar journals because none of the work had been done in humans.

An hour later, he had found three of them, in obscure neurophysiological periodicals, read them, and remained unimpressed. Sinclair, evidently in the latter half of his sojourn in London, had been poisoning baboons with various things that were known to give people Parkinson's disease, and then clamping their heads in metal frames, boring holes in their skulls and sucking out little pieces of the affected part of their brains, using the device, modestly titled the Sinclair probe, that Hadden had heard about in a lecture and reported over lunch. From a brief perusal it looked as if the business of stereotactic assessment might be bad for baboons and extremely bad for old ladies like Mrs Robson.

Campbell sat in the stuffy silence of the library thinking about all the problems Sinclair's proposed action raised, perhaps the simplest of which was the question of who exactly was going to do the operation. Although formerly a neurosurgeon, Sinclair had now been appointed to a distinctly non-surgical job as professor of clinical neurology. He would therefore have no access to the neurosurgical facilities required: the operating theatre, the stereotactic frame, and the various bits of electrophysiological kit needed to explore the deep structure of the brain.

Was this where Sinclair's previous association with Marcus Mackail might once more become useful? Mackail, known vaguely to Campbell as one of the more picturesque members of the surgical teaching fraternity, was an ageing and increasingly eccentric neurosurgeon based at the Southern, the hospital to which Mrs Robson was to be transferred as soon as possible. Campbell re-read a few of the more gruesome paragraphs about Sinclair's London baboons, and started to worry in earnest about a harmless old Edinburgh lady whose Parkinson's disease had been doing quite nicely on the tablets.

'Once a year is par for the course,' said Hadden. 'Ours was a wee girl, a quiet wee thing from Hamilton, totally unmemorable until half way through her surgical house job. Locked herself in her room and stayed in bed, wouldn't even answer the phone, until they came to take her away. Rays came into it somewhere, or possibly hydrogen bombs. A few kind souls went to see her down on the farm, for the first few months anyway. Bloody sad. She got out, but not back to medicine . . .' Hadden paused for a mouthful of beer. 'The more worrying ones are the kind that don't show up until they're fully registered. Wee Lena isn't going to do much harm, because she's not Dr Lena with the GMC.'

'This chap very nearly made it ... Just two months to go, but acting odd since last year. He'd gone from being pretty useless to actually being dangerous, then started saying odd things about Sinclair. How he had been getting at him, threatening him and blackmailing him by phone at funny times. It was all a bit weird, but in the end probably quite true, because Sinclair really had been trying to bully him into resigning, I think. Then the Sinclair stuff got progressively odder, too odd to be true, even for a nutter like Sinclair. Dennis was always talking about a year out of medicine he was going to take and spend in the Middle East, trying to make his fortune as a photographer. The second lot of phone calls were about that: how Sinclair was going to make it rough for him. When I asked him what he was going to do he came over all shy and said it sounded odd, but Sinclair was going to get in touch with the PLO and tell them about what Dennis was really up to. When I asked him about that he wouldn't tell me in the doctors' room, so we went for a walk round the car park, and he swore me to secrecy and it all came out. The CIA have been controlling our Dennis for months.'

'Ah well,' said Hadden, 'that explains why he's been such a bloody awful houseman.'

'I wasn't very sure what to do, so I tried to get hold of Dr Temple, our sane consultant, but before I could find him Dennis went right off his rocker, in the residency, oddly enough, at lunchtime today ... Stood on the table and told everybody Sinclair had poisoned the food to prevent him going to the Middle East and sorting out the PLO once and for all. Wullie was there, so he and the butler eventually got him down off the table and calmed him down a bit.'

'Yes, I can just see it. "Dinnae worry, surr . . . If ye'd prefer a biled egg I could dae ye one mysel' the noo".'

'No, he was pretty sensible, according to Wullie. Sat chatting to him about Suez and the Arabs until the duty psych arrived and took charge. He'd probably seen dozens of people go mad in the army. So Dennis is up the road in a comfortable modern professorial psychiatric unit, taking the pills and probably explaining to the registrars how nice Professor Sinclair's actually one of Yasser Arafat's leading hit-men.'

'. . . and not a clinical neurologist at all. Yes, it all figures. Another pint, lad?'

'Thanks.'

Hadden lumbered off towards the bar. Campbell sat back with the last inch or so of his beer. The club was busy, the regulars from the Institute and the University having been reinforced by people who came in only on Friday evenings. At a table on the left a little group of female academics were getting giggly on the gin, evidently because one of them was leaving. On the right a middle-aged and reputedly gay physiology lecturer was listening earnestly to a tale that he might have found tedious had it not been coming from a slender blond lad with carefully faded jeans.

Eventually Hadden returned. 'Sorry about that . . . Couldn't get near the bar for surgeons and lawyers.' He put down the two pints and set about his own. 'Bertie MacElwee's in full spate, with a polite audience of people who can't wait for him to retire. And Bill MacMillan's on the orange juice again, or maybe it's gin and orange. Where were we? Yes. Your poor mad houseboy. So they came with the van?'

'Not exactly, he went up to the department of psychiatry for a quiet chat and they took it from there. Admitted him for however many days it is, under an order. Kind of obvious, in retrospect.'

'Wonderful diagnostic instrument, the retrospecto-scope.'

'Seriously. He was slow, distracted, not up to it . . . And just . . . not really in touch. And he'd been not too bad as a student, according to Wullie. And then there was the marrow that went wrong.'

'God, was that him?'

'Yes.'

'Somebody had better tell the fiscal.'

'Sinclair has already. It was the first thing he did when he heard Dennis had gone.'

'Neat, really. Gets everybody off the hook. And the Institute can go on being the world's most wonderful museum of medical technology, or at least it's most complacent. After all, you can't guarantee that none of the housemen will go bonkers. Any family history?'

'Probably. He once said something to Wullie about getting away to visit his mother in hospital, but was a bit shy about the details.'

'Poor bugger. He probably knew, at a kind of cortical level, from doing his O level in psychiatry in fourth year, that he was at risk, but once the brain biochemistry took over it was all too real for him ever to question whether it was or not.'

'And then working for Sinclair . . .'

'That's interesting,' said Hadden. 'A case of "You're not totally paranoid, because somebody really is out to get you . . ." Poor chap.'

The couple on the right rose to go. Hadden had noticed them too and remarked, once they were out of earshot, 'Just popping back to the lab to do a solid evening's work on the pelvic parasympathetic reflexes, I expect. But of course we're not supposed to mind these days, as long as they don't frighten the white mice.'

The women on the left were having trouble sorting out who was going to pay for the next lot of drinks, the way women tended to, with two of them standing up and holding their handbags as though the matter might come to blows. Campbell started his second pint and thought about the Dennis business, settled at last that day. The unit had been relieved of a burden of uncertainty and risk, and Dennis now had a label and a prognosis other than that of an idle and bolshie junior doctor.

He would get better on drugs, in the sense that his odder convictions about the CIA and the PLO would soften quite quickly, first to suspicion then to memory, but the drugs would dull him, slow him down and probably give him the strange writhing movements that marked out the treated schizophrenic in the street to the knowledgeable observer; and despite all that the disease would almost certainly relapse again sooner or later into florid delusions, perhaps the same, perhaps unrelated. But undoubtedly the worst thing about the diagnosis was its long-term outlook: the gradual drift down to oddity and dereliction, the grubby and disorganized life of unemployability and vagrancy or its scarcely less ghastly alternative: the crowded, malodorous safety probably enjoyed already by Dennis's mother.

'Cheer up, lad . . . Friday, isn't it? And look . . .'

Campbell looked up in time to see Mhairi come into the club, glance quickly round the lounge as though in search of someone she was late in meeting, then go on into the bar.

'. . . our helpful little diabetologist. I don't know how we'd do without her . . . Your average orthopod knows as much about diabetes as your average blacksmith, so they call her in quite a lot. Mainly for things the patients could sort out for themselves if they were awake, but she's always terribly nice about it.'

Campbell, who was supposed to know more about diabetes than either blacksmiths or orthopods and therefore be less dependent on specialist help, said something vaguely approving about Mhairi anyway.

'Pity she's not going to be around much longer,' said Hadden.

'Really?'

'Well, not indefinitely. I suppose what I mean is that her husband is going to be out of a job quite soon and isn't going to get another one in Edinburgh. So they'll be off. Pity.'

'Hm. Hadn't heard, but I'm not surprised. He was in our year. Sort of ambitious but thick.'

'Yes, I think that's more or less the diagnosis. But he really got out of hand doing his orthopaedic rotation at Bavelaw. Went around giving the impression it was all a bit beneath him, as he was clearly destined for a chair in general surgery, then dropped himself in it by making such a mess of an old bird's hip that she lost the leg . . . *After* he'd got up everybody's nose, silly boy. So down trousers, smacked botty and stood in the corner. And of course Jock passed the word round the mafia, which is the real punishment. "So farewell then . . ."'

As a student Richard Kirkton had alienated about half the class by various crimes against good comradeship, the worst of which was claiming to be on first-name terms with most of the external examiners. While it was true he had substantial medical academic connections – his father and one of his uncles were professors of big departments in unimpressive medical schools in England – a wiser youth would have been more discreet about them. With an unflattering photograph and a quote ('As I was saying to the Dean . . .') which had been gleefully saved from very early in the course, the year book had duly taken revenge.

'Unless of course he just lets Mhairi get on with it and stays at home and does the housework,' said Hadden. 'She could probably be an SR quite soon if she let herself go.'

Somehow that did not seem Kirkton's style, but further

128

discussion was precluded by the approach of Mhairi, alone and carrying a dry sherry. Hadden moved along the sofa to make a space for her but she remained standing. 'You haven't see Andrea, have you? I was supposed to meet her here at half past . . .'

'Don't think so,' said Campbell. 'She's not round the corner chatting up the lawyers, is she?'

Mhairi smiled. 'I've looked . . . She's probably just even later than me.'

They chatted until about ten to six, when Andrea rushed in, looked excitedly around until she found Mhairi, who was sitting with her back to the general run of traffic through the lounge. After a flurry of wide-eyed courtesies she explained breathlessly to Mhairi that something had cropped up and she must dash. '. . . because one of Alastair's posh friends wants us up in Perthshire for the weekend . . . I suppose that's because somebody really posh had called off, but we absolutely must dash . . . Alastair's waiting outside, so I'm going to have to leave you with these dishy men, Mhairi . . . Have a nice weekend . . . Bye.'

Andrea swept fragrantly away. Mhairi laughed and then said, 'Shouldn't laugh.' Hadden, who had evidently not come across Andrea before, looked bemused. 'Alastair's an advocate,' Mhairi explained in an accent more rural and highland than her normal, 'and there are all these judges to worry about.'

'I see,' said Hadden. 'So a weekend swilling Lord Tacket's claret in a big hoose up by Auchterteuchter becomes a matter of stern duty. Hmph. I'm in the wrong job.'

They had another drink then Hadden muttered something about visiting in-laws and left, which rather surprised Campbell, because a pint with Hadden rarely stopped at three. Mhairi showed no signs of moving. Rather than reopen the topic of aketotic diabetes, Campbell asked politely about his former classmate, Richard. Mhairi looked at her sherry glass for a long time then said 'Interesting question . . .'

'Oh.'

Mhairi had slumped a little lower in her seat. She shrugged. 'Funny old business, marriage . . . One does one's best . . .'

'Problems?'

Mhairi lifted her glass to her lips and put it down again without drinking anything. 'You could say so. He pushed off.'

'Gosh.'

'About six months ago.'

'Sorry . . . I hadn't heard.'

Mhairi smiled. 'It's not the sort of thing people leap around talking about, David. For a start it's difficult to know what to say, because he might have just gone off for a weekend or a week or even a couple of weeks. But yes, he pushed off six months ago. With an enrolled nurse from theatre. Also called Mhairi, curiously enough.'

'Gosh.'

'It's odd . . . The thing that seemed to worry him most was mummy finding out. His, not mine. So when she finally did I knew he wasn't coming back. That was last week.'

Mhairi, whom Campbell had first noticed as a cheerful and decorative component of the student scene in the Medical Reading Room, sounded suddenly much older, and he realized that if marriage seemed to put a few years on people younger than himself, marital break-up quickly added a few more. She took a little sip of sherry then said, 'I shouldn't feel sorry for myself but I am a bit . . . and now Andrea's just stood me up with a couple of concert tickets. How do you feel about some Mozart and a great weepy chunk of Mahler, David?'

* * *

130

They ate at the club and went on to the Usher Hall. Though Campbell liked music, he was not a regular concert-goer. Soon the ritual and the civilized inactivity of it all took him over, as going to church or the launderette might, but more so, enforcing relaxation and giving generously of time for idle thought. The Mozart chattered agreeably and the seats were rather better than any Campbell had occupied before at a concert there: probably, he realized, the sort of seats middle-class couples took for the whole season because they thought their marriages were going to last at least that long.

At the interval they had ice-cream and saw, from a distance, one or two people they both knew from the Institute. Dimly Campbell realized that of such glimpses was gossip made, but did not unduly care. Only in the course of the Mahler did he realize, from an almost indefinable relaxation on Mhairi's part, mostly to do with their handling of the single concert programme she had insisted on buying, that the question of lending some substance to possible gossip might soon arise.

The last movement, something about souls from the earlier funeral march ascending heavenwards to judgement and bliss or whatever, seemed to drag a bit. Outside again, they walked quickly to Mhairi's car and only after they had got in discussed where they were going. Campbell's car was still in the serfs' car park at the Institute but, they decided, would be safe there overnight. Marchmont seemed closer than Duddingston, where Mhairi lived, for coffee.

To Campbell's surprise, Mhairi seemed to know, without asking, where he lived. As they went upstairs he began to worry about Bones, whose nights off duty, and hence whose presence in the flat, were a little unpredictable. He mentioned that to Mhairi. 'No problem,' she said. 'If he's there I'll just have coffee.'

* * *

On Monday morning morale in the unit had returned to normal or even something above it. No one mentioned Dennis, and Wullie, pending the appointment of a locum to cover the last few weeks of Dennis's contract, coped happily with the work of both wards, helped a bit by an ambitious male student who probably thought that conspicuous effort in a crisis would ensure him a professorial housejob and hence a glittering career in medicine.

Andrea, faintly weatherbeaten from her social duties in the country, shared in the general euphoria. In response to a platitudinous enquiry from Campbell she said she was feeling absolutely terrific and was sure the next few months would be bliss. He asked her about her weekend.

'Super, David. Some of these people are really bright, and not half as reactionary as everyone thinks. And we expected to freeze but it was all centrally heated. Must cost a fortune . . . How was yours?'

'Hm?'

'Your weekend, David.'

'Oh . . . All right.'

Andrea looked thoughtful for a moment. 'I felt terrible about letting Mhairi down like that . . . Sometimes it's so difficult.'

'. . . being a completely selfish woman in medicine,' thought Campbell, but said nothing.

'You know Richard's gone off . . .'

'Has he?'

Andrea leaned a little closer and lowered her voice. 'I just thought I should warn you, David.'

3

Though the baboon was presumably anaesthetised, it would have been hard to tell from a glance whether it was awake or asleep. If anything, it looked simply drunk, lying back in a thing like a miniature airline seat complete with arms and a headrest but equipped with unusually elaborate restraining straps. There was the customary adjustable webbing waistband, a similar strap encircling the animal's deep, rather narrow chest and four limb restraints, applied firmly but not, it seemed, uncomfortably. The overall impression given was one of excessive precaution, as though clear air turbulence had been forecast but not seriously expected.

As Sinclair worked the digits of the baboon's right upper limb began to move rhythmically, like those of a customer in a restaurant who felt his needs were being overlooked but who was not yet sufficiently incensed to resort to some more drastic means of attracting the waiter's attention. Dr Delatorre leaned closer towards Campbell, nudged him gently with her elbow and pointed at this oddly human gesture. Campbell nodded silently. Dr Delatorre smiled and imitated it on his forearm.

The left half of the creature's head and face was obscured by the solid left shoulder of Professor Sinclair, who sat, gowned and masked, on a stool close to the baboon's seat and within easy reach of a tray of instruments on a trolley to his right. An assistant, also gowned and gloved, stood on the other side of the trolley. Another male assistant, white-coated rather than green-gowned, stood idly beside a bank of monitoring screens and associated grey boxes.

No one spoke. Campbell, who had been suddenly instructed via Mrs Greenlees only five minutes previously, to escort Dr Delatorre from the clinical neurology office to a lab he had never visited, looked round and began to wonder how long he might be expected to stay. Had Sinclair, the ex-surgeon, summoned them across simply to form an audience for some tedious piece of surgical virtuosity of interest only to people actively involved? There was nowhere to sit, and nothing to see, but things like that did not seem to bother Sinclair.

The shoulder moved a little. 'Stand by,' said Sinclair, a little indistinctly from behind his mask. The green-gowned assistant held out a shallow stainless steel dish.

'Catch.'

An eyeball, bloodied and trailing stringy fragments of muscle and nerve, plopped into the dish.

'Nibblers.'

Steel passed from gloved hand to gloved hand, and the shoulder moved again. A moist crunching sound half-interrupted Sinclair's laboured breathing. The baboon convulsed briefly. Sinclair cursed it and threw the instrument back on to the tray.

'Diathermy.'

Sizzling noises followed, then a sickening burning smell that brought back for Campbell long hours spent in an operating theatre, weary and hungry, during his seemingly interminable surgical housejob. Sinclair muttered contentedly. Cauterisation of blood vessels controlled blood loss and improved the view. He picked up the bone-nibblers again and set to work, humming something so tuneless that it was probably to do with bagpipes.

Another ten minutes passed, with Sinclair doing routine things in the unseen operative field: nibbling, snipping, burning and tying, helped sometimes by his green-gowned acolyte. The tuneless humming rose and fell. The man in

134

the white coat, responding to some signal or simply to the stage that the procedure had reached, checked his screens and grey boxes and then busied himself with hanks of variously coloured wire. Eventually Sinclair got up from his stool and turned round. The front of his gown was disfigured by a star of blood like a martyr's wound.

'You took your time, lad. Get lost or something?'

Like a lot of Sinclair's questions, that did not seem to seek an answer. Campbell looked vaguely apologetic and waited. Sinclair duly turned his attention to Dr Delatorre. Speaking louder and more slowly he said, 'Dolores, this is where we do the animal work I told you about. Baboons cost the earth. You know, a lot. So I do most of them myself. You didn't really get a chance to see the first part of the procedure.' Sinclair paused to cast a disparaging glance at Campbell. 'It's an orbital exposure. Left eye. Marvellous access to the basal ganglia. A standard thing first described probably thirty years ago.'

Dr Delatorre nodded and smiled. 'I have seen. In Spain, we . . .'

'The next bit is the important bit. You won't have seen that in Spain.' He turned to his assistants. 'Five minutes to rig the frame and wire up. We're just going to look round the survivals.'

Sinclair led the way out and turned right into a narrow, windowless corridor ending with a blank metal door. He fished in his pocket for a key then opened it. The stench made Campbell catch his breath.

The three stood at the end of a gallery one side of which was formed entirely of animal cages, barred and netted right up to the ceiling. The other looked out on to a bare brick wall only a few yards away. A little daylight filtered in through high, grimy windows. Campbell looked into the first cage. It was empty.

In the second a baboon paced back and forward, rubbing

its side against the bars. Far less ape-like on all fours than its colleague had appeared when strapped in the airline seat, it resembled more a large dog or a small scrawny lion, with big, rather shaggy shoulders and disproportionately small hindquarters. Glancing sidelong at its visitors but not stopping for them, it looked bored and possibly hungry, but not unhealthy.

'Pre-op,' said Sinclair. 'Ah . . . Now here's one.'

In a back corner of the next cage was another baboon. Its left eye-socket was blank, having been filled with pinkish plastic material. It wore a tight-fitting leather helmet, like that of an old-fashioned motor-cyclist, perhaps to prevent it scratching at its various head wounds, and was curled up, half covered by a little heap of straw.

'You can't really see. Unless . . . Come on, beast . . .' Sinclair reached across the gutter with one foot and kicked the grille. The animal started then rose unsteadily to its feet. It paused, turned awkwardly to see the source of the disturbance with its remaining eye, then took a few shuffling steps forward.

'See that? Ever see anything like that, Dolores? A baboon with Parkinson's disease? You don't have those in Spain, now do you?'

'I'm sorry about that,' said Campbell.

The man smiled patiently. 'I put on my shirt again. Is that all right?'

'I'm very sorry. I wasn't expecting to be so long.'

'No problem. Medicine must be like that all the time. You have to go where you're most needed, and if there's an emergency . . .'

'Yes.' As Campbell sat down again in the chair at the desk it occurred to him that his clothes, especially his white coat, might still be carrying the smell of the baboon gallery: a rank, clinging odour combining the animals and their excreta. He sniffed the air of the consulting room. He was probably imagining it, the way that sometimes happens with strong, unpleasant smells.

'You were doing the pin-prick thing,' said the patient, taking off his shirt again and lying back on the couch.

'Yes. Thanks.'

'But while you were away I remembered something else. You asked me what the very first thing I noticed wrong was. And there's something else. I got up at night, to get a drink of milk because I'd been boozing, and after I'd closed the fridge door and it was dark again I was completely lost. I mean really lost. Like the middle of Rannoch Moor in a fog. I just hadn't a clue. I found a chair and sat down and then after a while my eyes began to adjust and then I saw the window, and then the door and the light switch and I put the light on and then it all came together again. The kitchen. That was months before the pictures started to go wrong. I blamed the drink. Departmental red plonk.'

The man laughed, rather sadly. He was a lecturer in Fine Art, a man in his mid-thirties whom Campbell recognized because he had been around the University for a long time, and had been a demi-god in the Drama Society when Campbell had been a freshman in the back stalls. He had gone to his GP with a rather unusual complaint: that pictures he knew were beginning to look odd. He had been referred to the neurology clinic at the Institute – 'A relief really. I was sure it was going to be the psychiatrist' – and Campbell had been half way through his assessment when the summons from Mrs Greenlees had come.

It was all rather odd. The man had described his symptoms with professional relish, talking about tonal dissonance and impasto effects like a programme on Radio Three that Campbell normally switched off, but undoubtedly he had something quite seriously wrong with him. The stuff about the fridge helped a lot. If you got lost in

137

your own house and were otherwise of sound mind it localized the problem within the brain quite nicely. Subtler, art-critic stuff would fit that too, but it was too unusual to get into the kind of textbooks that Campbell knew. The man had a brain tumour, probably in his parietal lobe.

'Has that happened often?'

'Getting lost in the kitchen?'

'Or anything like that . . .?'

'My sense of direction's not what it was. But I thought that was just . . . being nearly forty and over the hill.'

'Tell me about that.'

'Well . . . my wife drives me to work now.'

'I see. And definitely no headaches?'

'Everyone gets headaches. And peering at pictures . . .'

'But no oftener, and no worse, over the past few months?'

'Shouldn't have thought so.'

'How did you get here today?'

'My dear wife. Without whom . . .'

'How about drawing?'

The man looked at Campbell as though dealing with a point regularly raised by his dimmest first-year students. 'Fine art is knowing about it. Not, repeat not, doing it.'

'I'm sorry. I thought you might have noticed something with that. Like with the pictures.'

'I could try.' The man smiled. 'Something you'd recognize . . .'

Wondering if he were now being patronized, Campbell handed him a pen and an EEG request card, about six inches by eight and blank on the back.

'Best picture in Edinburgh. Those sugar-candy haystacks. An 1891 Monet in the National Gallery.' Campbell was being patronized. 'Good god . . . You know it, don't you?'

'Sort of.'

'So do I. Inside out and splodge by splodge and . . . Hm. Gosh, two stacks, receding to the left, lit from behind, blue shadows from about sixty degrees, overall pink and grey, with a highlight or two one sometimes wishes would go away . . . And now I can no more draw it than I could . . . Look.'

Campbell was handed a card with a couple of broken scrawls running across it. 'And I literally drew it once with my eyes shut. Gosh.'

Most brain tumours were secondaries from somewhere else, and most secondaries in middle-aged men originated from lung cancer. Campbell checked the hand holding the pen. The first two fingers were moderately stained. The next step towards a diagnosis was not to bother the man with the traditional pin-rituals, but to get his chest X-rayed. It could all turn out to be rather sad.

'How's your general health?'

'No use complaining. The main problem's what I've told you. The pictures, and my lousy sense of direction, and getting lost. Everything else is fine, thank you, doctor.' The man laughed nervously again.

'Can I just go back to a few routine things I should have asked you about earlier?'

'Go right ahead.'

Yes, the man smoked. Yes, he had a smoker's cough. No, he had not coughed up any blood. Yes, he had lost a bit of weight, but he was actually quite pleased to have done so. No, he didn't feel particularly well, now you've mentioned it, but being in fine art and having the pictures start to look funny on you was the oddest bloody thing. And then being interrogated by a chap who suddenly walks out on you and leaves you in your underpants for three-quarters of an hour is the sort of thing that gets the NHS a bad name.

'I'm sorry.'

'I feel a lot better now I've told you.' The man smiled like the professional performer he probably was. 'Circumstances beyond your control?'

'That sort of thing.'

'So what happens now?'

'Some tests. As an outpatient. But it might be best to get you into the ward for a few days once we've got some facts together . . . from the tests.'

'So can I put my trousers back on?'

Campbell filled out some forms for basic investigations and while he did so asked the man if he was indeed the Drama Society activist of a decade or so ago.

'That was me . . . and what a life. Not finishing my PhD and trying to decide between whether I was going to be the next Ian McKellen or would I just aim straight for the top and be the man who would sort out the National Theatre . . . A funny little world, university drama. It was like having the whole of the West End in a sand box. And the spotty chap I told to stick to physics, have you thought of teaching, etc . . . He's there for real, lucky sod . . . How long's all this going to take?'

'It depends. You know . . . what turns up.'

'Oh . . . I see. But nothing awful today.'

'This is for your chest X-ray, and this one's for something called an electroencephalogram. You won't actually have that until next week, probably.'

The man was pulling on his shoes. 'I'm sure you could run the National Theatre without a sense of direction.'

The remaining four patients had nothing wrong with them, or at least nothing wrong with them that could be much helped by attendance as an outpatient at the neurology clinic. There was a woman with tension headaches, a girl with some very odd symptoms that might have been neurological had she not been obviously anorexic, an old man who seemed to need new glasses and a normal fourteen-year-old schoolgirl brought along by a very over-wrought mother who thought she had been walking oddly.

They were the difficult patients. A man like the unfortunate fine art lecturer, the kind of patient for whom the clinic was intended, could be seen and processed quite quickly – other commitments permitting – and a short, clear letter despatched to the referring GP. The vaguely distressed about whom little could be done took a lot longer, and letters about them had to be worded very carefully indeed, at least if they were being signed by someone as junior as Campbell. He left the clinic at half past four with a bundle of case notes under his arm, heading first for the old Neurobiology Unit to leave his dictation with Fiona, then on up to the ward for some tea.

'Honestly, Wullie, it's unbelievable. Probably sixty of them – us, I suppose I should say – all roll up at two and at least half of them have a couple of kids already. So there are seventeen grubby toddlers in a sort of scrum for one pathetic sort of rocking horse thing, and half the mums smoke and keep nipping outside for a drag, and the place isn't terribly well ventilated and frankly some of them . . . well, stink. And that's not just the seventeen toddlers still struggling with potty training . . . So if you get the chance to do anything about those clinics, Wullie . . .'

'I don't think there'll be much an SHO can . . .'

'Jenny Gilmour was there too. Her second. Said that she only got through the last lot of clinics by pretending she'd just sent her bottom half along by itself, because that's all they're interested in, and her top half was somewhere else doing something nice. I tried that. Like self-hypnosis. Then someone fainted and I had to be all very efficient until the nurse arrived. They eventually saw me about twenty past three and some silly little man put one finger on me and told me everything was fine. Great, I thought, but has he *any idea*? Not just about pregnancy, I mean, but about sitting in that stinking zoo for an hour and a half and listening to teenage multipars shrieking "Darren, son, dinnae dae that, I telt ye already." about twice a minute the whole time except when they're out for a cigarette. Oh. Hello, David . . . I've just been to the ante-natal clinic.'

'Oh. How are things?'

Andrea laughed. 'I think I'm beginning to recover . . . But we've more or less finished the tea. There might be some coffee.'

Wullie got up. 'I'll fill the kettle. Anybody coming in from the clinic, Dave?'

'One chap. But not right away. He's having a few things done in his last days of freedom. A sad one.'

'A nasty?'

'Yes, but maybe a slow nasty. Quite a long history.' Campbell described the case briefly. Andrea said, 'Didn't Constable have something like that? Something in his eye that made the middle of his pictures funny? Or was it Canaletto? I can never remember.'

'But nobody today?'

'No.'

Andrea left, and Campbell and Wullie had coffee. Wullie, about to leave the unit at the end of his six-month housejob to move to the obstetric unit, was in philosophical form. 'I mean I'd try, if I thought it would do any good. Can you imagine old Wattie when I went to him. "Sorry about this, sir, but I'm going to have to sort out the ante-natal clinics. Habitat furniture, Vivaldi tapes, a wholefood snack bar and free Perrier water. On draught. Oh, and doctors with plenty of time. And ban all the toddlers. Right, sir?"

'Sounds fine.'

'I doubt if I can fix all that for Andrea this time . . . But maybe for her next bairn.' Wullie put down two coffees.

142

'Actually I don't mind her. She doesn't do much harm. I mean, compared to Barry or the boss.'

'What's Barry been up to?'

'Och, nothing special . . . Just his usual. "Would you mind, Wullie, wouldn't it be interesting to send off a smidge of blood for serum para-amino-marmalade? Fascinating paper in next week's *New England Journal*?" His usual bullshit. And this assessment of Parkinson's. He's never actually mentioned it to Dr Temple, but he's planning to try to put his patients in it too, to keep in with the boss. And he was so bloody stupid about Dennis.'

'Most of us were.'

'But Barry thought he'd cured him with his wee chat. What's happening with the marrow bloke, Dave?'

'Nothing definite yet, according to the best rumours. But they'll probably just pay up, for what it's worth. No defence, really. A mad doctor . . . and not very well supervised.'

'Terrible. I mean for his wife and kids.' Wullie yawned. 'I don't think I'm going to miss this place. When I left the surgical unit at Bavelaw I was kind of sorry to go. It was hard work, but you got on with it and so did everybody else. Helping folk. Here it's mostly looking after the boss, and if you're lucky there's time to look after the patients as well, but nobody seems very interested in that. Did you know that Mrs Robson's back from the Southern?'

'Today?'

'Just just now. I was going to see her when you came in.'

Campbell got up. 'Let's take a look. Any notes? Words of wisdom on what we knew already?'

'Don't know, Dave.'

They went into the ward and asked the staff nurse in charge where Mrs Robson was. The girl paused and frowned and said, 'Left six.'

'How is she?'

'You'll be able to see for yourself, doctor.'

'Oh.'

The lady in the sixth bed on the left was scarcely recognizable as Mrs Robson. For a start, she had a curious silvery crew cut, the presumed result of a couple weeks' growth following a scalp shave for whatever she had had done to her at the Southern. Her false teeth were not in evidence. Her face was haggard and sunken and there was crusting at the corners of her mouth. She was slumped against three pillows and gazed listlessly out into the ward.

'Mrs Robson . . . Hello.'

Mrs Robson groaned and made a wobbly gesture with her left hand. Only then did Campbell notice that the right side of her face was drooping and inert. The left hand continued to wobble but the right did not move at all. There was another wordless groan then a little cough, a sadly ineffective rattle that settled to painful wheezing then stopped.

'For God's sake,' said Wullie quietly. Campbell sat on the bed and asked Mrs Robson to put out her tongue. It was dry and brown and painful looking. The fact that she had put it out as directed meant that she could at least understand speech. The fact that she had not yet said anything was a little alarming. 'Can you hear me all right, Mrs Robson?' The patient nodded. 'Can you speak?' She shook her head and began to sob.

'Cough again, please.' There was another pathetic, fruity rattle. 'Can you move your right arm?' The left arm wobbled again but the right lay still.

Wullie shook his head. Campbell took Mrs Robson's right hand and held it a few inches above the bedclothes then let it go. It dropped limply. 'Move your legs, please, Mrs Robson.' The left moved and the right did not. 'Bloody hell, Dave,' Wullie whispered.

Campbell's bleep went off. He stood up. Mrs Robson stretched out her left hand towards him. The bleep sounded again.

'Excuse me, please, Mrs Robson. Better have a listen to her chest, Wullie. Like you said. Bloody hell.'

Campbell went to the phone at the nursing station and dialled the exchange. When he had identified himself he was connected to the extension of Mrs Greenlees, secretary to Professor Sinclair. 'You're to go across to the laboratory straight away, Dr Campbell. The professor says be quicker than last time, and you're to bring the Spanish doctor back to her office because she doesn't know the way. Right?'

Campbell put the phone down and went back to Mrs Robson's bed. Wullie had drawn the screens round and was stooped over Mrs Robson, holding her forward in a sitting position and listening to her chest at the same time. He shook his head when Campbell appeared, and pointed to the left of her chest. When he had finished and folded his stethoscope away he said, 'We better look at her pressure areas, Dave.'

There was a deep and malodorous pressure sore on the old lady's bottom and a smaller one on each heel. Wullie, now coldly angry, replaced the beclothes and drew the screens back again. Campbell worried for a few moments about what to say to the patient then said, perhaps without much conviction. 'Mrs Robson . . . I hope we can get you feeling better soon.'

'There's another one needs to sue this place,' Wullie muttered as soon as they were out of earshot. 'What exactly were they trying to do?'

'Not sure,' said Campbell. Hadden's account of Sinclair's enthusiasms in the field of stereotactic cerebral investigations was as much as he had heard from anyone. 'I think they're trying to use a stereotactic probe to get into the basal ganglia. And take a biopsy.'

'Not a lot of room in there for getting it wrong. I mean there's a lot of important things quite close together.'

For some reason Campbell recalled Sinclair's remark to the effect that baboons were expensive. Wullie shook his head again. 'She's as good as booked. No power on the right, no speech. And that's just her stroke. I mean, if they'd sent her straight back, we could probably have stopped her getting the bronchopneumonia . . . And those pressure sores.'

The staff nurse in charge was lying in wait as they left the ward. 'What are we trying to do for her, Dr Campbell? And did you know she came back from the Southern with a nursing transfer note saying her pressure areas were fine?'

'Gosh . . . Have you phoned them or anything?'

'Got a staff nurse who'd just come back from three weeks holiday and wasn't interested. Said I should get in touch with the nursing officer. Dr Campbell, what was she doing at the Southern anyway? Her daughter's been on the phone and wants to talk to somebody. She's coming in after her work. I thought you'd like to know.'

'Thanks, staff.'

'So what was she transferred for?'

'Well . . . investigations for her Parkinson's disease.'

'It was doing fine.' The staff nurse's tone was distant and angry. 'You put her on Parotrim and she was great . . . Talking about getting home.'

'Was there a doctor's letter with her?'

'No.'

'Oh. Perhaps I should ring up. What ward was she in at the Southern?'

'D.4.'

'Thanks, staff.'

The nurse remained suspicious but let them go. Wullie organized a chest X-ray and wrote a form for sputum culture. Campbell rang the Southern and asked to speak to the registrar on call for D.4. After a very long pause he was told the registrar could not be found. He asked for the houseman. After a shorter pause he found himself speaking to a medical student temporarily carrying his bleep.

'An old stroke? Oh. Yes. Sorry. Don't know much about her. Not doing too well, as far as I know. Pretty old and a bad stroke.'

'Do you know when it happened? Was she . . .?'

'Look, I'm sorry . . . I'm just carrying Dr Chotawallah's bleep for a couple of hours. Can you ring later?'

'Which consultant was she under?'

'Not sure about that Mr . . . Mr . . .'

'Mackail?'

'Yes. That's him. Mackail. OK? Sorry I couldn't . . .'

'Thanks.'

In the course of the various pauses on the telephone call Campbell had had time to think a little more about Mrs Robson and what they were now trying to do for her. Without vigorous treatment of her chest infection she would probably die. With it she might survive, but the prospect of her survival seemed to raise more problems than that of her death.

She appeared to be capable of understanding what was going on, but incapable, in any but the most general terms, of communicating any distress she might feel. Reasons for distress she had in plenty: she had suffered a major stroke, most probably as a result of an unnecessary and dangerous investigation; she could not move or speak; she had three large and painful looking pressure sores; she had pneumonia; and only two weeks previously she had been a newly diagnosed Parkinson's patient doing very well on the standard treatment.

Wullie had evidently been thinking in similar terms. He scribbled Mrs Robson's name on a couple of blood tubes then said 'Not a lot in it for her if she makes it.'

'No.'

'But we probably have to have a go . . . because it happened the way it did.'

'We don't know how it happened. Yet.'

'Come on, Dave. That test, more than likely. But that just makes it trickier. You know. If you've nearly killed somebody you've got to try a bit harder. But there's not a lot in it for her . . . Be interesting to see what Sinclair says tomorrow.'

'I doubt if he'll be very interested.'

'But for now?'

'I think we should treat her.'

'What's she like?'

'Short. Dark.'

'Pretty?'

'Vaguely. Works on it, I'd have thought.'

'Clever?'

'Hard to tell. Speaks ze charmeenk broken engleesh.'

'Rich?'

'I think so. Definitely well connected. Her uncle's something big in neurology in Spain.'

'What's she doing here?'

'Some kind of fellowship. But not actually doing any medicine. Sinclair's got her lined up to co-ordinate a study on motor neurone disease, but she's not actually doing that yet.'

'So what's she doing?'

'Following him around. She's the flavour of the week. I kept getting sent for today to get her from A to B, usually when I was doing something more useful. She's in the office next to mine.'

'Hmm. Not sure I like the sound of this.'

Mhairi, who was drying herself with a large pink towel, was smiling. Campbell, who had arrived while she was still

148

in the bath, was sitting on the bed with a fairly strong gin and tonic.

'Does she smell of garlic and gazpacho and things like that?'

'No. Something expensive I didn't recognize.'

Mhairi put down her towel and leaned across Campbell for some earrings on the bedside table. Campbell glanced at his watch and put down his drink. When Mhairi straightened up she found herself, as might have been her intention, in a loose embrace that quickly developed.

'David . . . We'll be late.'

'Not very. And for a good reason.'

'We just don't have hangups about that sort of stuff. Bill does nappies and bottles and everything. And he's terribly good.'

Bill's reaction to this testimonial could not be seen. He was on the other side of the room, going round with an earthenware bowl of nameless oriental fragments, heavily salted and spiced, that seemed to be on offer yet again instead of a second round of drinks. Having finished his drink, crunched his ice and eaten his slice of lemon, Campbell nursed a warm glass with fading hopes of relief and, when Bill came round, reached for another little handful of the stuff just for the sake of something to do.

'Take lots. There's tons more.'

Campbell took a few grams, spread it in his palm to check for mouse droppings and bits of insect, then started to eat it piece by piece, slowly and with continuing caution.

'You hear about men like that.' said the large red-headed girl whose name Campbell had not quite caught, '. . . but the first time I handed Eric a really stinky infant when he got in from work he made such a fuss it was hardly worth the trouble. And his nappies always leaked. I really can't think why.'

149

Eric, a man from the year behind Campbell's, chuckled roguishly, puffing a little volley of the Bangladeshi bazaar-sweepings down his tie. It was twenty-three minutes to nine. Campbell could have spent an additional sixty-four minutes in bed with Mhairi and still not missed anything of importance.

Bill and Jill, host and hostess, were contemporaries of Mhairi's and what she had called her oldest medical friends. Bill was a general practitioner, a downtrodden, prematurely grey man newly finished his training and now the youngest partner in a middle-class suburban practice. Jill, despite the rhetoric of equality, didn't seem to do anything. She had started training in psychiatry (Mhairi had quoted her as saying early in her first appointment, 'It's easy. All you have to do is be nice to people.') but had never passed any of the exams and had evidently become disillusioned at the continuing prospect of 'being nice to all these creepy people'. She had left to have a child and never gone back to work.

They lived in a big ground-floor flat in the posh end of Marchmont, in circumstances that suggested they had been affected deeply by a sojourn in the third world. Dusty cloth paintings and crude woodcarvings were all around. A huge indoor plant, more than filling the bow window and extending almost to the ceiling, reinforced the impression that the jungle was not far off. Curiously basic furniture, consisting mainly of poles and canvas and perhaps designed by missionaries with economy and mind-improving discomfort in view, might also have been thrown away with advantage.

Campbell sucked from his glass a further drop of warm ice-water faintly flavoured with tonic and lemon and peered to the left between the leaves of the pot plant at some bookshelves fashioned from planks and bricks. The first title to catch his eye was *Sewerage in the Tropics: a*

Household Guide. On either side were *An Introduction to the Dordogne* and *The Key to the Universe.* More worrying, there was a good half shelf's worth of vegetarian cookery books. Back to the right there was another worrying observation: Mhairi, sitting beyond Eric at the opposite end of the pole and canvas sofa from Campbell, was looking perfectly happy.

For something between the eighth and twenty-sixth time that evening, conversation flagged. Bill got up again and reached for his earthenware pot. 'No, dear,' said Jill. 'I think we're almost eating. We'll just give Andrea and Alastair ten minutes . . . Would anyone like another drink?'

Bill put down his pot and took orders. Eric and his wife both asked for fruit juice and Mhairi for a dry sherry. Campbell asked for a gin and tonic again, hoping vaguely that the state of his glass would indicate the need for a strong one, but before Bill had left the room the doorbell rang. Jill stood up. 'Well timed,' she said. 'They can just go straight in. Come on, everybody.'

'So where are you working now, David?'

Campbell explained. Jill listened as though the answer was both predictable and somehow unsatisfactory. She finished her mouthful of vegetarian savoury starter then said, 'And you have a new head of department . . .'

Campbell nodded.

'We hear he's a terrible chauvinist.'

Campbell in turn took his time with a mouthful of lentil goo. The observation was unfair to Sinclair, who treated the entire human and for that matter animal universe atrociously but quite without regard to the sex of the individual victim.

Jill put down her fork and turned towards Campbell. 'Of course it's a dreadfully chauvinist specialty. Can you think of a single female neurologist in Edinburgh?'

'Well, there's Hattie at the Southern, I suppose. And . . .'

'That's one out of about eight. And neurosurgery's even worse. They've got no one at all. No one. They're as bad as the orthopods. And of course the chap before him was one . . . What was his name?'

'Professor Aithie. Old school, of course . . . This is very interesting . . . tasty.'

'Bill made it.'

'Indian?'

'In the broadest sense. But people are incredibly patronizing and insensitve about that. No one talks about European cookery. People just don't want to know that there are as many different styles of Indian cookery as there are of European.'

'Really? I'd no idea . . . Have you lived out there?'

'Baroda. Just after housejobs. An incredible contrast to teaching hospital medicine in a country like Scotland. For a start . . .' Campbell relaxed and ate some lettuce and a bit of the cucumber-flavoured yoghurt smeared over the lentil goo.

Eventually, when Jill's attention turned to the supervision of Bill's clearing away of the first lot of plates, it became necessary for Campbell to converse with the red-haired girl on his other side, who seemed to think he was called Richard and wanted to talk about the promotion prospects in surgery.

'There really aren't a lot of jobs, are there? Eric says a lot of people end up in radiology and things like that. But that might be quite interesting, I suppose. Eric's lucky. There are lots of jobs in geriatrics and he really likes the grannies. And he's been practically promised a senior registrar job in the professorial unit, which doesn't happen very often in surgery, I suppose. Do you have children?'

Campbell shook his head.

152

'I suppose that makes it easier for you to keep trying in a difficult speciality. Fewer commitments. With four you have to be pretty certain something's going to turn up.'

'Four?'

'It was meant to be three, Richard. But . . . You know . . .'

'Quite . . .'

'Twins.'

'Oh.'

'A bit of a surprise, but a challenge too. Neurosurgery's the most competitive, isn't it?'

'Yes . . . I'm actually in neurology.'

'Oh.' The girl looked puzzled. 'Is that sort of the same?'

'Similar. How old are the twins?'

The conversation faltered on, with the girl whose name Campbell could not remember continuing to look puzzled, but not calling him Richard any more. Meanwhile, in a series of journeys from the kitchen Bill had conveyed to the table about a dozen variously large plates loaded with green, orange and brown things, and was returning again, this time with a two-foot platter heaped eighteen inches high with wet, greyish rice.

'No end of trouble.'

'I'd no idea.'

'Dry rot's the latest.'

'It's not what you're supposed to drink with curry, but it's all right.'

'Worse at night. Alastair's sure he's going to be a marvellous hooker. If he's a boy that is.'

'We actually get it cheap from the BMA.'

'Not promised exactly. More invited to apply. Eric says it's the same thing, really, and they basically haven't had any white men before.'

'Oh, yes. In fact lots of GP's only join for the cheap booze. And the sticker for parking anywhere with.'

'A tiny brown patch on the ceiling. But one of the removal men said he could smell it and he was right.'

'. . . still hoping to finish his MD, even though you hardly need one to get on with grannies.'

'On principle we don't use anything we didn't have in Baroda. So yes, it takes ages, but it's worth it.'

'Well, if you can call pushing him into large bowel research putting pressure on him, yes.'

'Gosh. Just the smell?'

'Yes, and about fifteen thousand, apparently.'

'Not sorry to be getting out. Well, not very . . .'

'And we always give Bill's mother a bottle home with her when she comes.'

'Carrots. And gherkins. Especially gherkins. I keep finding myself next to them at Safeways.'

'She likes what she calls a wine you can drink . . . Now, I think *someone* might just have forgotten to bring in the brinjals in ghee.'

Bill got up silently and shuffled off once more towards the kitchen. Campbell caught Mhairi's eye and she flashed him a tight little smile which might have been an exhortation to continuing social endurance. More constructively, in the temporary absence of her host she had launched a half-full bottle of BMA claret on its way down towards Campbell. Alastair, Andrea's lawyer husband, topped up his own glass with about half of what remained then smiled at the girl on Campbell's right, who pointed out that her glass, like Andrea's, contained orange juice. Alastair put the bottle down again within his own easy reach.

'A little more, David?' Jill asked. Campbell smiled and nodded. Jill pushed towards him the huge platter with its still substantial depot of sludgy grey rice. 'Take some of this and a little of everything else on top. And be sure to leave some room for the brinjals in ghee ... when they arrive.'

'Oh ... Thanks.'

'Andrea?'

'Delicious, Jill, but I really mustn't ...'

'Eric?'

'Why not? Look what it did for Mahatma Gandhi.'

At the end of the meal Jill announced that the men would do the washing-up. Eric, who was evidently familiar with this arrangement, took charge, appointing himself to the sink, Campbell and the lawyer to drying and Bill to putting away. Somewhat to Campbell's surprise, the twenty or so minutes thus spent turned out to be the most enjoyable part of the evening.

A fair amount of claret required to be tidied up, including two bottles in the corner of a case, and in the markedly more relaxed atmosphere conversation blossomed. Bill continued to have little to say, but seemed happy that people were now enjoying themselves, and even after the work was done the four sat in the kitchen talking about the kind of things that men talk about at times like that, until they were interrupted by Jill with some enquiry about coffee.

The move back to the lounge marked an irretrievable decline. The pole and canvas sofa seemed more uncomfortable than ever and conversation never became general. When Mhairi made noises about having to go shortly she found she had precipitated a kind of race for the coats, with Eric's wife muttering about baby-sitters and extra bean penalties for being late, and Andrea patting her bump and saying that sometimes she felt she was sleeping for two as well. Within twenty minutes of having hung up his dishcloth Campbell found himself sitting thankfully in Mhairi's car.

* * *

'Well done, Dr Campbell. You sure you're feeling strong enough for another lot?'

'I think so.'

'Not for long. I said I'd look in, and that's literally all we're going to do. And there won't be any brinjals, I promise.'

'Are they like that all the time?'

'Bill and Jill?'

'Yes.'

'They used to be quite normal. Well, fairly normal, before Baroda.'

'I remember them from the library. Young love and all that. Now he looks about fifty, poor bugger.'

'Keeps pretty fit though. He runs.'

'I bet he does.'

'David. They're quite happy really.'

'Really?'

'Really. He even likes her being horrible about his mother, because he can't stand her either. And he's besotted with their kid. And he likes being bossed about.'

'Oh.'

'His mother again. Funny old business, marriage. Anyway, thanks for putting up with them, and I really did my best to get you a drink when you were dying for one, but that won't be a problem where we're going now, I promise.'

'Ciamur a tha thu, Mhairi.'

'Tha go math.'

'Agus co tha seo?'

The man who had answered the door turned and Mhairi and Campbell followed him into a dark and noisy flat. Campbell must have looked anxious, because Mhairi came close to him and said 'Don't worry, David. Most of them

156

speak perfectly good English. They just prefer Gaelic when they're drunk.'

In the kitchen there was more light. About a dozen people stood or leaned or sat, most drinking, a few eating. The oldest was around forty, a fleshy, bespectacled man in a suit. The youngest looked far too young for the large whisky in her hand. Mhairi led Campbell towards someone he vaguely recognized. 'David, you must have met Ian . . . Ian Maclean . . . He's at the Institute.'

'Hello, David.' Maclean, whom Campbell had last seen in a white coat at lunchtime that day in the hospital dining room, was now only vaguely recognizable partly because he was, to Campbell, out of context, but more so because he was now wearing voluminous sandy-coloured tweeds of immense style and antiquity, which seemed to transform him from a tidyish junior hospital doctor into a kind of caricature of genteel highland decrepitude. Shiny dark leather protected the cuffs, turn ups and elbows. Horn buttons like ancient ivory, perhaps a dozen altogether, decorated the jacket at various points and there were a couple of salmon flies, boutonniere-style, on the left lapel. 'D'you like my suit?'

'Marvellous. You should wear it to work.'

'I might, you know. If they make me a consultant. How are things with you?'

'Not too bad.'

'D'you know a lot of these folk?'

Campbell shook his hed. Mhairi said, 'Ian, have you seen wee Alastair?'

'He's somewhere around, still walking about. At least he was a few minutes ago.'

'The one who's twenty-one,' Mhairi explained. 'A wee cousin. Hello, Ewen.'

Ewen was the middle-aged man in the suit, who turned out to be a senior lecturer in linguistics and another cousin.

157

He and Campbell exchanged polite noises while Mhairi went off to find a couple of glasses. His accent, perhaps fortified by whisky, was stronger than either Mhairi's or Maclean's but his conversation standard Edinburgh and perfectly easy going. Eventually Mhairi returned with drinks. She handed him something without ice or lemon that was nonetheless a gin and tonic and said closely in his ear, 'Cheers, Dr Campbell.' Ewen smiled and nodded.

'David, this is Alastair Beag. Alastair, David.'

The cousin in whose honour the party was being held was a slight, dark youth with a mop of glossy hair and bright, drunk eyes. He hiccoughed and said something that might have been Gaelic. 'Happy Birthday, young Alastair,' said Mhairi, and moved Campbell on gently by the elbow.

'He's in something called machine intelligence, half way through a PhD, for what it's worth. Clever, when he's sober. Let's go in here.'

A large sitting-room was lit only by two candles on the mantelpiece. Perhaps twenty people sat around, most of them on the floor. Hand in hand and careful not to tread on people's legs, Mhairi and Campbell made cautiously for a vacant space against a wall. Drinks glinted here and there, and as Campbell's eyes adjusted a curiously seance-like picture established itself. Bearded men with their eyes shut and their mouths open and wild-haired girls huddled under their arms sat in an irregular candle-lit semi-circle, listening intently to a tape of a solitary piper deep in a pibroch.

A world away from the vegetarians of Marchmont, Campbell relaxed against Mhairi and let the gin and the piping take over. He knew no more about pibroch than sufficed to recognize it, but was drunk enough for its weird, austere progressions to have acquired the hallucinatory resonance of late Beethoven or even Beatles. Mhairi put an arm around him. He closed his eyes.

158

When he woke up someone was singing. One of the girls had moved from the floor to sit on one end of an old-fashioned club fender. Almost motionless and lit from above, eyes shut as though in a trance, she sang slowly and softly in Gaelic, to drunk murmurings of approval from her audience. When she finished the murmurings became louder and more emphatic, and her audience, expanded by a cluster of people standing around the door, seemed to want more. She looked round then beckoned to Mhairi, who shook her head, then, after a bit more crowd noise, got up and went across the room to sit on the other end of the club fender.

Programme notes of some kind would have been helpful. In their absence Campbell could only guess that their duet was some sort of work song, perhaps to do with a traditional domestic skill of the islands, in this performance simply hinted at by rhythmic hand movements, such as making intoxicating liquor from seaweed. The tune was quick and pretty, the singers undoubtedly skilled and in close rapport. When they stopped suddenly, together and, as it were, in mid-air, there was loud, drunken applause.

They sang again and then, despite a fairly determined effort to avoid it, again. Mhairi, pink and happy, eventually returned to the space beside Campbell and took a little sip of her drink. 'Sorry about that. These things have a way of happening. They can all sing, just about, but we don't have to stay for the full programme.'

They stayed long enough, through a half-hour series of progressively less talented and more drunk performers, and left shortly after midnight, stepping over a few more cousins, the birthday boy among them, on the way to the door. By half past twelve they were back in Duddingston.

Mhairi lived in a substantial mid-Victorian house opposite a pub which claimed to have been in business since

159

1386. To Campbell, who shared a rented Marchmont flat with Bones, her four bedrooms and three public rooms were more than a little daunting: the kind of house he associated with prosperous young consultants rather than registrars. For a variety of reasons, he sometimes felt uncomfortable there.

The front door was solid and glossy and bore a formidable brass plate engraved simply 'Kirkton'. When they went in Mhairi switched on the hall light and said, as usual, 'Hello, house'. Campbell followed her into the kitchen knowing what was coming next. Without asking him whether he wanted any or not, she set about making two large mugs of cocoa. Campbell sat on his usual stool, worrying as usual about the tiles.

The kitchen was a large one, with a twenty-foot worktop running down one side. Above it were three rows of tiles, only the first of which was complete. The second was three or four tiles short, the third less than half finished. The overall effect was that of a powerful silent statement about the human condition or something. To Campbell it was always thought provoking, but never more so than after this recent period of enforced vegetarianism and the subsequent excess of whisky and cousins.

Mhairi flicked two teaspoonfuls of cocoa into each of the matching mugs. The smell of warming milk filled the kitchen and she went back across to the stove to check the saucepan. Her eyes rested for a moment on the rough grey of the untiled wall. She smiled and said, 'I really must get something done about those tiles.'

That night Campbell slept badly. In the morning Mhairi's car would not start. They rang the AA and got a rather discouraging estimate for the time of arrival of help, so Campbell walked from Duddingston round the park and in towards the Institute, not hurrying but in good time for

160

Sinclair's Saturday morning ward round, which usually began at half past ten.

'I'm sorry, Dr Campbell, I really am.'

'It's all right.'

'It's just with it being my mother, and nobody at that place ever saying anything about what was going on, and me thinking it was all some kind of experiment, you know, the kind of thing you see on late night films . . . I sort of lost my temper . . .'

'How is she this morning? I haven't seen her yet.'

'Much better. Well, her chest is. Her arm's much about the same. I'm really sorry I shouted at you yesterday, Dr Campbell.'

'I can understand why you were upset.'

'It was mainly that place. Even wee things, like them not covering her head when she was bald. My mother? Bald? I mean, even that itself . . . But yes, she's doing better. And you think this Professor Sinclair would have time for a word this morning?'

Towards the end of the most unpleasant interview with a relative that Campbell had ever experienced, Mrs Robson's daughter had insisted on seeing what she called 'the top man' immediately. Campbell, who had little idea of how to get in touch with Sinclair at six o'clock on a Friday evening and even less about how his chief might view being asked to come in to discuss basal ganglion biopsy with an enraged shop assistant, had eventually negotiated a compromise: Professor Sinclair would almost certainly be available for a few words the following morning.

'I'd still like to see him. Is he a nice man?'

Campbell smiled. 'I think you'll find him very sympathetic. Probably the best thing would be to just wait around here. He usually goes round the other ward first and gets here about eleven o'clock. I'll let him know you want to see him. All right?'

'Thank you very much, Dr Campbell.'

Campbell went on into the ward and talked to the staff nurse in charge. Officially, Mrs Robson was 'settled'.

She looked better, if only because her silvery crew cut was concealed by a deep purple bandana. A glance at her temperature chart was also encouraging. Her fever had dropped overnight, within twelve hours of starting on the antibiotic. Her pulse too had fallen to something more like normal. She was breathing more steadily, without the rattle of the previous afternoon.

'Hello, Mrs Robson.'

'Eeeegh.' The old woman grimaced unevenly and gestured at Campbell with her left hand, alternately shaking her fist and making as though to push him away. It was not obviously the behaviour of a patient who was glad to see her medical attendant and delighted by the results of his life-saving efforts on her behalf. Campbell drew the screens round her bed then went off to get a nurse to help him examine her chest.

When they tried to sit her up she fought them off with her good side, shouting wordlessly and scratching the nurse's forearm. As Campbell listened for the various signs that had been present low in the left of the chest the day before the old lady suddenly snatched at his stethoscope and pulled it briskly from his ears, hurting him quite a lot.

'She was like that all night, apparently. Kept the whole ward awake with her shouting,' said the nurse as they retreated. 'There's a woman who's in with cirrhosis whose nerves are bad and she says she's going to get her husband to write to her MP about it.'

In the male ward downstairs the new houseman, new not only to the job but to graduate medical life generally, having qualified only a few weeks previously, was waiting

162

for his first professorial ward round. As Campbell came in to the doctors' room he jumped from his chair and stood by his trolley of case notes with an eager, rather servile expression that went quite well with his brand-new white coat but was probably wasted on someone of Campbell's lowly status.

'William, isn't it?'

'Yes. I was here as a senior student last year, Dr Campbell.'

'Yes. Everything all right?'

'Yes, thanks. I sort of know where things are because I did a locum for a week last year. And Dr Swift's going to talk to us after Professor Sinclair's ward round.'

'Good.' Campbell went to the trolley and fished out the notes of one or two of the Sinclair patients. Wullie, organized to the last, had written a short summary of the current problems of each of them for the benefit of his successor. He would be sorely missed.

'Is Professor Sinclair usually on time on Saturdays, Dr Campbell?'

'Sometimes.'

On this particular Saturday he was not. At quarter to eleven Barry Swift, the senior registrar, breezed in. 'Morning, Dave ... William ... Lovely morning. Stress of medical life not too bad so far, hm? Not to worry, William, it just goes on getting better and better. Seriously, any problems so far, or has Dave here been over everything, including those important little details like where the staff loo is? Very good, is Dave, about things like that. Shall we just get on then? A quick whistle round the patients, sort out the problems, heal the sick, comfort the dying, that sort of thing, hm? And then perhaps some coffee upstairs ... Oh. Haven't you heard, Dave? Hamish asked me to stand in for him this morning, and just take you and the

163

new people round on his behalf, he sends his apologies and all that.'

'Is he unwell?' William asked.

'Not in the least. In fact he's in cracking good form is Hamish. He just thought it would be nice to show our lovely Spanish colleague a bit of Scotland, what with her being new here, and the weather being so conducive, so he's asked me to stand in and do the needful. So now then, young William, what seem to be the problems? Or have you just gone straight ahead and sorted them all out?'

Swift pirouetted round the male ward, generally upsetting people, with William, Campbell and a mutely resentful nurse plodding in his wake. A man in the final suffocating grip of motor neurone disease was told that it was probably a neuritis, a pretty unpredictable condition that often just seemed to stop in its tracks and leave you feeling quite OK. A moribund stroke victim was uncovered, prodded and scratched in the vain hope of eliciting for William's edification a curiosity of clinical neurology known as the crossed extensor response. A youth just back from the neurosurgical management of a moderately nasty brain tumour was told that a crew cut suited him.

Upstairs he was just as embarrassing, chatting cheerfully, patting hands and making much of what he probably thought of as a boyish smile but when they came to Mrs Robson he stood back and looked grave. 'You've certainly got yourself a problem here, Dave . . . I can't be sure what Hamish is going to think about how you've handled this, but my gut feeling is that he's not going to be too pleased. I wouldn't go so far as to recommend stopping the antibiotic now, not if you've essentially snatched her from the jaws, as you seem to have done. But a tricky one . . . Shall we say leave it till Monday? I know it's difficult sometimes, when you get too closely involved, as you might have done here . . . We can all do that. It's one of those things we have to watch for, William. But let's say tincture of time, at least until Monday, when we get a chance to run it past our head of department. OK, Dave? But that's definitely a tricky one you've got yourself there.'

When they had finished the round Campbell went to apologize yet again to Mrs Robson's daughter. Barry joined them uninvited and was mistaken for Professor Sinclair, a misunderstanding he seemed to regard as perfectly natural. 'Yes,' he said when they had got things straight, 'it's all been terribly unfortunate, but you must realize that strokes are very common, and can happen at any time around this age. But fortunately most of them do quite well and that's what we're all hoping for in your mother's unfortunate case. So don't hesitate to get in touch again if there's anything you want to ask about. Grand . . . Grand . . . Good morning. And I'll let Professor Sinclair know you came up. It's just unfortunate that something even more urgent has cropped up for him at short notice, but I'll certainly tell him we've spoken. Good morning. Lovely to have met you. Goodbye, ma'am . . . Yes, Dave . . . Definitely a tricky one there. Now how about some coffee?'

'I remember him well. A perfect shit. Forever greasing around making himself helpful to people who might be useful to him. How would you like your ward round today, sir, merely subservient or grossly obsequious as usual? That kind of thing. And always fancied himself as one of the last of the great bedside teachers. What's he been up to now?'

Campbell sketched a few of Swift's recent offences. Hadden frowned. 'He'll be in his element with Sinclair. Do most of his doctoring for him and leave him free to get on with empire building and the slaughter of innocent wildlife. It all figures quite nicely, and perhaps what's in it for Swift is some kind of soft-money job with an easy MD on the side once the empire gets properly off the ground. So our lad sets himself up for a nice teaching hospital consultant job with enough sessions to spare to get both front legs into the BUPA trough in earnest. And he probably fancies himself as quite good with duchesses, despite his 'umble origins.'

That was a cynical but perfectly plausible version of how Barry might spend the next few years. Sometimes, and usually in a pub, Hadden displayed an unsettling percipience about things, as though he was some kind of tweedy surgical soothsayer who could foretell much simply from staring into a pint of export, and of whom it might be dangerous to ask questions the answers to which might prove disturbing.

They were drinking in the Wee Man, a pub once near derelict but now restored as a temple of the real ale cult. Around them were moustachioed arts faculty lecturers in dinky leather jackets and young solicitors in daring week-end denims. A cat lying on top of the TV was reaching down from time to time in vain attempts to claw up items of interest, mainly jockeys, from some sports coverage with its sound turned down. 'How's Mhairi?' Hadden asked out of the blue.

'All right.'

'I see her around the wards, adding just that dash of insulin that seems to make all the difference. We'd be lost without her.'

Campbell looked down into his glass and saw only export. Hadden watched the cat for a moment then said, 'I hear her husband's off to Saudi.'

It was actually Oman, but Campbell let that pass. 'And the best of luck to him,' said Hadden. 'I gather it's got from the thirteenth to the seventeenth century as recently as April. Public beheadings are more or less confined to rural areas and most of the Edinburgh graduates can get their hands on whisky somehow, so he should get by. And he's in good company, given what was happening to his career. All the Brits out there are on the run from something.'

Campbell thought of the tiles in Mhairi's kitchen but said nothing. The cat lunged half-heartedly at a top-hatted man patting a horse then curled up with its back to its audience. Mhairi the second had lasted a lot less well than Mhairi the first, and Richard was now off on a contract job as GP to a multi-national labour force grubbing for oil in the Omani desert. A man on the run. After a long pause Hadden changed the subject. 'So tell me about recent advances in Parkinson's disease, Campbell.'

'As diagnosis improves the patients do worse. Of the five patients who've gone across for what we laughingly call assessment, two are doing nicely thank you, two died at the Southern, and one's dying back at the Institute.'

'Ah, the price of progress. But they'll probably get better at it. I once worked for a cardiothoracic surgeon who used to say that he and all his colleagues had had to climb to competence over a mountain of corpses. A mountain of corpses, my boy. And he probably meant it.'

'Some of the relatives get upset.'

'Funny, isn't it. No respect for medical science. And he's not just killing people. There's something kind of fishy going on about lab work.'

'Really?'

'One never listens to servants' gossip of course, but I have a brother-in-law in Dundee who's a clinical chemist. Interested in CSF assays of this and that, and been talking to his opposite number in Edinburgh. They've been getting samples for obscure assays that normally come in at the rate of about one every six months, to do with motor neurone disease mainly, but since the new chap's arrived the local incidence of motor neurone disease seems to have quadrupled at least.'

'He's doing repeat assays.'

'Why? If you've got it you've got it.'

'He's bringing people back to see if things change.'

'Dozens of them?'

'No, but quite a few.'

'The clinical chemists aren't too impressed. And the old chap in charge is beginning to wonder.'

'He's trying to set up an international multi-centre study.'

'If you invite people to dinner you have to tell the cook. And he hasn't. And they think he might be up to something. Oh, it's not the sort of thing where you get Mr Plod in to take statements. What the hell would Mr Plod know or care about the more rarefied immunochemistry of the cerebrospinal fluid? But people are beginning to wonder. It might simply be a question of manners, an area in which your leader has a fair amount to learn, as I understand it. You know. If you're setting up a big multi-centre trial you at least let the bottle-washers know and promise you'll put their names on the resulting learned papers. Simple politics, really. But for sure they don't like him.'

'Not many people do. It doesn't seem to bother him.'

'Exactly. That's why psychopaths have more fun. And when you think about it, academic medicine's full of them. That old chap who used to dress like a stage magician and call himself a gastroenterologist. Beattie. And the psychiatrist who was eventually run in for wife-beating. And half the surgeons in town, Mackail to name but one. And there's bugger all you can do about them, unless they beat their wives and leave marks, because if they're clever they never go far enough beyond the limits of normal in any one area to get the chop. They're just a little bit beyond the limits in most areas most of the time, and the chaps say

168

yes, rough diamond, a bit of an enthusiast, terrific energy, takes all sorts, be dull if we were all the same and all that, and there are enough of them around to take care of each other, like the masons. And since it's medicine and not the Strategic Air Command we're talking about, the death toll never gets much beyond double figures. Really, there's no serious problem and the public ought to be duly grateful ... So long live the professor of clinical neurology and may he succeed in eradicating Parkinson's disease without eradicating all the patients first. Thanks, lad. A pint.' Hadden had lowered his voice towards the end of his peroration, because the lawyers were listening.

'So who's teaching them now?'

'No one. I was, and I've just sent them off for coffee. Hamish has them at quarter past eleven.'

'What are they like?'

'Average. I'm sure they don't know things I'm sure I knew at their stage, like feeling for a spleen. And there's a chap with a waistcoat who really fancies himself, so I put him through it on the common causes of abdominal swelling. Even with me standing right there large as life he didn't think of pregnancy. The girls rather enjoyed that.'

Andrea, who had read something about a possible risk to the foetus from the consumption of coffee, was sipping a glass of milk and had her feet up, thus occupying the only two comfortable chairs in sister's room. Campbell asked her how she was feeling.

'All right, generally. A bit funny after Bill and Jill's on Saturday. Made me wonder about all the things that go into Indian food that might, you know, upset things. But Alastair's very sensible, even at three in the morning. Told me that India had the most horrendous population explosion even though they ate stuff like that all the time, and just to go back to sleep. Yes. An interesting evening, in its way. D'you know them well?'

'Not really. Jill used to be vaguely into student politics when . . .'

'And wasn't Eric hilarious? All that joys of geriatrics stuff, when everybody knows he's really had the heave from gastroenterology and is desperately stuck for a job.'

'Oh?'

'Gosh, David, didn't you *know?*' Andrea went into gleeful details of some crisis in the Large Bowel Studies Unit at the Southern, making it sound like a place it would be wise to leave on any pretext. Since Campbell's own past included a brief misguided spell in gastro-enterological research he found himself fairly sympathetic towards Eric, who, it appeared, had been pressganged into evaluating faecal incontinence in an institution for the mentally subnormal, having been originally recruited on the understanding he would be doing a questionnaire survey on a new proprietary preparation of peppermint water.

'. . . so if it's a choice between grannies and the dole and they've got all those children to think about, you can see why he's a born-again geriatrician. And it might turn out to be not *too* awful . . . Once you got used to all those old wifies saying "Whit?" all the time.'

Andrea finished her milk and got up to go. 'An interesting evening, altogether.' She paused at the door. 'And if you don't mind my saying so, David, you've been awfully *good* for Mhairi.' If Campbell had minded it would have been unlikely to have made any difference. Andrea smiled and went on, '. . . because, when you think about it, most of the single men in Edinburgh medicine are either hopeless boozers or wildly gay . . . David, would you mind telling Hamish the students might be a wee bit late because the first session went on a bit . . .? Super. Thanks awfully. Gosh, David. Look. Hamish will be *so* pleased.'

170

Campbell stood up. From the window of sister's room they had an excellent view of the last remaining south-facing green space in the Institute's grounds. A few labourers looked on while a bright yellow tractor shovel, like a twenty-five ton poisonous steel insect, stripped the turf up in huge green and brown swathes to make way for much-needed facilities for research into Parkinson's disease.

'Right, lad. Swift says you've got a stroke up here for me to teach on. A right hemi with dysphasia. He said her name but I've forgotten it. You better come with me, lad, and show me where she is. And don't be all day about it. The students have been hanging about long enough.'

It had not been necessary to explain to Sinclair why the students had been delayed, since they had come back at twenty past eleven and then spent ten minutes or so standing around waiting for him. They were clustered at the door of the doctors' room when Sinclair and Campbell emerged. Sinclair strode through them as though they weren't there, with Campbell hurrying after him and the students trailing untidily down the ward in his wake.

'Roberts? Robertson? Something like that?'

'Mrs Robson? She's not exactly a straightforward stroke, sir . . . She was the lady who went across . . .'

'She's got a right hemiplegia, hasn't she? So Swift said, anyway. And some kind of speech disorder. It's the clinical signs that matter at their stage, Campbell. We're not doing a bloody post-mortem. Is this her? Ah, yes . . . Right, my dear, got some young doctors here who are very interested in your condition. All right to bring them along and let them talk to you? Good. You'll get your lunch when we're finished . . . Come on, closer, she's not got bloody rabies . . . You, girl . . . What do you see?'

A spotty blonde girl went pink and opened her mouth but did not succeed in saying anything.

'Too slow. Pathetic. You, boy.'

'Well, sir . . . An oldish female . . .'

'What's wrong with calling her an old woman, eh? And let's get on with it. She's in bed. We can all see that. She's got a pink nightie and a purple headscarf but we're not going to go into all that. From the end of the bed you can see that there's something pretty serious wrong with her . . . You, boy.'

'She's a bit pale, sir,' said the youth with a waistcoat showing under his white coat.

'Fright, probably, at the thought of you lot getting on to the medical register. No, she's not pale, boy. Look again. Lips are fine . . . Come on . . . End of the bed stuff. Yes?'

'Her face, sir . . .'

'Yes? Yes?'

'It's a bit sort of asymmetrical.'

'Well, that's a start. Yes. She's got facial weakness. What side's the lesion then?'

'The weakness, sir? The right.'

'The lesion, lad. Come on, come on. Basic neuroanatomy. Ever heard of the decussation of the pyramidal tracts? They cross over, don't they? The lesion's what we're interested in. We're neurologists now and it's a very precise discipline. So where's the lesion?'

The group consisted not of neurologists but of very junior students attached to the wards for three mornings a week to pick up the most basic of clinical skills: how to talk to patients and how to do simple clinical examination. For the moment they were learning neither. Campbell stood at the back reflecting that some of the most useful sessions of his own undergraduate career had been those spent in silent embarrassment watching someone doing something so badly that a simple resolution never to get like that was an education in itself.

Sinclair had concentrated so far on Mrs Robson's facial

asymmetry. There were other aspects of the case he could have taught on: the laboured breathing, the temperature – displayed on an easily visible chart and rising again – or the confusional twitchings of the left hand, a phenomenon known to clinical science as carphology. Mrs Robson, having been a little better on Saturday morning, was now very much worse and in all probability dying: a small matter that need not of itself detain an enthusiastic teacher of clinical neurology.

'All right. We're somewhere in the left cerebral hemisphere, since we're now agreed that the decussation of the pyramids, first described at least a hundred and fifty years ago, is a fact of neurological life. And if one of you were to go a bit further and suggest that the lesion was in the carotid territory and probably in relation to one of the striate arteries I'd be nothing short of bloody astonished, but there we are. So what's gone wrong?'

'A stroke, sir?' said the waistcoat.

'Good lad. So let's take a proper look at her . . .' Sinclair whisked the screens round and, with the students crowding inside, variously tapped, scratched and tugged at Mrs Robson's limbs to demonstrate the signs of upper motor neurone damage caused by her stroke. There was no fight left in her now. She lolled on the bed as Sinclair worked, her eyes half-closed, her tongue hanging loose and her breathing sometimes so faint as to suggest that her troubles might all be over very soon.

'See? And you can elicit exactly the same reflex by flicking the second and third toes. Like that. See? Or just scratching there. Downwards on the shin. Right? Try it, boy. Harder. You won't hurt her. That's better. Now you. Good . . . Next . . . Come on, come on, we haven't got all day.'

By twelve o'clock most of the students had been bullied through some little fragment of routine neurological examination. Sinclair waved them away, threw the bedclothes back up over Mrs Robson, bent down and shouted 'Thanks, my dear' in her ear then straightened up and snatched the drug chart hanging from her locker.

'Campbell? What's this?'

'Sir?'

'She's on a bloody antibiotic.'

'Yessir . . . On Friday we found she had a chest infection. I thought we should start . . .'

'This is Monday, Campbell, and we're going to stop it.'

'Sir.'

Campbell drew a line through Wullie's prescription for ampicillin, hung the drug chart back on the locker and accompanied his chief up the ward. 'She could linger for months and bloody months, blocking a bed,' Sinclair grunted. 'Is that what you want, Campbell? No turnover and a quiet life, eh? Well I bloody don't. Not now the motor neurone disease study's under way, and assessment for Parkinson's is beginning to get on to some sort of rational basis. We need all the beds we've got. Now let's get a hold of Dolores and go and have some lunch.'

In the queue for the lunch counter Sinclair suffered visible agonies, grinding his teeth, moving from one foot to the other, drumming his fingers on his tray and rattling the change in his pockets with the other hand. It was, Campbell realized, verging on the intolerable for him to be delayed in anything he wanted to get on with. A queue of lowly hospital functionaries, served politely but slowly by amiably dim catering staff, might immobilize him for only three or four minutes, but seemed to cause him the kind of distress experienced by ordinary mortals only in twenty-five mile traffic jams on warm bank holidays.

When eventually he reached the serving point he grunted and pointed to indicate his order, and when he had got it he pushed his tray along so briskly that a plate of soup on

174

the tray of a student nurse just ahead of him juddered and slopped messily around, a disturbance of which he was quite unaware. Behind him Dolores was coming to grips with Scottish institutional cuisine, whispering fragrantly in Campbell's ear, 'Daveed, what is this bleck pudding? Good, yes? Or maybe no? OK . . . And this yellow thing . . . Feesh, perhaps? OK?'

From the cash register Sinclair led them resolutely across the dining room to a table at which sat a middle-aged consultant physician half way through a pink blancmange. 'George, we're going to join you,' said Sinclair setting down his mince and mashed potatoes. 'You're not just going, are you? Dolores . . .' he raised his voice a little. 'This is George MacKay, one of our leading cardiologists.'

MacKay, properly surprised to hear himself so described, looked up at Dolores and grinned foolishly. Sinclair dumped his tinned fruit salad and ice cream down beside his mince. 'Dolores Delatorre. Just joined us from Madrid to co-ordinate the international motor neurone disease study. And you'll know Campbell . . .'

MacKay nodded and grinned a bit more. Dolores put down her fish as though having second thoughts. 'George and I graduated together,' Sinclair announced. 'A few years ago, we'll say.'

To Campbell that was surprising information. MacKay, a slavishly conventional dullard who behaved more like a registrar running into the end of his contract than a teaching hospital consultant in a prestigious specialty, he would have guessed to be at least ten years older than Sinclair.

'And how are things, Hamish?' The question had taken some time to formulate but was answered very promptly indeed.

'Pretty good, George. New building started today. Be finished by the end of the year or there'll be trouble. We'll be in it as soon as this place wakes up from its New Year and gets its porters organized.'

'I saw them working. On my way back over from the Haig Memorial Maternity Pavilion this morning. One of those really difficult ones where whatever you do is going to upset somebody. A girl of fourteen, twelve weeks gone. Makes you wonder . . .'

'No it doesn't. They're all at it. No way to stop them. The secret's the penalty clause.'

'The penalty clause, Hamish?'

'Every week that building's late costs the builder three thousand pounds. So they'll bloody well have to get themselves organized if they're going to make a penny out of it.'

Sinclair was using his fork to beat mince and potatoes together into a kind of pale mud whip. MacKay had finished his blancmange and placed his spoon the way his mother had probably told him to. 'Nice enough wee girl,' he said. 'Catholic, of course, but probably wanting an abortion anyway.'

'Only way to deal with them. And the way trade is just now they just have to put up with it.'

MacKay nodded again then sat silent. Dolores smiled at Campbell, perhaps to indicate that the fish was edible after all. Sinclair ate purposefully, finishing his main course in seven or eight large forkfuls and eyeing his pudding even as he did so. 'People want results for their money,' he announced with his mouth full. MacKay looked puzzled.

'No point in telling people you need money and then leaving it in the bank. I want to take this chap round the building the same year he gave me the money. Tells him I needed it and even lets me go back for more. When's cardiology going to get out of those rabbit hutches?'

'Well, Hamish, that's a very difficult question. You know we were pencilled in for the original phase one of the new Institute, but for some reason it's been decided venereology's more urgent. And then the fallback was for us to be first in a plan for what they call rolling refurbishment, but the floor of ward four's apparently a structural risk they're not prepared to take meantime, so it's all in the melting pot yet again until the lower corridor scheme's either approved or shelved, and even then we're up against the new intensive care area, and the surgeons are quite keen on that so there's really no saying. I don't think I'd be breaking a confidence, Hamish, if I told you . . .'

'You can see why I'm organizing my own bloody buildings, George. You wouldn't catch me leaving it to that bunch of wet hens at the Board.' He threw down his pudding spoon. 'We'll have you along for the opening. Show you how it's done. End of the year at the latest. You'll see.'

'Very good, Hamish. Look forward to it. Now I really must go. Another of those wretched committees. I've got the outpatients' secretarial services subgroup of the ancillary staff co-ordination committee and you've no idea the depth of feeling. They'll be at it . . . hammer and tongs . . . all afternoon, I expect. So . . . Nice to meet you, Miss . . . Dr . . . Very nice to meet you.'

MacKay got up, still grinning sheepishly, and left them.

'Look at that,' said Sinclair. 'Last time I had a suit like that I must have been a fourth-year student.' MacKay's suit, dark, shiny and crumpled, was certainly unimpressive from the back. 'Poor old George. Another one who's never been away. Been skulking around this place not offending people for about twenty-five years, poor bugger, and always talking about patients he's just seen because he hardly sees any. But if you want a volunteer for the outpatients' secretarial services subgroup of the ancillary services co-ordinating committee he'll be there and he'll take it seriously and he might even enjoy it, God help him.' Sinclair shook his head. 'Would you believe that for the first three years in medical school he won all the prizes? We thought he was brilliant, but he was just the middle-aged schoolboy then that he still is now. You wouldn't believe how little he's changed.'

'It muss be very deefficult, the obstetrician in the permissive society . . .'

'He's a cardiologist.'

'Oh . . . I thought he was saying . . .'

Sinclair switched to English for foreigners. 'He was saying that he had been seeing a young girl, pregnant, in the obstetric unit, with a cardiological problem.' He put his right hand on the left of his chest. It occurred to Campbell that it would have been even more helpful if he had also held his left hand eighteen inches in front of his waist, but perhaps that point had been established already. 'Deefficult,' said Dr Delatorre, picking again at yellow fragments of fish. 'And he too is having a new department?'

'He is hoping to. But he is too slow.'

'Hameesh . . .' Dr Delatorre glanced fondly at Sinclair and showed her teeth in a throaty giggle that made Campbell wonder how far their tour of scenic Scotland had taken them the previous Saturday, or perhaps weekend.

'So what's anybody doing about it?'

'There doesn't seem to be much anybody can do.'

'There must be something.'

'That's what everyone thinks, but there isn't really.'

'Hm. That sounds pretty feeble.'

'Yes. If you thought about it, you'd probably think there would be some quite simple way of stopping somebody mad from killing people, but there isn't.'

'Because he's a doctor?'

'Partly. But mainly because he's a professor.'

'Yes . . . That makes it a bit special.' Mhairi moved a little, allowing the circulation to return to Campbell's right leg. 'You can get rid of mad housemen quite easily, but that's because they're only housemen. Professors are different. So it probably boils down to something to do with academic freedom . . . Coffee? Or . . . shall we . . .?'

'Mmm . . . Coffee, please.'

'Oh.'

'Well, coffee first, please.'

Campbell lay in a pink sea of tastefully contrasted Laura Ashley textiles, yawning and stretching and contemplating the gradual return of normal sensation in his right leg. Mhairi got up, took a pink dressing-gown from the back of the door, put it on, gathered the cocoa mugs of the previous night from the matching bedside tables and went off downstairs.

It was all very difficult. In the past few weeks there had been other dinner parties, some less gruesome than the Baroda revisited scene at Bill and Jill's, and Mhairi's cousins, of whom there seemed to be about twenty around the University and in central Edinburgh generally, seemed to have loosely adopted Campbell as one of their circle. One, the most drunken, even seemed to think he spoke Gaelic.

Duddingston nights had become so common that Bones had taken to readdressing Campbell's mail and scrawling things like 'Come home, all is forgiven' and 'Where did you put the peppercorns?' on it. Only Campbell's clothes, thrown over a chair and defiantly untidy in a very tidy bedroom with ample spare wardrobe space, seemed to express even token resistance, but their symbolic disorder, stage-lit now by early morning sunlight, seemed, if he were honest with himself, to be tolerated only by the gracious permission of his hostess. Mhairi returned with coffee.

179

'Wasn't there a chap a while ago who got sort of sacked? A surgeon?'

'A professor?'

'No, but a teaching hospital surgeon.'

'Oh. A. J. somebody. Lorimer. Quite a long time ago.'

'Yes. They got rid of him, didn't they?'

'That was a bit different. He was a kind of gifted but appalling drunk, quite a nice chap, according to Hadden. And it was all very informal. The two most senior surgeons went round to see him, told him to stop operating and three days later he cut his wrists in the bath.'

'Gosh.'

'So it's not really the same.'

'Does Sinclair drink?'

'A bit. Holds it quite well, and it doesn't affect his work at all. So they'll have to think of something else for him.'

'What about the three wise men business.'

There was said to exist within the Health Service a shadowy system of informal tribunals which could intervene on receiving information about wayward doctors. No one seemed to have heard of their being active in a specific instance, which might either be a tribute to their discretion or a demonstration of their utter ineffectiveness. Hadden, with whom Campbell had briefly discussed the matter, inclined to the latter view, and had quoted an instance from somewhere in England where a physician had sought to shop a highly dangerous senior colleague, made some enquiries and discovered that of the local three wise men one was dead, one demented and the third the chap he wanted to complain about.

Campbell quoted that and Mhairi laughed then said, 'That's awful. But somebody's got to do something.'

'It's practically impossible. There's nothing he's done that he couldn't argue about. He could say people have strokes all the time, and it's just tough if they have strokes while you're doing something that's probably going to help in the precise diagnosis of their illness.'

'You don't really believe that, do you?'

'No, but it's what he'd say. And it's the same with his loony ideas on treatment. You can't say that his triple therapy is wrong just because it's not what everybody else is using. He'd say that the stuff everyone else is using has got its drawbacks, and what he's using has probably got some advantages. All he's doing is giving three established drugs in combination and there's a certain crazed logic in it. A bit of L-dopa because that's what your brain's run out of, some benzhexol to allow you to use as little L-dopa as possible and an anti-depressant because an awful lot of Parkies actually are depressed, and . . .'

'You sound as if you've finally succumbed, Dr Campbell. You'll probably get a permanent job in November.'

'I haven't and I won't. And I was going to say that the only trouble with triple therapy is that it doesn't actually work.'

'So he's a dangerous lunatic.'

'I agree, but there's nothing that says we all have to prescribe the same thing for the same disease. Teaching hospitals are full of rugged individualists with lists of nevers and alwayses that you have to learn the first week you work for them, half of them being violent prejudices for and against drugs. Clinical freedom. So that won't work.'

'Well, what about his teaching?'

'He's rude and awful, but so are a dozen other people in God's own teaching hospital. Think of Bobby MacElwee, even on a good day.'

'I suppose so. There must be something else. Does he beat his wife, like that mad psychiatry professor who had to go to Ireland?'

'I don't think so.'

181

'What's she like?'

'I haven't met her.'

'Does he have mistresses?'

'Probably. But no one minds that. Think of the consultant vacancies there would be if . . .'

'What about the money side of things?'

'Hmm. Hadn't really thought about that. I suppose he does a fair bit of entertaining that's sort of semi-departmental, and I suppose if anybody asked about it he would say it was departmental, full stop. No. It's like Hadden said. He's a bit over the line all over the place, but not far enough over it anywhere for anyone to do anything about it. And he probably knows all that, because whatever else people say about him he's actually pretty bright.'

'So we're stuck with him until he moves.'

'He won't. Why should he? He's a professor at his old teaching hospital, and people don't usually move from that.'

'A chair of medicine somewhere?'

'Possible, but I don't think so. The next bit of the plan seems to be to conquer Europe. He keeps slipping off to see people here and there, and it's all to do with lining things up so he can be vice-president of some European association of neurologists, so he can be president the three years after that.'

'I see. Tomorrow the world.'

'Probably. Even having that Madrid woman here is something to do with fixing the Spanish vote. And he spends hours on the phone to faraway places. It's all quite interesting to watch. And it keeps him away from the patients.'

'Can't be bad.' Mhairi put down her coffee cup, smiled and lay back with a purposeful air.

182

'Another one that doesn't take his tablets.'

'Thanks, nurse.'

Campbell took the case notes offered and flicked through them. The last few entries were brief and discouraging, with only the date and 'DNA', signifying 'did not attend'. A copy letter a bit further back recommended to the GP that the patient's dose of phenytoin be increased as a blood test indicated that his previous regime had been insufficient to achieve therapeutic levels etc, etc. That happened quite a lot in the epilepsy clinic: a patient would be found to have too low a concentration of the drug in his blood to control his fits, and someone would double his dose instead of sorting out the real problem, which was that the patient had decided, for whatever reason, to ignore advice and take himself off his drugs.

'D'you want him in?'

'Yes, please.'

The nurse opened the consulting room door and shouted 'Williams . . . Hurry up, please. Doctor hasn't got all day.'

Mr Williams was short and unprepossessing, with lank, greasy hair receding enough to show a couple of dimples in his skull from previous neurosurgery. Campbell glanced at the notes to check the man's address. It was that of a hostel in the Grassmarket perhaps just one step up from vagrancy.

'Hello, Mr Williams. Please sit down.'

The man glanced at the nurse then sat nervously on the edge of the chair at the side of the desk. 'Eh . . . Hello.'

'How have you been keeping?'

'Eh, to let you understand, doctor, a wee job came up in the farming line . . . Out of town, you understand . . . So it's been kind of hard to come up, losing a day's work and that . . .'

'Well, I'm glad you could come up today. How have you been?'

'Well, that's why I came up. Not so well, really. And the boss . . . You can understand it . . . He wants things sorted out.'

'So you've had a few more turns?'

'One or two.'

'Often?'

'Well, you know. Too often for my liking. And, like I said, the boss . . .'

'And had you made some arrangement to get the tablets, Mr Williams? While you were out of town.'

'Like I was saying, that's why I thought I'd come up.'

'So you're off the tablets, and having turns again.'

'Sorry, doc . . .'

'Where are you working?'

'Just West Lothian. Out by Tarbrax, a nice wee job.'

'What kind of thing?'

The man hesitated. Campbell glanced again at the notes. Under 'Occupation', 'driver' had been scored out and replaced by 'labourer'. 'It's, well . . . a kind of labouring job.'

'With machinery?'

'Sort of, doc.'

'Tractors?'

'Not on the roads, doc. Just fields, honest. And really not very much.' In the background the nurse was rolling her eyes. Campbell asked her to leave. She flounced out and slammed the door.

'Mr Williams . . .'

'Man to man, doc . . . when I take the pills I don't have them, and if I had the pills I'd be fine. But if I'd asked for time off to come in he'd have asked me what it was for and I would have had to tell him, and it's a great wee job. A wee room tae myself, and nice work, and he's nice enough, but . . .'

'Did he see you having one?'

184

'Found me after one.'

'Driving?'

'No. In a byre. Shit everywhere. Sorry, doc.'

'Well, what about starting the tablets again? What were you taking when you were all right?'

'One in the morning, two at night. And I was fine, honest.'

'What about a doctor out there?'

'My doctor's in the Canongate.'

'You know you can go to another doctor, and just sign something to say you're not permanently with him?'

'Oh. Well . . .'

'So you can get your tablets, and not run out of them.'

'Eh, right.'

'And what about driving?'

'Well, like I said, it's not really driving if you don't go on the roads, and I don't really have turns if I take the tablets. So . . .'

Campbell scribbled in the notes to give himself time to think. If the man had a job and wanted to keep it he would have to take the tablets, and he probably would if he could get them, and good luck to him. And if an upland farmer somewhere had a willing wage-slave probably making less than the legal minimum because of the peculiar circumstances, then good luck to him too. The driving aspect was marginal, one of those things it would have been more convenient not to know about, but if the man stayed off the roads and took his tablets and didn't have fits it would probably all turn out right in the end.

There was a list of GPs in the heap with the telephone directories, and they found the one nearest Tarbrax and agreed that Campbell would write to him and Mr Williams would go to him for his tablets in future. It all took rather longer than the ten minutes allowed for the appointment.

When Mr Williams left the nurse was looking distinctly disapproving.

The next patient was a little old lady of ninety or so who probably didn't have epilepsy and certainly hadn't had any fits since she started on medication. Campbell took blood for a level and talked to her only briefly. She was followed by a girl of twenty who had started fitting only a few months before and might or might not have a small and slowly growing brain tumour, the plan according to the notes being that she should be reinvestigated at six months.

It was not clear from the notes whether or not this had been discussed with her. She did not raise the question and Campbell felt under no obligation to do so. What concerned her was the effect of the drugs on her appearance. To Campbell, who had not seen her before, she was an averagely good-looking girl with a touch of acne. In her own eyes she had become emphatically ugly.

'I'm sure it's the tablets, doctor. I've got a friend who works in a chemist's and she looked it up in a book and she says it's more or less bound to be. I've never had acne in my life and my face has really changed. Not just the acne, it's sort of coarsened my features. That sounds silly but it's true. Look.'

She pulled from her bag a photograph of herself as one of a pair of bridesmaids, and she had undoubtedly changed since it had been taken. 'Look. Six months ago. And I'm sure everybody I know has noticed, but it's not the sort of thing they're going to say to your face. See. I look like my own ugly sister. And the worst thing is my gums.'

She drew back her lips in a kind of emotionless snarl. Like many patients on phenytoin, she had developed something called hypertrophic gingivitis, a disfiguring overgrowth of the gums. Thickened and deep pink, they encroached upon her teeth, seeming to shorten them and giving her mouth a curiously simian appearance. 'I'm

186

frightened to laugh, and I even have to be careful when I'm smiling. Honestly, Dr Campbell, I'd rather have the occasional fit and look the way I did before.'

Her friend from the chemist's was right. Campbell wondered about switching her to another drug, perhaps less effective but probably less distressing to a self-conscious and recently pretty female in late adolescence. 'And another thing . . .' She put the picture back in her bag. 'Do they make you hairier? I've got hair now in places I never had hair before.' She rolled up a sleeve. Not only her smile was simian.

Campbell hesitated. 'How much are you taking?'

'Four a day.'

Keeping her on the same drug but trying to get by on a bit less of it was at least a theoretical possibility. Campbell tried to remember what impact, if any, that was supposed to have on the side-effects of which she complained.

'Honestly, they're a lot more trouble than they're worth. I went for a herbal consultation, about the hair, mainly, but I asked him if he had anything for people with funny turns. He said he could probably help, but it might be quite expensive, so I said I'd think about it.'

'Hmm. Might be a bit difficult.'

'Herbalism?'

'Yes.'

'My granny never went to anyone else.'

'But with your complaint . . .'

'And she never had a day's illness in her life.'

'I'm sorry about all this. But these tablets don't seem to suit you.'

'You're telling me.'

'. . . so we should try to get you on something else. Another tablet.'

'Will I get my looks back?'

Campbell wasn't sure, but felt the best thing to do was

to say he thought so, sounding as confident as he could. 'Oh, yes . . . Yes, of course. We'll start you on something else, swapping the tablets over gradually, so there are no problems with your . . . fits. And things should return to normal but might take, well, weeks or even a couple of months.'

Resolving to find out as soon as possible whether or not what he had just told her was true, Campbell scribbled a prescription for some sodium valproate. 'That'll get you started . . . I'll write to your own doctor telling him all about this and asking him to prescribe it for you from now on. And we'd better make your next appointment a bit earlier than it would have been normally.'

Whatever second thoughts Campbell had about what he had just done receded when he considered the possible alternative: the girl paying twenty guineas for a bottle of dandelion water, stopping her pills and firing off a series of uncontrolled fits that might kill her. He wrote a longish note because it was all a bit unusual. As she left the girl smiled cautiously and thanked him.

It was ten past three and the clinic was more or less back on schedule again. The nurse came in with another batch of case notes and put them down on the desk. She was a tense, dark little woman in her late fifties, with a hook nose and an old thyroidectomy scar like a pink necklace. A regular and on the whole unpleasant feature of neurology outpatients, she had become if anything worse of late: tetchy with patients and abrupt with staff, clumsy and difficult when required to help with procedures and generally behaving as if even part-time outpatient work was too much for her.

She had been discussed over coffee up on the ward, with Andrea defending her, Swift wondering how long she had to go before retirement and Campbell, himself probably a transient in the department, having no strong views. The discussion, which had stopped abruptly when the ward sister had come in, had been occasioned by a report that she had had a brief but highly acrimonious exchange with Sinclair on the subject of which consulting room he should use; after which he had made enquiries about how to get rid of her and found to his distress that he was unable to influence the matter.

As she retreated from the desk Campbell focused suddenly on a specific aspect of her general unpleasantness. Throughout the clinic, in the course of which he had seen around fifteen patients so far, he had been intermittently aware of the smell of stale alcohol, attributing it variously to such likely patients as the near-vagrant farm labourer and a decrepit lawyer of doubtful habits. Now there were no patients around and the smell was as strong as ever. He looked up and the nurse paused by the door.

'Yes, Dr Campbell?'

'Um. Next patient, please.'

'Certainly, Dr Campbell.'

As he waited he tried to remember her name. Bird, or Birt or possibly Burton. She was wearing a name badge that would allow him to check in due course, and Fiona, the secretary who organized the NHS end of things in the unit, might know a bit more about her. Burton.

'Mr Gahagan.'

'Thank you, Nurse Burton.'

Mr Gahagan turned out to be an epileptic above reproach, of the sort junior hospital doctors in neurology dream of: the sort, in other words, who in a well ordered world would not be attending an outpatient clinic at all. He was a railway clerk of sober and meticulous habits. He took his tablets, did not have fits and did not complain of side effects. As he reported cheerfully on all this it occurred to Campbell that although the man could probably be discharged from the clinic without coming to any harm he might take it as a grave affront; and, besides, patients like that afforded the chance of a few minutes' rest and agreeable mutual congratulation amid a sea of troubles, so, like everyone else over the last fifteen years, Campbell gave him another appointment for six months ahead.

Of the remaining half dozen patients, two failed to attend and the rest were fairly straightforward. Campbell tidied them up and rattled through his dictation so as to finish comfortably before Fiona went off at five o'clock. He arrived in her office with his armful of casenotes at quarter to. Her typewriter was covered and she was folding the last of the afternoon's letters for the post. She looked up as he came in, and made a face.

'Not urgent. Tomorrow or the next day will do.'

'It'll have to.' Fiona smiled. 'I'm not playing busy-secretary games. It's just there's a fair amount of work around. Unless any of them are urgent.'

'Nothing special.'

'How's things?' she asked, continuing to fold her letters.

'Average fitters' clinic.' Campbell took the tape from his dictaphone and laid it on top of the heap. 'No use complaining. And you?'

'No use complaining. He wouldn't listen.'

'Prof Sinclair?'

'Who else. Probably the world's worst dictator. Definitely its most impatient. And he keeps thinking of things and sticking bits in the middle of his letters that have to go off in memos and other letters, and then losing track and going over the same bit of the letter but saying something different, as if he weren't actually thinking about the patient.'

'That's possible.'

'And he expects all the letters to be finished the day before he dictated them. Apart from that, he's fine. No. That's nonsense. He talks to me as if I were that woman upstairs, and gets upset because I can't read his mind. And *she* treats me as if I were a temp she couldn't wait to get rid of, and altogether I'm pretty fed up.'

'Oh . . . Sorry.' Fiona, who was young and pretty and sensible and efficient, had been around the department longer than Campbell and had been consistently sane and helpful through the troubled last weeks of the Brown regime. She was quietly observant and sometimes a valuable source of information. If she were to go it would be unfortunate but hardly surprising. 'Is there anything . . .?'

'Oh, I'm just having a bit of a moan. More thinking about looking for something than actually splashing out good money on the *Scotsman*. But he really is pretty horrible. What about you?'

'About the same. Sort of thinking about getting out. But nothing very definite.' Campbell was still on a locum contract with nothing certain beyond November, which was still too far away to stimulate active job-hunting.

'I'd sort of heard you were thinking about proper jobs.'

'Oh?'

'Settling down and all that.'

Campbell picked up a blank tape and slotted it into his dictaphone. Fiona smiled and said, 'Your letters will be ready tomorrow, sir. Unless that madman wants another instant upheaval organized in neurology outpatients, with letters to everyone and copies to everybody, like last week.'

'Oh?'

'Had words with nurse. Took the matter further, then the nursing officer as good as told him to get stuffed, which was quite refreshing and probably very good for him. But he doesn't give up, so half a dozen letters to all and sundry and a number of acrimonious telephone calls later we're still not sure.'

'Nurse Burton?'

'That's the one.'

191

'Drinks?'

'Yes. But he doesn't seem to have noticed that.'

'She isn't always drunk.'

'No . . . But more so lately.'

'Yes . . . I suppose so. I mean I've never noticed it before. Are there problems?'

'You could say so.'

'Oh?'

'Just a small matter of a shoplifting charge.'

'Gosh. Still to come up?'

'It's next week. So I think the nursing officer thinks she's got enough without that horrible man being nasty to her.'

'What was the . . .?'

'The details are very squalid, Dr Campbell. Most men wouldn't be interested. Poor Nurse Burton needs our sympathy.'

'That's a bit sad. But they hardly ever lock them up these days.'

'I should jolly well hope not. And I've only told you so you'll be nice to her, Dr Campbell, not so you'll tell him.'

'Noted, Miss Davidson. Gosh. Poor woman . . .'

'And you haven't signed your last lot of letters yet. They're in your tray.'

'Thanks, Fiona.'

Campbell sat down as directed and signed a dozen letters from the general neurology clinic earlier in the week. Fiona, who kept her finger on the pulse and could spell words like dysdiadokokinesia without a moment's thought, was better to have around than not to have around, even if, as it now appeared, her sources were not always one hundred per cent reliable.

'Sorry I'm late, Campbell. Had a small crisis over something that was supposed just to have been a routine bit of water-doctoring. Old boy with a prostate the size of a Victoria plum, as the boss puts it, in-and-out stuff, chipping and washing, but he bled like a pig from this Victoria plum, even when all that should have been left of it was the skin, so a long capillary-hunt up there in the dark at the end of the tunnel. Usual story. Blood stops play, people panic, and start to flap about everything else and want ECGs and what's his clotting time anyway and could he be getting himself into a bleeding-out situation and he's a pretty important chap, like most of the Victoria plum brigade, so I'm sorry. But now I'm here I'll have a pint, thanks. The eighty shilling. And some peanuts. Ordinary peanut-flavoured ones . . . Well. Good to see you . . . How have you been lately? It's been some time now since we last met, but I'm Bones, your flatmate . . . And I have several messages for you.'

'Oh?'

'Nothing that can't wait for that pint.'

They were in the second-nearest pub to the Institute, a place of complex pretensions with a clientele comprising, in approximately equal proportions, tourists, people from the world of folk-music and academics banned from the University staff club. It was busy and service was slow.

'And what am I supposed to tell people?' said Bones when Campbell returned. ' "David doesn't live here any more? Have you tried Mrs Kirkton's place? Oh. Sorry, Mr Kirkton . . ." I mean, I'm your flatmate. People expect me to know.'

'Messages?'

'Mainly women. None of them your mum.'

'Yes?'

'A foreign one. Speaks like zees. No message.' Bones took a long sup of beer. 'Ah. Just the job after our plum friend. Here. Have a peanut . . . Go on. Take lots. And the last married one. No message there either, but it sounded as if she wants to talk to you again. And someone trying to sell fitted kitchens and a chap who said he knew you from the navy but was probably just looking for somewhere to stay last weekend. I thinks that's it. No. There was another one ... Oh, yes. Mhairi. But I think she's probably got you by now. Cheers.'

'Cheers.'

'And are you getting your letters all right?'

'Yes. Thanks.'

'Great. Oh, and the peppercorns turned up ... Well, Campbell ... Good to see you ... It's been a long time.'

4

'Is it all right?'

'Yes. But you know you're about the third this morning. So all right, but don't stay long.'

'Thanks, staff.'

'She's in the third single room on the left.'

Campbell went along the corridor as directed. It was fiercely clean and gloomy and had not been repainted since he had been there as a student at least five years previously. As then, the floor-covering was glossy and deeply sprung, so that normal footsteps were reduced to a muffled squeak, a sound which further revived unpleasant memories of a dull subject badly taught. The first room was empty. In the second a crowd of relatives seemed to be having a party. He knocked softly on the door of the third.

'Come in.'

Andrea lay in bed looking simply awful: pale and ill and exhausted, hollow-eyed and far more wasted than Campbell would have believed it possible to become in the time since he had seen her last. Her arms, white and bony, were bruised and pock-marked at the recent sites of half a dozen intravenous infusions and a temperature chart behind her head logged a long and still unfinished struggle against infection. Barry's report from the day before ('A bit peaky maybe, but basically back to her robust and cheerful self') was clearly nonsense. 'How are you?'

Andrea shrugged and smiled. 'Come in, David. There's a chair somewhere behind these flowers. Honestly, I feel like a Latin American funeral.'

There were twenty or thirty bunches of flowers, most of

them fairly impressive, ranged on the bedside locker and the window-sills and a long coffee table, behind which there was indeed a chair. Campbell moved it carefully, so as not to upset anything. Andrea brightened up. 'People were being so lavish I was sure I wasn't going to make it, but it's beginning to tail off so I'll probably be all right.'

Campbell, by now embarrassed by his offering of half a dozen skinny carnations from the hospital shop, sat down. Thirteen weeks before her baby had been due Andrea had gone into sudden, forceful labour. A tiny child, a boy, had lingered four or five days in the intensive care nursery and then been allowed to die. There were rumours of malformations, but even without them so premature an infant would have had limited chances of survival.

Andrea herself had suffered a series of misfortunes attributed by all who heard of them to the fact that she was a doctor. She had lost a lot of blood and then developed a transfusion reaction. She had needed some complicated surgical tidying up and subsequently acquired a series of infections with exotic and resistant organisms. She had become septicaemic and gone on to acute renal failure, requiring dialysis for several days and then, just when she seemed to be getting better, had complained of a sore leg. A deep venous thrombosis and pulmonary embolus had added another two weeks to her illness.

'So how are you?'

'Better. And much better than I'd expect to be if I were just somebody I'd heard about. You know. A case presentation or something. D'you want the whole story, David, or have you heard?'

'I've sort of heard . . . in general terms . . . And I was sorry to hear about . . .'

'Adam . . .'

'Oh . . .'

'Adam Logan Scott. Poor wee thing.'

196

'Gosh.'

'Yes. Christened and buried . . . in nine days.' Andrea bit her lip and frowned in an effort to stop herself crying.

'How awful.'

'And when I was really ill I thought he was alive again. The worst bit was getting my head together and realizing he wasn't. Alastair was super, and so was Andrew Gordon . . . the chaplain.'

'Yes . . . Good bloke.'

'Super . . . and people generally.' Andrea waved vaguely at the banks of flowers half filling the room. 'They've been really super . . . And carnations, David . . . Thank you very much. They . . . sort of sort them out in the afternoon.'

Campbell put his flowers down with some relief. 'I'm not ill now,' Andrea announced suddenly. 'It's mainly about Adam. You know . . . being bereaved . . . really bereaved. Andrew said something very sensible about it. "Being bereaved is like being in love. You want to talk about it all the time." So I'm glad you asked about him.'

Adam had had blue eyes and the sweetest little tufts of dark hair behind his ears and had weighed some pathetic sum of kilograms that would have made more sense to Campbell in pounds. His hands had been barely large enough to grip Andrea's little fingers and his usual facial expression throughout his short life had been one of calm concern. Everyone had tried very hard but he had been just too little to live, and when he had died he was still and white and almost transparent. Everyone had loved him. '. . . so a lot of these flowers are more for him than for me, David.' Andrea had tears in her eyes. 'People have been really super . . .' She smiled again. 'How's the unit?'

'Oh, all right.'

'Sorry about the rota.'

Andrea's absence meant Barry and Campbell had been

197

on call alternate nights for more than six weeks. 'No problem . . .'

'How's Hamish.'

'Much the same. Beginning to get a bit wound up about his conference. Not in the wards much.'

'Poor old you.'

'We get by . . . Simpler, in some ways.'

'I know what you mean . . . But he's awfully stimulating, and a marvellous diagnostician, of course.'

'Quite.'

'And his research means a lot to him.'

'Seems to.'

'How's it going?'

'Well . . . we don't actually see him much . . . but one or two of the patients . . . seem to have had problems.'

'I actually meant his baboons, but I did hear a sort of a rumour. Alastair says I shouldn't, but it's hard not to . . . One of his legal friends had an inquiry from someone who's dad had been assessed . . . You know, for Parkinson's, at the Southern . . . David, you won't gossip about this, will you, because Alastair really insists *I* don't, but this chap's apparently done badly . . . I mean very badly indeed. Like, basically he'd be better to die and be done with it, and the chap who's wondering about the law is in two minds because of that, because he still doesn't know what's going to happen, and how he'd feel if his dad actually didn't make it. Suing won't bring him back, all that stuff. But it's touch and go whether he's going to or not. And you know I do sometimes wonder about Hamish. It's all very well being dedicated, but . . .'

'That's interesting. What's his name? Did you happen to . . .'

'Gosh, are there lots of them?'

'One or two. And some old ladies too.'

'And he's still doing them?'

'Well, he just sends them . . . Marcus Mackail actually does them.'

Andrea paused on the brink of further indiscretion. 'You know, David, I hadn't realized just how mad he is.'

'Mackail?'

'Yes. It's odd. Lying here week after week I get people coming in who'll talk about anything other than Adam, and they just sit where you're sitting rattling on about this and that. Barry was in yesterday, and chatting away the way he does, and a bit of it was about Mackail. He seems to ring Barry at home, in the morning, and I mean really early, like seven o'clock sometimes, to ask him if there are any more assessment patients on the way, and to tell him it's a lovely morning and he's just been out for a walk on the Braid Hills, and sometimes he tells a joke before putting the phone down, and would be quite happy just to chat until it was time to go to work, which I gather he does at about half past seven. All a bit odd, even for a brain surgeon. He hasn't always been like that, has he?'

'Hmm. I don't think so. In fact . . .' In the course of Campbell's brief and compulsory undergraduate sojourn at the Combined Neurosciences Clinic at the Southern his group had been taught by Mackail, who arrived twenty minutes late and discoursed gloomily on glioblastoma multiforme and how badly patients with it did, quoting desperate cases and heroic interventions with variously futile outcomes. If anything, he had seemed to Campbell, who happned to have just done his six weeks' compulsory psychiatry, to be more than a little depressed, and people who got depressed sometimes went straight through the normal bit and off the top into hypomania. Perhaps Mackail and his protégé had more in common than their interest in the biopsy diagnosis of Parkinson's disease. He briefly recounted the occasion for Andrea, who seemed to agree.

'Manic depressive, from the sound of things, and through the roof just now.'

'Sounds like it. So for the time being up there with Hamish . . .'

'Oh no, David. Hamish is nothing like that . . . He's just naturally energetic, and people resent that, but he's not mad. He's tremendously hard-working and forceful and organized, and also really kind when it matters . . . He sent me these.' Andrea nodded towards a vast bunch of mixed orange and white lilies, '. . . and an invitation to a drinks thing with a note to say he would perfectly understand and all that. No, David, people don't understand Hamish, what he's like and what he's trying to do, but he's completely sane and really one of the . . .' Her eyes filled with tears and she reached towards a box of paper hankies. 'I'm sorry, David . . . Would you mind . . .'

Campbell muttered sympathetically and got up to go. As he opened the door the staff nurse was waiting outside, glaring disapproval and reproach.

As a gesture towards academic activity in keeping with his status as a locum lecturer, Campbell had begun, in the weeks since the fine art lecturer had turned up with his odd symptoms, to read up about the more unusual presentations of cerebral tumours, particularly those involving disorders of visual perception. The big old neurology textbooks contained rich but vague accounts of these clinical curiosities, and some dusty hours in the basement of the medical library had been rewarded by a couple of good pre-war papers, strong on lyric description but limited by the crude investigative techniques available at the time; then Dr Temple, with whom Campbell had discussed the topic briefly, had pointed him in the direction of a monograph published in Sydney in 1956 and obtained eventually on loan from the national neurological library in Queen Square.

It was all quite interesting. In the absence of any easily accessible recent review or series, Campbell had half decided to try to go through the unit's records to find some more cases, possibly with a view to writing them up. He sat in his office on the ground floor of the old Neurobiology Unit, browsing among the collected oddities of a lifetime's neurology in New South Wales and hoping vaguely for something colourful and local, like a man who mistook his wallaby for a didgeridoo, to turn up; so far without any luck.

Meanwhile, the fine art lecturer was doing badly. He had been admitted to the ward for a detailed clinical assessment that had added nothing to what Campbell had already discovered at the outpatient clinic. He had then been transferred to the Southern for specialist radiological investigations and a biopsy. A subsequent short course of radiotherapy had made him drowsy and confused, temporarily much worse, and would at best only slow his overall decline. He was now blind.

Bloated by high-dose steroids, he shambled round the ward from Monday to Friday, guided by a nurse and talking with curiously muddled authority about things he had once been able to see, going home at weekends to the care of his wife, who, having three young children to cope with as well, usually looked at least a little relieved when she arrived back on Monday morning to turn him in again.

'Hello, Daveed.'

'Come in.'

Dolores smiled round the edge of Campbell's door. 'You are not too busy?'

Campbell moved a heap of Xerox copies and offered her a chair. She sat down and arranged the folds of her skirt in a manner that Anglo-Saxon society would have regarded

201

as verging on the hysterical. 'You are a naughty boy, Daveed.'

'Oh?'

'You are never at home.'

Campbell put down his book. 'Oh, have you been trying to get hold of me?'

Dolores smiled even more broadly. 'No, Daveed ... Only talk to you. And perhaps ask you to help me ... There are so many things. You know your ... electricals ... here are like nowhere in Europe or perhaps on earth. And in my apartment there are even two different kinds, so I wonder, and think who can help me ... Daveed, perhaps, so I phone you ... And you are not in, once, twice, even three times.'

'I'm sorry.'

'It's OK. In another apartment are helpful men, boutique men, very practical and so on. They explained everything and now it's OK ... And sometimes just to talk ... Edinburgh is not Madrid. I know so few people.'

'Yes ... It must be difficult.'

'And my Engleesh, that does not help.'

'It's very good.'

'Well, perhaps ... But not the Engleesh of some people here.'

'In the department?'

'Oh no. The shop people, the bus people. "Come on, hen ..." Is this possible? Hen?'

'It's just an expression. Nothing personal.'

Dolores thought about that and was reassured. 'There are so many things, in a new place.'

'You'd lived in London ...'

'Not for long. Edinburgh is much better, believe me.' She looked from side to side then leaned forward. 'No Arabs, Daveed ... You know in Spain we have them too, very very big ones, in certain places ... They drink, they corrupt the youth, with their big money. No . . . Edinburgh is fine.'

'And your work?'

'Good, Daveed, very good. An interesting topic, and a study that will count. A big disease, certainly in neurology. The study is good . . . But . . .'

'Problems . . .?'

'Not problems, Daveed . . . A problem.'

'Oh?'

'A . . . secret problem. Secret? Confidence?'

'Confidential?'

'Yes . . . Confidential problem, like the magazines . . . "Dear Abby, I have a problem . . ."'

Campbell was torn between a strong inclination to keep his distance from a possibly dangerous hysteric and a natural curiosity about her sex life. 'What sort of problem?'

'"Dear Abby . . ." In this case, "Dear Daveed . . .' I have a problem with my boss . . . He wants to . . . sleep me.'

'To . . .?'

'You know, Daveed . . . To fuck with me . . . And he is of course married . . . As usual, Dear Abby . . .'

It occurred to Campbell that if she really had such a problem her best plan might simply be to write to one of the standard authorities, and that his contribution should be confined to making sure her letter was in reasonable English, without too much in the way of upside-down question marks at the beginnings of sentences. It was likely, however, that the true problem was not the one presented. Dolores was probably simply intimating that her charms had not gone unnoticed in the department, and if there was dilemma at all it was not the moralist's one of what to do but the hysteric's one of how many people should know.

'Daveed . . . You must not speak of this . . .'

'Of course not.' Campbell nodded vigorously and reached for the Australian monograph.

'You Engleesh ... Daveed, I think you too have the upper lip.'

'What's happening with the motor neurone disease study?'

'We are getting lots of samples, and from many places, but Hamish is not completely pleased, and we will need more ... You too are doing research?'

That was putting it a bit strongly, but talk of clinical curiosities among doctors is a universal pastime, and Dolores too had seen some odd things in Campbell's area of interest. They chatted until it was time to go to coffee.

'There you are, Dr Campbell. That's you up to date. Sad about the chap with syringomyelia. And please get yourself some new batteries because you are getting fainter and fainter. I might even have some here.' Fiona reached to the back of a drawer in her desk and found a couple of dictaphone batteries. 'Here. Put them in yourself. They're bad for my nails.'

'Thanks. What's all that stuff?'

'Hers. Well, his. Conference bumf, and it's getting worse. She's doing the personal assistant to the managing director bit. You know. I'm policy, you're typing, and here's another three days' worth. If I weren't looking for something else anyway I'd just leave today and dump it all back on her. And she's so completely ghastly to deal with. "Ah, Fiona, my girl ... Been lookin' for you ... What you been up to, eh? Well, I've got just the job for you ... Another three hundred envelopes with five enclosures for the professor's conference, that'll keep you out of mischief, eh? Ho ho. Just joking, my dear. The professor really appreciates what you're doing for 'im. He was telling me so 'imself only the other day". Honestly. It's like being the

204

office junior in a fifties movie. I could strangle her. Or pinch her dentures and give them back to her mounted as costume jewellery.'

'Odd, isn't she?'

'God knows where he found her. Or him.'

'Him?'

'This morning, over the two hundred and fiftieth envelope or so it occurred to me that she was probably a female impersonator. You know. One of those ghastly gay men that hate women and send up all the ghastliest things about them. To do it properly he'd really need curlers and one of those wrap-round pinnies, artificial fur-trimmed slippers and perhaps a mop and bucket. But for an office version of same, I suppose he's got the general idea. Hair like a fright wig, Edna Everage specs, audible check skirts, the dreaded flounced blouses, seamed stockings and feet bulging over the patent leather . . . But he must really hate women.'

'Hadn't thought of it.'

'Obvious once you do. Malevolent camp caricature of office cow, possibly too overdone for general theatrical use. "Nice try, Adrian, thanks for coming along . . . We'll let you know, dear . . . Next!".'

Campbell was impressed. Mrs Greenlees would be just a little harder to take seriously after all that, or Mr or whatever.

'And the conference really is a mess, David. I've done one before, for the ENT lot. Just a UK one, but it comes to the same thing . . . Accommodation, circulars, tours, entertainment, transport and all that as well as the basic nuts and bolts of the scientific programme. It should take eighteen months and he's throwing it together in six. Cursing poor Bobby-baby every inch of the way.'

The proper organization of the Thirteenth European Conference of Clinical Neurologists had been another victim of the disorderly transition between regimes. Perhaps Bobby, in his heart of hearts not believing that he would get the chair, had neglected things for a crucial period of planning on the grounds that his successful rival would suffer more than he would as a result; or perhaps the knowledge that he had laid the foundations for an embarrassing international debacle had simply added to Bobby's already substantial list of reasons for doing away with himself.

It would be interesting to know but impossible now to find out, and in any case it hardly mattered, since Sinclair had taken the business of the conference in hand with characteristic zeal, lack of regard for others and general effectiveness; a successful Edinburgh conference being an essential precondition of his plan to dominate Europe.

'And I think she's up to something else,' said Fiona. 'Not sure what it is but she's gone extra charming, sure-you're-all-right-dear this morning, and something fishy is obviously just round the corner.'

'Fishy? Financial?'

Fiona paused over her envelopes. 'Shouldn't have thought so . . . No . . . He might, she probably wouldn't. No, some office ploy, more than likely involving a bit of extra donkey-work for Fiona-my-girl. We'll see . . . Haven't you got any work to do, Dr Campbell.'

Campbell, who had read and signed his letters in the course of their conversation, handed them back to Fiona, thanked her and left to go on up to the ward. William, even after more than two months in the job, needed a lot more supervision than ever Wullie had.

'Nothing new, doctor . . . Just the awful weakness, and I suppose it's a bit worse. It's like being tired, but more tired than you can ever imagine having been before. I'm always having to think what I'm going to use my pathetic little store of energy on this morning: blouse buttons or cleaning my teeth? And I know I can't do both without feeling completely exhausted until lunchtime, and then it's time for another decision.'

'You know you can get special easy fastenings.'

'I've seriously thought of getting a nightie that looks like a dress. Or even just staying naked and turning up the central heating.'

The lady spoke softly, because her thoracic muscles were beginning to be affected. She was in her early forties and had been diagnosed as having motor neurone disease only eighteen months previously. She was unlikely to last another six months.

'There are sort of Velcro things that go on normal clothing. Some people think they help quite a bit. How's your back?'

'All right, thanks. Dr Swift's awfully good. He says it's because he's done hundreds just practising to do me. And he says people all over Europe are collaborating to find a cure for . . . to find a cure. Did you know I've given five samples now, Dr Campbell?'

The lady, an intelligent and sensible administrator from a polytechnic in Leith, was beginning to sound like the simpler sort of blood donor, the kind that collected badges and probably thought of themselves as being in credit at the blood bank. The collaborative study in which she clearly placed her hopes offered nothing to science or medicine other than a slightly more detailed picture of what was known before. It was a redundant exercise in biochemical and immunological description, dismissed by Hadden as being about as useful as collecting stamps in the hope of improving the postal service.

There was nothing in the study about finding a cure, and absolutely no hope of anything that might change her short and dreadful prognosis. And something she didn't know about it was that the study protocol also included as one of its aims a post-mortem rate of one hundred per cent. When the time came her husband would be approached for a signature on the appropriate form, but with unusual and quite unseemly haste, because the pathologist wanted everything nice and fresh for his clever but useless enzyme assays.

'The twitching's better, Dr Campbell. That's one thing I've noticed over the last month or two.'

'Let me see.'

Campbell lifted a skinny forearm to confirm the patient's observations, flicking it with his finger because that helped to elicit the sign. True, the tiny irregular muscle movement had diminished, but that was not encouraging. Dying muscle twitched, dead muscle did not and there was hardly any left still to die. Campbell nodded and made as though to go.

'So I'll come in again as usual, Dr Campbell.' She smiled wanly. 'A few more times at least.'

Campbell hesitated. Terminal care by investigation was still terminal care, and there are certain courtesies to be observed, such as not rushing away when the patient seemed to want to talk about something serious.

'It's all very tiring.' Her voice was weaker even than when she had first spoken. 'And one begins to wonder . . . You know. How long it's going to go on, for example.'

Campbell sat down on the edge of the bed. 'It's a bit difficult . . . It varies such a lot between individual cases.'

'My husband's a vet and he says what you say, but it'll be either years, or months . . . or just weeks.'

Campbell hesitated again then said, 'Well . . . I don't think years. Not from the way things have gone. But not weeks either . . . so . . . months?'

The woman smiled again, more confidently, and nodded as well. 'That's what we think . . . my vet and I. So perhaps I can help . . . a few times more.'

William was standing a little apart and busying himself with his notebook, perhaps out of respect for the privacy of the occasion, more likely because he was not yet reconciled to the fact that neurology units lost more people than they cured. They moved on.

'And Mrs Robson?'

'No change, Dr Campbell.'

'And no word about her moving on?'

'No.'

Campbell said good morning and Mrs Robson waved. Her speech was as bad as ever but her mood had improved a lot. Sinclair's decision to stop her antibiotic had been the turning point in the case: suddenly she had rallied, reminding all concerned that a ruling to 'let nature take its course' meant just that. Nature had been around a long time, and people had recovered from pneumonia, sometimes, for centuries before the invention of modern drugs.

Sinclair had taken it badly, glaring at her on his ward rounds and grunting about the inadequacies of the geriatric service. A series of increasingly intemperate letters had been written and somewhere Mrs Robson's name was on a waiting list that did not seem to move very fast. Meanwhile she blocked an acute neurological bed, which in practical terms meant that she slightly diminished the numbers participating in the futile and meddlesome motor neurone disease study, and grinned unevenly as he passed. With good nursing care her pressure sores had healed, and she had developed no further life-threatening infections. Short of strangling her with his stethoscope there was nothing Sinclair could do, so now he tended to ignore her.

'What's she on?'

'Panadol as required for pain, and a laxative.'

'Daughter coming in regularly?'

'I think so, Dr Campbell.'

'Good.' Mrs Robson grinned and waved again. They

moved on. She would be around for some time. The rest of the round consisted of the mixture as before: multiple sclerosis patients in various states of resentment, resignation and despair; a couple of quietly hopeless victims of cerebral tumour in its last stages; a woman with a strange wasting illness that did not fit into any known diagnostic category but which appeared to be destroying her inexorably anyway; a youngish woman in for investigations and hoping probably in vain for a diagnosis that would permit her to see her children grow up; the epileptic girl whose fits had, as earlier suspected, turned out to be caused by a tumour.

Disfigured as much as ever by her anticonvulsant treatment, no longer an outpatient briefly subject to the thraldom of the hospital but a herded captive of the ward, without dignity or privacy and almost without possessions, she was subdued and quietly grateful for the passing attention of the power that had put her there. No talk of herbal remedies now, only an awed and fearful submission to the rules of the game: uncertainty, investigation, a revelation perhaps incomplete, a little hope, then more uncertainty and perhaps less hope. And she was not yet twenty-one.

At the end of the round William walked closer to Campbell than he had done at the beginning. As they went into the doctors' room he said, 'She's younger than I am. When I filled up all her forms it struck me. Same birthday actually, and just two years younger. A bit spooky. And she probably won't . . . live to be as old as I am now.'

'Probably not.'

They had coffee, and Campbell went back to his office to read a bit more from the wilder shores of neurology. After the ward the cases reported took on a darker hue. Blotchy photographs and post-mortem specimens were more visibly human remains, the residuum of a series of people who had it in common that their last illnesses had begun in a fashion that had tickled the jaded palate of a busy Antipodean neurologist. 'Flickering lobulated patterns of rainbow light spreading radially from the right upper quadrant of the visual field' were explained only a few months later by an ugly smudge of tumour in a slice of brain, and a thirty-one-year-old Australian stockbroker had got his, with only the little immortality of a case report as a memorial.

Campbell put the book down and rang the orthopaedic outpatient department to find out if Hadden felt like some lunch.

'Is this going to be posh, David?'

'Don't know . . . Probably, a bit.'

'OK . . . Something semi-posh, summery, with just a hint of respectable adultery. This, do you think?'

'Ideal.'

Mhairi put it on. Campbell too had had to think about what to wear, and had decided on a pale corduroy jacket, now comfortably run in, that had only a few years ago been regarded as too louche for wearing on student attachment to old Creech's wards: 'The sort of jacket,' Bertram had remarked, 'that should only be worn among consenting adults in private.'

Mhairi's dress was a simple silk or silkish thing in a colour that fashion folk might well call oyster. Among its other virtues, it went quite nicely with Campbell's consenting-adults jacket. Perhaps that was what she had meant by a hint of respectable adultery. Campbell sat on the bed and watched her at another cupboard, deciding what shoes to wear.

The final effect was quite stylish. Campbell took a mouthful of gin and told her so. She smiled and said, 'And you, Dr Campbell.'

'Thank you, ma'am.'

'Yes . . . Did I know you always worried about your shirts?'

'What?'

'Yes . . . I knew you weren't married, but because your shirts were always nicely ironed I thought you must be living in sin . . . already.'

'I owe it all to the Boy Scouts.'

'Really? Do they teach ironing?'

'Yes. And not living in sin.'

'But you did, didn't you. With Jean.'

Campbell drank some more gin and tonic. Jean, with whom he had not strictly speaking lived, had been quite discreet about things, as had Campbell. He had, after all, been involved only briefly with her when her husband was dying; or rather, as James Thurber might have put it, when everyone had thought her husband was dying. When her husband recovered Campbell's services were no longer required, and everyone continued to be very discreet. It was odd that Mhairi knew about it. 'Jean?'

'Jean Moray . . . When her husband was ill . . . Ages ago. I was doing my medical housejob when he was in as a patient. Everyone seemed to think you were doing a fine job, Dr Campbell.'

'Thanks,' said Campbell, finishing his drink. 'And I did all my own ironing throughout.'

Mhairi laughed then said, 'I knew quite a lot about you, David. Before . . . That sounds awful, but you were somebody interesting in the year above, you know, with a lot of capital letters. So I knew more about you than you knew about me.'

'I used to see you in the library. You worked awfully hard.'

'Richard sometimes mentioned you.'

'We were in the same group in fourth year. We used to disagree in tutorials.'

'And when you cropped up that night with the hyperosmolar lady I'd just been thinking about you. I'd seen you in the dining-room, and decided if I did again I'd sort of join you. Which I did anyway, the day the jolly green giant rolled up.'

'Gosh. And I never suspected.'

'Women are more methodical than you think, David. Come on . . . You're not senior enough to be really late.'

They drove from Duddingston round to Grange in evening sunlight. Sinclair's house stood on the corner of two broad, leafy streets, a mellowed Victorian villa with a front garden of neat lawns and shoulder-high rose bushes. Outside it were enough cars to make Campbell wonder if he were indeed insubordinately late. They parked half a block away and walked back.

'Barry's here. That's his go-fast Escort . . . And I think the Scimitar is Dolores.'

'The Spanish temptress?'

'That's the one.'

'Hm. Raven-haired, I suppose?'

'Yes . . . Just now anyway.'

'And what's Mrs like?'

'Mrs Sinclair?'

'Yes.'

'Haven't met her. Said to be couth, and rich, and a psychiatrist.'

'That makes sense . . . the psychiatry bit.'

'A child psychiatrist.'

'Even more so.'

Campbell rang the doorbell. They waited in a porch with a gleaming brass boot-scraper and an equally well-cared-for brass umbrella stand. 'It's all a bit more civilized than I . . .'

'Hello, lad. Good to see you . . . Even if you did take your time. Come in. Hello . . . Good to see you . . .'

Campbell began to introduce Sinclair to Mhairi but they were already being led through a large entrance hall done in pale greys and pinks and fragrant with cut roses and on into a lounge from which a party comfortably in progress was spilling out through French windows on to another set of lawns. They halted by a sideboard and Sinclair handed them glasses which he filled from a jug, one of several standing at the ready and filled with gin and tonic.

'Here, lad. You must know Fraser Ratho. If you don't it's time you did. Fraser . . . Young Campbell here's supposed to be working for me. And . . .' He waved his jug of gin and tonic at Mhairi and moved on.

Campbell knew Fraser Ratho and rather disliked him. When Fraser looked pointedly at Mhairi's ring finger, now vacant, and then at Campbell that seemed at least to indicate that further introductions were unnecessary. There was a pause in which Campbell sipped his gin and tonic and found it to be strong.

'I must say it's awfully good to have Hamish back in town,' said Ratho when their host was almost out of earshot. 'Edinburgh's lost far too many good people in the last ten years. Awfully nice to see at least one of them coming back . . . And things really had begun to slide under old Aithie, and even more so because of poor Bobby, of course.'

Campbell recalled a corridor conversation with Ratho a little less than a year previously, when Bobby had been 'awfully go-ahead, just what neurology needs next, although that's not to say that Professor Aithie isn't terrifically progressive on the clinical side'.

'And are you working for Hamish too, Mhairi?'

Mhairi shook her head. 'Still trying to be a diabetologist.'

'Of course. Of course. Awfully interesting, isn't it, and

lots of scope for research . . . And you're still . . .?' He glanced again at her ring finger. 'You're still in Duddingston?'

'Yes,' said Mhairi firmly, 'You're quite near here aren't you?'

'Next door but one, actually . . . so we're tremendously pleased to have Hamish as a neighbour.'

'How's gastro-enterology, Fraser?' Mhairi asked. 'Anything coming up?' Campbell stood back and enjoyed his gin. Gastro-enterology was a field crowded with brilliant young men but Fraser Ratho was not one of them. Mhairi, if she knew him at all, must have known that. 'Isn't there a senior registrar job soon at the Southern?' Mhairi sipped her drink and smiled and waited. Fraser looked thoughtful. Campbell had a feeling that the post had been filled a few weeks before and was doubtful if Ratho had even been short-listed. Perhaps under some provocation, Mhairi was playing it rough.

'An awfully good field, I understand. Of course I've been concentrating on finishing my MD thesis . . . Time enough to look around when that's out of the way. And one gets so . . . absorbed in an MD.'

Mhairi pursed her lips and nodded sympathetically, as though Ratho had just confessed to a lifelong fetish for being caned by sailors in black frilly underwear. 'I see,' she said, sounding a bit more highland than usual. 'I see, Fraser . . . So that's the way of it.'

Ratho looked frankly shifty then muttered something about Hamish having a lovely garden. Mhairi nodded again and he went off in the direction of the French windows. Campbell laughed sooner than he would have done had it been anyone other than Ratho. 'That wasn't very nice.'

'He isn't a very nice man. I can't be bothered with his genteel bad manners. He was one of my husband's sillier

215

acquaintances. The golf, you know ... A kind of silly game.'

In a corner Sinclair was working hard on a suave and swarthy man in a dark suit, with Dolores looking on admiringly. 'Is that your Dolores, David?'

'That's Dolores.'

'Hm. Has she got something going with our host?'

'Not sure, but she wants everyone to know she's been asked.'

'And who's the chap who looks like Mr Aristotle Onassis?'

'No idea. Who's that with Barry?'

'No idea. But it's usually Miss A. Nurse, isn't it?'

The girl with Barry looked wrong, in a very Barryish sort of way. She was a tall, bleached blonde with a yellow headband, a leathery tan and a low-cut short white dress with a shiny white belt. Barry, in a pale green safari suit and red silk cravat, was talking animatedly to an older woman. The blonde was no longer paying any attention, but looking vacantly out over an empty glass as though trying to remember where she had parked her chewing gum. The older woman Campbell recognized eventually as Miss Pittendreich.

'Let's go outside, David.'

'Fine.'

They went down a few steps on to a lawn. Groups of people stood around on the first two terraces of a long south-facing garden ending in a little orchard and stone wall. It was still sunny, even warm. From another garden the chatter and tasty smoke of a barbecue drifted over. Campbell identified a few more people from the Institute: Mackay the cardiologist, holding his glass as though elders of the kirk should not be seen drinking out of doors even in secluded gardens in Grange; an obstetrician who might be a neighbour; a commercial urologist whose white

Mercedes was by far the grandest of the cars parked outside.

A woman in blue was going round with a jug of gin and tonic. Seeing Campbell in need she stopped and smiled. 'Dr . . . Cameron, isn't it? I'm Elspeth Sinclair. Can I top you up? And . . .?'

Mhairi introduced herself and accepted a couple of millilitres in a still almost full glass. Mrs, or Dr, Sinclair did not appear to be in a hurry to move on. Mhairi asked her about coming back to Edinburgh.

'London's all right . . . for people who haven't lived in Edinburgh.' Mhairi seemed intrigued by that, and perhaps about to say that Edinburgh was all right, for people who hadn't lived on Raasay. 'Neither of you are from London, obviously.' They nodded. 'You have to be a millionaire to live decently anywhere near anywhere, and I hardly saw Hamish through the week. And I was at school here, and medical school, and it's jolly nice to be back.'

Campbell asked her about her work. 'A bit of good luck there too. I've sort of inherited an MRC job from a girl who's off having babies. Following up families of crazy, mixed-up kids. It's wild but interesting.' She looked down the lawn to sunlit backs of a row of houses similar to her own. 'The other side of Edinburgh, in all senses. I must just splash this jug about a bit. We'll be pushing you all in to eat shortly.'

She smiled and went off. Mhairi made a puzzled face. 'She must be mad or incredibly sane. She probably thinks of herself as . . .' She was interrupted by the arrival of Barry, steering his blonde by one brown elbow. 'Hello there, folks . . . Lovely do, n'est-ce pas? Dave, Mhairi, can I introduce Meryl? Meryl isn't anything to do with medicine so there's to be no shop and no Institute gossip.' Meryl smiled back with her mouth open. She had beautiful teeth, all the way back. Somebody had to ask Meryl what she did. She was in travel, which turned out to mean she was an air-hostess, which everyone thought was really glamorous, but was really hard work.

Up above the world so high, like a waitress in the sky, Campbell mused, as she went over the rigours of the Lagos route and the state of the beaches in Nigeria and how a bottle of soda water cost about two pounds and probably had dysentery, but at least you got out somewhere with decent weather once in a while.

In the north-west the sun was setting and purple dusk gathered between Arthur's Seat and the Pentlands. An aircraft, a sliver of gold leading a stately trail of vapour high and westwards, passed silently overhead. Four miles below it swallows squeaked and swooped around the idle chimneypots of Grange in summer. Forty feet under them, bees nuzzled at Sinclair's lupins and snapdragons. 'You know what I mean,' said Meryl. Mhairi nodded and Barry grinned. 'We're all green with envy, love . . . I think they're trying to get us inside now. And I believe the eats tonight are really something special.'

There was a genteel conversational queue in which Campbell found himself next to a man who admitted to being in the printing industry, then to managing a large part of it locally, and finally to being on the Health Board, which presumably explained his utility to Sinclair and hence his presence. Behind them the commercial urologist was enumerating, for the benefit of an unidentified middle-aged man who evidently drove a Lancia, the multitudinous defects of a Lancia he had once owned himself.

By the time Campbell and Mhairi drew level with the three whole salmon which formed the centrepiece of the cold buffet two of them looked as if they had been mobbed by a flock of seagulls and the third not much better. Suddenly two girls in black with white aprons and frilly caps parted the queue, removed the remains and brought

218

in two more whole poached salmon on arm-long platters, rearranging the various supporting dishes so that, apart from a few pink crumbs here and there, all was as new. The urologist growled with satisfaction and further back in the queue morale picked up visibly.

After the food table another girl in black dispensed a wine that seemed to Campbell probably the best he had ever drunk standing up. With glass and plate he followed Mhairi back into the lounge, which was too full now for them to stop, and on into a little sitting-room overlooking the terraced garden at the back of the house. On a sofa behind the door Dolores was deep in an evidently intimate conversation with Sinclair. A few people seemed to have taken food out into the garden, which now seemed as good a place to eat as any. They went back through the lounge and outdoors once more.

'Interesting,' said Mhairi as they sat down on a stone step. 'He really is a shit.'

'She seems quite nice.'

'Mrs?'

'Yes.'

'Keeps the show on the road, I imagine. Being nice to all the people he's horrible to and generally being more grown up than he is . . .' There was a pause and Campbell wondered to what extent her comments were based simply on observation of the Sinclairs, but she did not elaborate. As they ate their salmon Campbell recalled Wullie's remark about the bones and false teeth, and thought of telling Mhairi about it, but decided against it on account of Andrea's recent troubles.

'A beautiful evening, no?' said a deep voice behind them. The man who looked like Onassis lowered himself down on to the curved step beside Mhairi. 'May I join your picnic, yes? Such a pity to lose the wonderful long evening of the north inside the house.'

The sentence sounded so thoroughly rehearsed that Campbell feared for the man's fluency in further conversation, but he need not have done. A neurologist and a Madrileno, as he had introduced himself, he was in Edinburgh in connection with the forthcoming European conference, staying the weekend with Professor Sinclair and going back to Spain on Monday. 'Today your castle and palace, tomorrow your highlands, the next day home, alas, and so much unseen. But maybe in September . . .'

Relaxed perhaps by gin and tonic and a few toppings-up of white wine from the catering girls, who were circulating dutifully in the dusk, he was good, amusing company, a successful and probably quite powerful man at home, a confessed naïf but a formidably intelligent one abroad. He talked of the recent politics of his country and its oddly rushed assimilation to the rest of Europe, and of the protracted dying of Franco: 'not punishment, I think, but at least some kind of comment . . . As though heaven could wait.' Eventually they went in for pudding.

They were directed to the kitchen, a large and lavishly modernized one with a central island laden with various gateaux, mousses, trifles and fruit salads. Another agreeable white-trimmed girl in black lay in wait with rows of fresh glasses and a dozen bottles of posh pudding wine. Mhairi took a spoonful of fruit salad and half a glass of wine and, by way of allowing Campbell to relax a little, offered to drive on the way back.

In the hall a small bald man was standing by himself. He smiled and raised his arms, spilling some sauterne, as Mhairi emerged from the kitchen. 'How are you, my dear? How very nice to see you . . . And you, sir, I don't believe we've had the pleasure.' Campbell had been around long enough to have gained a little experience in the delicate art of dealing with his superiors when they were more drunk than he was himself. Mhairi, with vast exposure to highland culture, was presumably just as well prepared. She smiled and said something about the party then introduced Campbell. 'Mr Mackail, this is David Campbell ... He's with Professor Sinclair.'

Mackail did not seem interested. He took a large mouthful of sauterne, smiled broadly and looked down the front of Mhairi's dress. 'A wonderful year,' he announced.

Mhairi sipped from her glass and nodded. 'Nineteen seventy-one?' Campbell was impressed that she had noticed such a detail. Mackail looked simply puzzled then shook his head. 'I may have had a bit to drink but I am totally oriented in time and space. This is nineteen seventy-five. It is Saturday the ninth of August and if I told you our position was three degrees west and approximately fifty-six north I doubt if you would be in a position to contradict me, young lady. It's the west that puzzles people. You are clearly unaware that Edinburgh is, for example, west of Bristol.' He looked up at her face and smiled again.

They were not to discover what had made nineteen seventy-five, or what had passed of it so far, so wonderful for Mackail. For some reason he began to talk about the metabolism of deep-sea Arctic fish, having read recently of a species without haemoglobin and hence without conventional red cells to store and transport oxygen. He seemed to want to debate the question formally, and although Campbell said virtually nothing he found himself cast in the role of counsel for the red corpuscle. 'You might argue,' a wet-lipped Mackail pronounced, 'that the partial pressure of oxygen that can be achieved by haemoglobin would outweigh all conceivable problems of its manufacture and sequestration. But no ...' There was a forensic pause. 'Not in the icy depths of ninety north, where metabolism is a matter of chilly care and maintenance, where predator and prey may take months to achieve that fatal rendezvous, and where a momentary lunge, anaerobic but sufficient, can provide for years of survival and growth. You might argue the economy, indeed the elegance of the red cell in almost any terrestrial and most marine contexts, but your red cell is a meaningless extravagance, an irrelevance to the problem in hand, a colossal overkill of the oxygen transport remit three miles under the ice. You simply haven't got a case . . . and think of all the problems raised by the existence of red cells . . . things we put up with because we've simply never begun to contemplate the alternative.'

'Marcus, darling.'

'Mackail turned and looked down Elspeth Sinclair's front.

'Marcus, darling . . . You're getting terribly serious . . . You probably know Barry, but I don't think you've met Meryl.'

'Hello, my dear. This is indeed a wonderful year.'

Mackail ogled Meryl's tanned expanses. Mhairi and Campbell retreated into the lounge and spent twenty minutes in the company of a middle-aged lady with a remote nursing background and strong opinions on practically everything. She was Mrs Mackay. She talked a lot and her special subject was schooling in Edinburgh. By the time an opportunity arose to go for coffee Campbell had begun to feel quite sorry for the lacklustre cardiologist last seen shyly sipping a gin and tonic on the lawn.

By eleven it seemed time to go. They made a brief search for their host but did not find him. Mrs Sinclair, upon whom the strain of the occasion was perhaps beginning to tell, accepted their thanks as one with a great deal on her mind. They walked down the rose-scented path into cool, comfortable suburban dark and made for their car. A fair proportion of the previous row of cars had gone, but Dolores' Scimitar was still there. That was interesting. On the quick and fruitless look around for Sinclair Campbell had not seen her, and wondered if these observations were in any way connected, and if Mrs Sinclair's preoccupation when they had said goodbye was perhaps thus explained.

As agreed, Mhairi drove, zig-zagging through Grange then making neat use of a one-way street Campbell hadn't known about to get across Newington and into the park. At the roundabout there had been a minor accident, with one car angled on the verge and another still on the road but crumpled round the front and surrounded by fragments of glass. There were three police cars, flicking blue light in ragged unison, and as Mhairi was waved past they saw a number of dazed youths assisting a sergeant and half a dozen constables with their enquiries. For the moment no one seemed to need a doctor, although of course that might change quite quickly once they all reached the cells.

Campbell, glad not to be driving even though it was his car, sat back as the road wound on through the park and round the outworks of Arthur's Seat towards a strange geological formation, a system of huge serried pillars of red basalt known as Samson's Ribs, looming high and threatening on the left immediately above the road and signposted beforehand with a graphic warning about rock fall. For two hundred yards or so a suburban journey offered risks a little out of the ordinary.

Sometimes, walking back from Duddingston to Marchmont in the morning, and especially if it were misty, Campbell experienced moments of anxiety passing the place, as though the otherwise more or less forgotten god of his childhood, an emblematic figure combining features of Michaelangelo's Moses and a rather sterner Kirkudbrightshire primary school headmaster, might be waiting up there to remind insect-like transgressors below of his existence with a couple of tons or so of condign rock.

Travelling by car under cover of darkness seemed somehow less provocative. They passed beneath the looming pillars. Nothing happened. Duddingston came into view, the church tower silhouetted against the lights of the village beyond, the little loch gleaming to the right. Campbell found himself looking forward to cocoa in Mhairi's half-tiled kitchen.

'Is that everyone?'

William hesitated. Campbell ran through the previous Friday's ward round in his head, modifying it in the light of the weekend's events. One of the multiple sclerosis girls had been discharged, and an oldish woman with motor neurone disease had been admitted as an emergency on Sunday, it appeared for the home straight. There was still a gap.

'Girl with fits and probably a tumour. Hairy from her phenytoin.'

William pulled out a notebook and flicked through it. 'Barbara somebody?'

'MacIlwraith. Same birthday as you.'

'Gosh, yes ... Her ... Don't know, Dr Campbell. Sorry. I was off for the weekend, and nobody said anything about her. I'm sure they'd have mentioned if she'd ... died.'

William, after a fair start lasting a couple of months, was beginning to sound like Dennis. 'Let's see if we can find her notes.'

They went back to the doctors' room. There was still a slot in the case notes trolley labelled, in William's neat hand, 'MacIlwraith', but it was empty. They looked round the worktops and the desk. 'I suppose I could ask the nurses.'

'Might be best.' That seemed to acknowledge a certain lack of grip on the part of the ward medical staff but it was probably the quickest way to sort things out. William went off into the ward again. Perhaps the girl had indeed discharged herself against medical advice for another flutter with herbalism, but, if she had, somebody ought to have told somebody about it first thing on Monday.

William returned. 'The Southern. Went across on Saturday. Come to think of it Barry muttered something about it on Friday . . . Biopsy?'

'Barry?' Strictly speaking Barry was now responsible for Sinclair's male inpatients, Campbell for the females. Though Campbell's superior by virtue of his senior registrar post Barry did not, in the ordinary course of events, supervise Campbell's work or, as in this case, meddle with it. A biopsy of the by now strongly suspected cerebral tumour might or might not be a good idea, but the decision was Campbell's or, should he choose to do one of his increasingly infrequent ward rounds, Sinclair's. The problem was that Sinclair's ward rounds were now very infrequent indeed, and Barry, as the next in line of clinical succession, had taken to playing locum consultant more or less at will. 'I'm not sure she really needed a biopsy. The scan seemed to tell us what we needed to know, and on clinical grounds we'd probably just wait and . . .'

William was looking shifty again. 'I don't think he meant a tumour biopsy. He sort of chatted her up and got her to sign a form for the Parkinson's assessment.'

'Bloody hell.'

'They'd been talking about it over tea in sister's room earlier last week. Getting some normals, now the technique's been perfected.'

'You're kidding.'

'And I think one of the MS chaps from downstairs might have . . .'

'Thanks, William.'

Campbell rang the exchange and asked them to bleep Dr Swift. After several minutes of waiting he rang exchange again and was told that Dr Swift had not been in touch

225

that morning, and that Professor Sinclair's secretary sometimes took messages for him. Campbell rang Mrs Greenlees.

'Yes . . . And who is it wishes to speak to him?'

'Dr Campbell?'

'Dr who? Ho, ho. Oh, you know what I mean. Who are you?'

'Dr Campbell, Professor Sinclair's registrar.'

'I do beg your pardon, Dr Campbell . . . I just didn't recognize your voice . . . An awfully bad line, isn't it . . . And who did you want to speak to?'

'Dr Swift.'

'I'm sorry, Dr Campbell. I don't think I've seen him this morning. But as you probably know he sometimes goes over to the Southern on Mondays. He didn't tell me exactly whether he was intending to go across there this week or not, but I know for a fact he sometimes goes over in connection with the Professor's work, with that Mr Mackail, you know, at the Southern.'

'Thanks.'

'Don't mention it, Dr Campbell . . . Goodness, isn't this an awful line?'

'Mrs Greenlees, is Professor Sinclair . . .?'

She had hung up. Campbell decided to have a cup of coffee before ringing her again.

'Operating with him was a sort of Ealing comedy done by Hammer films, except that the show rarely lasted less than four and a half hours. He would start out to do some weird bloody procedure he'd just been reading about in the Transylvanian Journal of Head and Neck Circulation, and then it would turn into another of his one-off tales of mystery, horror and neurosurgery. "Hmm . . . We could join this to this and then sort of plumb in a bit of this . . . Yess . . . Ah, yes . . . Splendid . . . We should probably write it up for one of the journals. Oh ... Now what's going on here? We seem to have this rather large end to spare ... I wonder where that came from ..." And the gasman was usually Habib the cryptic Copt, nodding off over his stocks and shares and saying, "I have seen zese people ... Zey die." And of course most of them did.'

Hadden sketched a respectful little cross in the air with his fork. 'Then he rather lost interest in the surgical approach to problems of the cerebral circulation.'

'Because of the results, or because somebody complained?'

'Neither. Boredom. The referrals kept coming in because there's bugger all else you can do for strokes, and sections of the middle classes appear to prefer a quick, clean kill. He just got bored, and asked Santa for a stereotactic frame and when it came he unwrapped it, glanced at the instructions and set up in business as the man who could find the globus pallidus the way a pig finds truffles, first shot and every time ... as was sometimes confirmed at post-mortem the following day. God knows what he'll think of next. And he's still a couple of crazes at least from retirement.'

'I met him on Saturday. At Sinclair's.'

'Maybe a revival of psychosurgery. Dust off his phrenology charts and start chopping out the neural centres associated with dole scrounging, football hooliganism and double parking. Or perhaps he'll just revolutionize the treatment of dementia by implanting forget-me-not seeds in the cerebral cortex. In summary, my lord, my client pleads insanity, grievously aggravated by the tragic temptations of his unfortunate neurosurgical background, and throws himself on the mercy of the court.'

'Hmm. As bad as that?'

'Just about. What was he like on Saturday?'

'Drunk, and mildly strange about Arctic fish. And looking down people's dresses a bit.'

227

'The sane doctors over there worry about him from time to time, but there's not much you can actually do. The whole of brain surgery's a dangerous experiment, if you think about it, but some experimenters are more dangerous than others.'

That was not encouraging, but Campbell described Sinclair's latest initiatives anyway. Hadden looked thoughtful then said 'Baboons maybe, people probably not. And there's no suggestion either of these bods has got Parkinson's?'

'Not as far as I know, and I've seen them both.'

'He might say you weren't much of a diagnostician.'

'He might, but people seem to have been talking about getting some normal controls, or at least patients who aren't Parky.'

'And those two have given what we laughingly refer to as informed consent?'

'They both seem to have signed something.'

'And they've both survived?'

'Don't know yet. They've only been over there a couple of days.'

'That might be worth finding out. But you can just imagine Swift going in there with his oily charm and telling them that the whole future of medical science depends on them helping with just a little test that we're developing, and it doesn't take any time at all and Professor Sinclair will be so grateful and it's really less trouble than going to the dentist and when you think about all we've done to help you the least you could do is think about helping us to help other people . . . Smarmy shit.'

'I've tried to get hold of him this morning. At the Southern, but not available on the phone.'

'He'd be helping Marcus twiddle the knobs, and making notes for his MD thesis.'

'Probably. He's getting generally worse . . . Swift, I

mean . . . Becoming a sort of Sinclair clone, talking like him on ward rounds and even eating like him and spending hours chatting up his ghastly secretary just to keep in touch with everything.'

'Smart chap. Should go far in medicine. Coffee?'

In a slow queue for the coffee till Hadden asked, 'How's Mhairi?' just as Campbell asked, 'How's orthopaedics?'

Hadden answered first. 'Oh, jogging along. A hundred and twenty patients is probably too many for a morning fracture clinic, but no one seems to have noticed that attendances have doubled in the last ten years. I suppose I mean no one senior enough to do anything about it. But the patients are terribly sympathetic. An old wifie this morning gave me a tube of Smarties and told me not to work too hard, because her father had been a doctor and it had killed him.' Hadden rummaged in the pocket of his white coat. 'Here . . . have a Smartie.'

'Thanks.'

They took their coffee out on the lawn. In the distance the rumble of construction machinery marked the continuing progress of Sinclair's new building, now two storeys high and still growing. Eventually Hadden asked again about Mhairi. Campbell answered in general terms. 'A remarkable young woman,' said Hadden. 'Very good with orthopods. Makes allowances for their rather primitive grasp of medicine with amazing tact. Has Bill MacMillan eating out of her hand. You know he's between wives again?'

'Didn't know that.'

'He really ought to try to give up physiotherapists. Many of the other health care professions offer charm, tact, physical fitness and even the ability to finish quite complex sentences.'

That seemed less than fair to the various Mrs Mac-Millans. Hadden warmed to his speculation. 'Occupational therapists, for example. All those activities of daily living, as they call them ... Kitchen practice, dressing and undressing, getting in and out of bed. And such fetching green uniforms, just like the Royal Company of Archers. But he seems quite besotted just now with little Mhairi's casual mastery of the sugar diabetes. Going on about her throughout an Exeter total hip replacement the other day. She's clearly made a considerable impression ... But you're still ... involved there?'

'We keep in touch.' Campbell finished his coffee and so did Hadden. As they walked back across the lawn Hadden started to hum a bouncy little tune. Only as they climbed the steps to go inside again did Campbell recognize it, a highland ditty from a long-forgotten school song book, something about stepping we gaily, on we go, heel for heel and toe for toe, that had once been used for the musical equivalent of square-bashing by a teacher with red hair and terminal acne. Only as Hadden strolled off in the direction of orthopaedic theatre did Campbell recall its title: *Mhairi's Wedding*.

On the way back from the library in the early afternoon Campbell went up to Sinclair's office with the vague intention of trying to make an appointment to see him to clarify, among other things, the policy for assessing patients with Parkinson's disease. The outer office was empty and the inner office closed. With no reply to fairly persistent knocking, Campbell waited, listening for any sound, such as heavy breathing, that might indicate that Sinclair was continuing the discussions on motor neurone disease last seen in progress on the sofa of the little drawing room at his home.

The inner office was evidently unoccupied. Campbell decided to wait a little longer and put down his briefcase. The outer office had changed somewhat, in keeping with a settled tenancy. The long worktop was now cluttered with files, books, and a selection of pot plants, Mrs Greenlees's pillarbox-red office cardigan hung over the back of the chair at the desk and a pair of stout black lacing shoes sat just behind the door, presumably in case of unseasonal rain. The smell was worse than ever.

Campbell was standing by the desk with half an eye on some correspondence in French which seemed to be mainly about money when Mrs Greenlees came back from lunch, breezing into her office humming breathily to herself. Seeing Campbell at her desk, she let out a little indignant shriek, rushed towards him and tripped over his briefcase, teetering clownishly then falling to the floor backwards with a satisfying thump and a seaside-postcard flash of black stockingtops, pudgy thighs and lurid underwear.

In a proper pantomime the moment would have rated applause, a drumroll and probably some kind of loud raspberry noise as well. Campbell did not even smile, but moved solicitously forward to help her up. 'What are you doin' in 'ere while I was out?' she shrilled from an undignified sitting position. 'And leaving that damned briefcase for me to trip over.' Scrambling briskly and unassisted to her feet she glared afresh at Campbell then marched towards her desk again, stopping suddenly a few feet short of it in a posture of extreme agony, mouth open and hand clutching her side, as though posing for one of Goya's more explicit torture etchings.

Campbell waited politely. The Goyaesque pose lasted fully half a minute, then Mrs Greenlees, a crouching, broken woman, limped forward with tiny, agonized steps until she could cling to her desk for support. With little whimpering breaths she turned to Campbell. 'Me back . . . You've done me back in, that's what you've done, Dr Campbell. Just wait till the professor hears about this.

You've no idea the agony I suffer with me back . . . and you've brought it all on again.'

'Is Professor Sinclair around this afternoon?' Campbell enquired, having come to the conclusion that the only rational way to deal with a performance like that was to ignore it entirely. 'I'd quite like to talk to him fairly soon.'

'Just let me think . . .' Mrs Greenlees lifted one hand painfully from the supporting desk and applied it to her brow. 'No. You can't . . .' Her voice had become even fainter. 'He's . . . abroad.'

Campbell watched and waited and thought of several other people he probably ought to talk to about the affairs of the Sinclair empire. The longer Sinclair was abroad the better. 'Thank you, Mrs Greenlees. Sorry to disturb you. Now if I can just pick up my briefcase . . .'

'Great party, n'est-ce pas? A really lovely home and Hamish knows such marvellous people. We spent a lot of time with a nice chap from the board, and of course there was that lovely lady who's paying for the new labs, and isn't Elspeth a sweetie? Meryl really enjoyed herself, which she doesn't usually do at medical parties. Jet lag caught up with her in the end of course . . . Hazard of the job.'

Campbell wondered in a Mackailish way about the longitude of Lagos and decided that Meryl's indisposition – she had last been seen coughing drowsily and slumped against Barry's shoulder in the queue for the Sinclair's downstairs loo – probably had more to do with the evening's wines than with the occupational risks of flying. 'Oh. Did it? I'm sorry.'

'Absolutely grand the next morning. Always is. And wasn't Mhairi looking lovely?'

'Barry . . . You know Barbara MacIlwraith . . .?'

'Big girl . . . One of Elspeth's friends?'

'Not the party, Barry. Barbara MacIlwraith from the ward.'

'Run it by me slowly, Dave . . . Barbara somebody . . . A female inpatient?'

'Early twenties. Fits.'

'Oh yes . . . I know the one . . . Hamish was a bit upset when he found she'd been switched to valproate.'

'She's been moved.'

'Right,' Barry nodded slowly and smiled. 'Right . . . I'm with you now, Dave.'

'I wasn't aware of any plans to biopsy her, Barry.'

'All discussed, Dave. All fully discussed. I'm just sorry nobody let you know. Hamish is very keen, very keen indeed, on tissue diagnosis. You must have picked that up, Dave, you've been working for him for six months. So she gets a biopsy. I spoke to Marcus about it on Saturday . . . Chez Sinclair, actually. He was very interested and promised to fit her in on Monday if I could get her across on Sunday for the usual preliminaries. The little trim and fasting from six the night before . . . So she's the lucky girl. No hanging about. I'm just sorry that what with one thing and another and mainly with it all happening at the weekend the communication side didn't quite keep up. I certainly would have mentioned it to you if I'd been able to be around this morning.'

'Thanks . . . And what's he going to biopsy?'

'Oh, Dave . . . come on. There's got to be progress in medicine. I know you're not as keen on research as some people round here but there's such a thing as being that and not being a dog in the manger about it. She needed setting up in the frame, she needed a biopsy of that suspicious stuff in the left temporoparietal bit on the scan, and while she was all set up, well, yes we did take a tiny peek at her basal ganglia.'

'And how is she now?'

233

Barry did his sincere thing. 'Well, yes. A problem or two. Not in the basal ganglion department, I hasten to add. And with a tumour like that she basically wasn't going to do anyway ... but she's comfortable, you'll be glad to hear, and she'll be over at the Southern for ... some time to come. So that gives you a female bed to play with.'

'And there was a chap from downstairs.'

Barry frowned. 'You're not really involved, are you, Dave, with the Sinclair male inpatients? But we've got a chap down there just now with the most fascinating variant of MS. Predominantly deep central involvement, very little of his cord's been chewed away so far, but the most fascinating collection of olivopontine signs and quite definite hypokinesia, so though he's technically an MS in all probability, there are things going on in and around his basal ganglia that really need to be explained, and now we've got the technology ...' Barry paused and winked triumphantly. 'Why not?'

'I see.'

'So we get a tissue diagnosis before the post-mortem. In a syndrome so rare that it's just got to be documented properly, with a biopsy of course, and written up. You've no idea how much of an advance the Sinclair probe is proving, Dave.'

'So you're not expecting an early post-mortem on this chap.'

'Go on, Dave ... He's doing brilliantly. The whole thing went like a dream from start to finish. I shouldn't really talk too much about this, you know, but Marcus is a very keen teacher, and basic stereotactic technique's pretty simple provided you know your neuroanatomy. Yes ... in all modesty, Dave ... I did him. With Marcus right there, naturally, in the left-hand seat, as they say in the airline business. And you'll be pleased to hear the lad's doing extremely well. We'll be having a preliminary look at the

234

fixed specimens tomorrow. A real breakthrough, Dave . . .
It's just about going to revolutionize the whole of
neurodiagnosis.'

'And where's Hamish?'

'Come on, Dave . . . don't you think he's earned a
break? Works longer and harder than any of us, and
doesn't really ever take holidays. He's just off on a quick
swing round the main neurology centres of Europe, doing
his fieldwork as conference anchorman. A spur-of-the-
moment whistle-stop thing, starting today in Madrid.
Doing two jobs, in fact as usual . . . Tying up some loose
ends on the motor neurone disease study while he's at it.
Was there something you needed to discuss with him?
Maybe I could help, Dave, n'est-ce pas? You know I'd be
glad to.'

The following afternoon, at the end of his outpatient clinic,
Campbell took his casenotes and dictaphone along to Fiona's
office. She was not there. The desk had been cleared and a
note on it directed 'All dictation etc., to Room 13, old NBU'.
With some misgivings he made his way to Mrs Greenlees's
office, where Fiona sat with most of the windows open
sorting out a vast heap of letters and cheques.

She smiled as he went in. 'Well, Dr Campbell, you've
certainly got a lot to answer for.'

'Sorry, Fiona.'

Fiona put on her Mrs Greenlees face. 'It's all that Dr
Campbell's fault. Me back hasn't bothered me for months
and months and then he as good as trips me up deliberately
with that briefcase of his and it's gone again.'

'Not quite what happened.'

'Of course not. She's a scheming, lying bitch who was
going to work out some way of taking time off when her
boss was off without losing any of her holiday, whatever

235

the excuse. Lots of secretaries do that, Dr Campbell. Well, the nastier ones. But it's all been very interesting.'

'Really?'

'I had to spend most of the morning working out where she keeps the keys to the places she keeps the keys to the places she keeps the keys, but I think I've cracked it. How urgent are those letters?'

'The top two a bit . . . the rest can keep.'

'I'll do my very best and see what I can do for you, Dr Campbell, but you mustn't expect miracles and I've got all the professor's conference to organize, you know . . . so probably tomorrow.'

'Fine.'

'And you know he's taken La Pasionara?'

'I didn't, but I'm not surprised.'

'Dirty bugger. His wife was on the phone earlier, sort of trying to find out without actually asking. She sounds quite nice.'

'She is . . . Psychiatrist. The sensible kind . . . Met her on Saturday.'

'Oh. Yes . . . Good party?'

'Pretty good.'

'Should have been, at that price.'

'Oh?'

'Bill for about five hundred from Just a Crust . . . and since the deposit came out of the European Conference Number Two account I suppose that's where the rest's going to come from too.'

'Bloody hell.'

'So I'm glad you enjoyed the party, Dr Campbell . . .' Fiona waved at a heap of cheques on the desk with an airy finishing-school gesture. 'There seems to be just enough here to cover it.'

Campbell recalled the endless gin and tonic and the spare poached salmon and a subsequent discussion with Mhairi along the lines of 'whatever else you say about him he's an extremely generous host', etc. 'That's a bit odd.'

'Well, I'm not an expert on international conferences, but it's not the way the ENT lot did it.'

'Hmm.'

'Hmm indeed. And there are some quite interesting American Express chits nibbling away at the Number One Account. We seem to be very fond of first-class air travel to Madrid. Not just yesterday's free trip for two.'

'Is that in there? Barry said it was a spur of the moment thing.'

'Booked at least two weeks ago, according to my records. What's going on in Madrid?'

'He seems to be working on the Spanish connection. Something to do with a committee. Anything from Zürich?'

'Dr Campbell . . . how could I possibly divulge such information even if I knew about it? Yes, he seems to like going there too.'

'What about his . . .?'

'And eating in some quite expensive places. I just hope he's left himself enough to actually run this wretched Thirteenth European Conference. Although of course it's really none of my business. I'm just the office junior. And I'll do my best to get your clinic letters done tomorrow or the next day, Dr Campbell.'

'Thanks.'

'Drop in again . . . I'm sure there's a lot more here that's pretty suspicious, if you're interested.'

'Dr Bertram.'

'Hello, Ronnie. David Campbell here. Sorry to bother you at home.'

'No problem, young Campbell. What can I do for you? And how are you anyway? Never see you these days.'

'Not too bad. Do you have a minute to . . .'

'Go right ahead.'

'A sort of problem . . . about things up at the Institute . . . Departmental, and a bit tricky . . .'

'Tell your uncle Ronnie.'

'Well, it's to do with Hamish Sinclair.'

'Oh yes.'

'You know about it?'

'Well, I'm at the Southern. Some of his patients don't seem to do too well when they come over here. Marcus Mackail doing his white man's acupuncture in the middle of their brains . . . that stuff?'

'Partly.'

'Yes. One or two people are a bit worried about that. Dodgy, but probably safer than what he was doing for strokes. What else?'

'Well, Hamish generally. Do you know him?'

'He was a kind of boy wonder in neurosurgery when I was a student. Seemed to have written more publications than any of us had even read. And an international star now, so everyone's jealous. How's he making out as a prof?'

'Well . . .'

'Come on, Campbell . . . come to the point. Is he buggering those baboons of his, or what?'

'Not as far as I know. More the money side of things. I'm not sure even if . . .' Campbell briefly outlined some of the uses to which the funds of the Thirteenth European Conference were being put. Bertram listened, grunting sagely from time to time. When Campbell had finished he said, 'So?'

'Well . . . Isn't it . . .?'

'And you're still a locum lecturer, young Campbell?'

'Yes . . . Probably not for much longer.'

'Son, even if I was a senior lecturer or for that matter a

238

vice-chancellor I would play it fairly carefully if I were you. Think about it. What do you want to happen? Not just to you. Sure, it's all a bit grey, but are you really going to get the cops in? They would have you up for wasting police time. "Of course there are expenses involved in running an international conference. You have to travel, dammit . . . it's international." All that stuff. And you would be left looking like an office boy with a grudge . . . and no job.'

'But . . .'

'I'm not saying that what he's doing, if that's what he's doing, is right . . . or even that I like him. I don't, really, and I don't like the sort of name the Southern's getting because of what he and Mackail are up to. But a guy like that . . . You've got to be sure you're right and that what you're saying will finish him, because sure as hell he'll finish you if you're anything less than about two hundred and fifty per cent certain of what you're on about.'

'And the thing at his house?'

'Lots of professors do that, young Campbell. Even the honest guys. So that's your uncle Ronnie's advice – keep your eyes open if you want, but definitely keep your mouth shut, and maybe let me know if you actually catch him committing an unnatural act with a primate, or any other member of the senior clergy for that matter.'

'Is there any point in asking . . .'

'Dave, son, I'm probably going to have to read Thomas the Tank Engine another fourteen times before I get anywhere near my marquetry tonight.'

'Sorry.'

'It's all right . . . Keep in touch . . . OK?'

'Thanks, Ronnie. Sorry to . . .'

'Nae bother . . . Cheers, son.'

'Thanks, Ronnie.'

Campbell put the phone down. Mhairi, at the other side of the kitchen, took off her oven glove and said, 'Drink?'

'Yes, please.'

'Large one?'

'Yes, thanks.'

'So Ronnie wouldn't make a fuss.'

'No.'

'Didn't get where he's got to today by making fusses.'

'That's more or less it . . . and he's got a sort of a point. If Sinclair got nasty, as he undoubtedly would, he's in quite a good position to make things look good for himself and very bad for me.'

'And you don't feel your career would benefit from any pointless heroics?'

'Not just at the moment. Thanks. Gosh . . . difficult, isn't it?'

'The problem is,' said Mhairi over the top of her glass, 'that Sinclair doesn't see any conflict of interest . . . because what's good for him is, by definition, in his terms anyway, good for neurology, and whatever society whose money it is, and the conference, and even his dollybird, especially if she happens to be a neurologist from Spain.'

'Where the votes come from.'

'So he does exactly what he wants, and for him it's OK, even altruistic, to go off round Europe making sure that the best man gets to be the next vice-president of the society or whatever . . . and even a good party is good for neurology, and money well spent.'

'Is that what the law would think?'

'Nobody's going to get the law in. What did Bertram think?'

'Waste of police time.'

'He's probably right. Is there anyone else worth talking to about it?'

'I was thinking about old Creech.'

'Creech?'

'Well, he's been around for a while, and he's very old-fashioned about money. And he's actually quite sensible and he's older.'

'Older?'

'Than Sinclair. Bertram's younger, and a bit overawed.'

'I suppose so. Isn't medicine hierarchical?'

'And anyway I quite like old Creech.'

'An acquired taste, I think. He was on the committee that made me a registrar. Asked me if Raasay was the Whisky Galore island, and if the whisky was still drinkable.'

'Any word of her coming back?'

'Not so far ... She did phone in. "You managin' all right, dear? Just leave all the difficult conference stuff for me ..." I made a polite inquiry, and she suddenly sounded as if she were bravely having her toenails pulled out by the Gestapo. "Don't worry about me, Fiona ... Just do your best ... I'll be back as soon as ever I can ..." It was quite hard not to laugh. Your letters are over there.'

'Thanks.'

'I'm sure she overdoes the overwork stuff. Just looking through the files there's not actually that much. Sinclair rarely dictates anything longer than about a page and all the conference stuff is just forms. Does your wife want to go to the Zoo? The theatre night? The short scenic tour? The long scenic tour? Shoplifting on Princes Street? Please tick boxes appropriately. God knows what she does with all her time. Even the slush funds are basically simple.'

'Oh?'

'They're not actually called that ... Motor Neurone Disease Study, brackets Administrative close brackets ... That's a nice little earner. A twenty-five dollar handling charge on every specimen from the international collabo-

241

rative study. He really ought to give the lab a box of Black Magic at Christmas, since they're doing all the work.'

'They might be getting a bit suspicious.'

'Well, two boxes of Black Magic . . . And you know about the conference accounts.'

'Yes.'

'Weekend for two at Gleneagles? Plus travelling expenses of course . . . and a fair amount of souvenir Edinburgh Crystal, small tokens of respect and gratitude to distinguished foreign neurologists, one presumes. Honestly, the cheek of the man. And God knows what this week's little jaunt is costing. Nothing but the best will do for Dolores. But I suppose it's worth it if the specimens keep rolling in.'

'It's all very difficult.'

'It looks very easy.'

'I mean there's probably not much anyone can do.'

'Really?'

'Not without a hell of a fuss and a messy inquiry that might come out all wrong.'

'Who says?'

'Well, I've been sort of asking around. It depends a lot on how broad a view you take of expenses. He would say that he's spending money for the good of the conference, and even if he weren't he could make it sound as if he were . . . or make it so unpleasant for anyone who wanted to argue. You know what he's like.'

'Yes. An arrogant shit . . . lying, cheating, stealing . . . and even killing, come to think of it . . .'

'Probably.'

'. . . from the comfort and security of his own academic department.'

'That's more or less it.'

Fiona looked round the office and frowned. 'Makes me wish I'd got two more 'O' levels and done medicine at the University.' Campbell laughed and Fiona stuck out her

242

tongue at him. 'Or one less and joined the police . . .
"Professor Sinclair, we have in our possession information
that leads us to believe . . . As a medical man you will no
doubt wish to come quietly but I must warn you that
anything you say . . ."'

'That'll be the day.'

'With the notorious Lemmy "the Smell" O'Fagan, a.k.a.
Gladys Greenlees, conman extraordinaire and master of
disguise, pulled in as an accomplice before, during and
after the fact . . . Another triumph for the Festival City
Conference Crime Squad. Really, I'm just wasting myself
as a typist . . . but I did those clinic letters for you anyway.'

'Thanks, Fiona.'

Waiting in Creech's office for his former chief to finish a
ward round, Campbell reflected on how simple the struc-
tures of medicine had seemed when he was a houseman: if
you weren't completely sure about something you asked
your registrar, in his case Ronnie Bertram, now translated
to consultant authority at the Southern, and if he wasn't
completely sure (which wasn't often) old Creech, as a sort
of tribal elder of the Institute, pronounced on the matter
and that was that.

In only a few years the difficulties seemed to have
become more complex and the sources of authoritative
advice more diffuse and less reliable. Barry Swift, Campbell's immediate clinical superior, had been utterly cor-
rupted and was more clearly part of the problem than
anything to do with the answer. Bertram, formerly an
approachable colleague, was now a circumspect and rather
remote consultant at another hospital, but probably
reflected a proper professional caution about accusing a
senior colleague of major impropriety. Perhaps Creech, a
white-haired Presbyterian godfather on the scene, would
say much the same and if he did Campbell would then

leave it there, having done everything that could reasonably have been expected of him.

Having made an appointment for which he knew old Creech would almost certainly be at least ten minutes late, Campbell sat in a sagging leather armchair in the oddly old-fashioned office-cum-laboratory, agreeably idle and watching the patterns made on the carpet by sunlight through the trees outside. No one, he reflected, seemed very interested in Sinclair's invasive and sometimes lethal investigation of patients with and without Parkinson's disease. His appalling aggression and rudeness to patients, students and staff were likewise agreed to be hardly noteworthy, at least in a teaching hospital context. Adultery with a colleague, in these enlightened times, and perhaps fortunately for the profession at large, was no longer of much interest to anyone, but financing it from conference funds might just be considered improper, and that seemed to be the charge with the best chance of sticking.

Campbell began again to wonder about how precisely to phrase all that for the forthcoming interview, but had fallen to imagining a savage interrogation of Sinclair by Fiona dressed as a police inspector when old Creech came in. He got up. 'Morning, sir. Thank you for . . .'

Creech, older and more stooped than Campbell had expected, waved him into the armchair, walked round his desk and sat down looking preoccupied and even a little suspicious, as though wondering whether someone might have moved his office furniture about while he was doing his ward round. 'Yes . . .?'

'Dr Campbell, sir . . .'

'Yes.' There was a tiny, mournful smile. 'I remember . . . David . . . What can I do for you? A reference or something?'

'That might be quite helpful, sir . . . Fairly soon, maybe

. . . But meantime I wanted to discuss something – fairly confidential – to do with my present job.'

'Sinclair?'

'Yessir.'

'A horrible little man.'

Although another 'Yessir' was tempting, Campbell hesitated. 'Um . . . there seem to be one or two things going on that I find a bit difficult to square with . . .'

'He just parks anywhere.'

'. . . and I wondered . . .'

'Old Aithie always used to park in the little space by the oxygen tanks. Welcome to it as far as I was concerned. Never fancied going out one evening and finding my car burned out or supercooled or something. But Sinclair, not having worked here for ten years or so – and I remember him as a student of course – just seems to be more or less ignoring the way we do things. It's not a question of rules – you shouldn't need them for something as trivial as parking. Convention, I suppose – or even basic good manners.'

'That's one of the . . .'

'At least three times in the last two weeks I've come in at my usual time – within a few minutes of eight forty-five, as you know, as I've done for years – and found that foreign car of his in my space without so much as a by your leave.'

'He seems to be fairly . . . single-minded, about a lot of things, and I was . . .'

'There's nothing can be done, of course, but with only a year or so to go before I retire I would have thought a certain . . . courtesy, consideration, you might call it . . . might be in order.'

'Very much so, sir. He's a difficult man, I think it's generally recognized. But in some things, sir, perhaps as important in their way as . . .'

Creech shook his head impatiently. 'He's created a great

deal of ill-feeling, and perhaps the saddest thing is that I've no reason to believe he's aware of it ... I know John Temple's getting pretty fed up with him.'

Dr Temple, the NHS consultant neurologist who shared the wards of the unit with Sinclair, was a mild and well-mannered man who had so far dealt with the Sinclair problem by courteously ignoring it. Like Creech, he was due to retire within the year. He had no academic appointment, though he taught sometimes and was much valued for his long experience and common sense in diagnosis. He worked part-time, spending several sessions as consultant physician to the Army in Scotland, a post that seemed to suit him quite well, not least by taking him away from a thoroughly unsatisfactory colleague several times a week. If he were beginning to jib, then perhaps something could indeed be done. 'I wasn't aware ...'

'Yes,' said Creech mournfully. 'He sometimes parks in his space too.'

'So what the bloody hell *have* you been up to for the last two weeks, Campbell?' Sinclair was standing too close and shouting too loud. The students, more frightened than embarrassed, shrank back leaving their seniors a generous circle of floor space just at the entrance to the ward. The staff nurse who was about to accompany them on the round looked pointedly out of the window. Sinclair glowered even closer. 'Parkinson's disease hasn't just bloody disappeared off the face of the earth just because I've been out of the country for a couple of weeks. Don't try and tell me that, lad. It's common and it's not difficult to diagnose. The average fourth-year student can find half a dozen cases from the top of the bus on the way in from Dalkeith Road in the morning, and you're spending your week in neurology clinic and you haven't found one. I bloody despair of you, Campbell. You're only here because you were here when I came, I wouldn't have appointed

you and I'm bloody well not going to reappoint you.
You're idle, you're dim and you're not even doing what
you're paid for. I've been keeping tabs on you, closer than
you think, and I've had enough. When your locum finishes
you're finished, and don't even pester me for a reference
because you won't get one, at least not one that'll do you
any good . . . Right? Now, what *have* you got to show for
your two weeks' idleness?'

Despite standing close, Campbell listened only distantly,
as though to a television set turned up too loud in a pub:
an unpleasant but half-expected noise about which sensible
people did not on the whole complain. He turned to the
first patient as if Sinclair had simply said good morning.
'Mrs Hughes, sir . . . A thirty-eight-year-old lady with
recent onset grand mal epilepsy. Nothing sinister on investigation and stabilizing on medication.'

'Phenytoin?'

'Yessir.'

'Home today.'

'Yessir.'

'Next?'

Mrs Hughes smiled wanly at Sinclair's back as the round
moved on. Campbell would, as usual, go round again fairly
soon explaining and not quite apologizing for what had
happened. The next patient, an unconscious stroke, was
beyond misunderstanding or embarrassment but was
pulled about a bit for the benefit of the students. The third
patient was Mrs Robson, who grinned unevenly and yet
again heard but was unable to join a discussion about her
continuing presence in the ward.

'Still here?'

'Yessir.'

'I thought maybe while I was out of the country for a
couple of weeks she might have got on her way. What the
hell do the geriatricians think they're playing at, leaving

people like her silting up an acute unit? God knows I've written enough letters about her. What else do I have to do?' Sinclair turned from Campbell to the students. 'Bed-blocking . . . This sort of nonsense . . . is one of the greatest threats to medical education today. How am I expected to teach neurology in a ward full of ancient strokes who aren't doing anything. What's the point in having teaching hospitals if the geriatric service is so bloody awful that they're indistinguishable from nursing homes? Nothing like this in Spain, I tell you. If you're in a teaching hospital you're worth teaching on and that's it. And if you're not there are plenty of nuns about to do the social stuff. Switzerland's even better. No pissing about, straight off to a cosy little clinic in the mountains . . . And what have *we* got? Geriatricians who are so bloody slow . . .' he lowered his voice slightly. '. . . that they usually don't get there before the bloody undertaker. Next?'

A couple of motor neurone disease study patients were prodded and perfunctorily thanked and a girl with recently diagnosed multiple sclerosis was left in tears. The ward round ended with further injunctions about the importance of finding more patients with Parkinson's disease who might contribute to the advance of diagnostic methods. The students drifted off. As Sinclair was about to leave Campbell attempted to discuss with him the case of the girl who had gone over to the Southern and failed to return.

'Of course I bloody well remember the case. And even if I hadn't I don't need you to remind me, because I've been through it in detail with Swift already this morning. Interesting case. The Sinclair probe proves its worth again. That girl had a very diffuse glioblastoma multiforme, the diagnosis of which you seemed to have cocked up pretty comprehensively. In my absence Swift took her over and sorted her out, and he's shown that she had far more tumour than your half-baked attempts at diagnosis ever began to come up with, and he did it using the probe . . .'

'You know that she's . . .'

'Yes. She's dead because her head was full of tumour . . . that you failed to diagnose. Right, Campbell? So I've asked Swift to keep a much closer eye on you for your remaining weeks with us, because I don't trust you and with the European conference coming up I can't be over here all the time. Just do what you're told, pull the finger out, find some cases of Parkinson's and at least you'll stay out of trouble. I'm sorry about that, but after all the business with that poor schizophrenic bugger of a houseman I just can't afford to take any more risks. Right?'

The corporal stood to attention and said, 'Good afternoon, sir. Can I help you?'

'Dr Campbell. To see Dr Temple.'

'Oh, yes, sir. Colonel Temple's expecting you.' The soldier stepped smartly from behind the desk, revealing the full glory of his boots, opened a door and said, 'Colonel Temple, sir . . . Dr Campbell to see you, sir.'

Dr Temple stood in front of the fireplace in a large office decorated with a set of prints of gallant deeds in the Flanders mud. Campbell had contacted him by phone half an hour earlier asking if he could at some time see him to discuss a confidential matter, and had been surprised to be instructed to come straight across to something called the MRS. This facility, of whose existence Campbell had been only vaguely aware, turned out to be a villa in Grange, as it happened not far from Sinclair's house, and some kind of satellite clinic of the RAMC.

Had Campbell anticipated in detail the circumstances of the interview he would probably have stopped off in Marchmont and polished his shoes. A big old-fashioned drawing-room with leather armchairs, a leather examination couch and a mahogany desk and chair looked south across the rooftops and trees to Blackford Hill. Dr Temple, smiling from the hearthrug, pointed him towards one of the armchairs. 'Our corporal makes a good cup of coffee.' He pressed a bellpush by the fireplace. 'Sugar?'

The corporal reappeared, there was a ritual exchange and he left again. 'It's another world, David,' said Dr Temple. He sat down in the armchair opposite. They chatted generally for some minutes, in the course of which the function of the MRS was explained. 'As the RAMC had gradually faded out in Scotland, we're the smile of the Cheshire Cat so to speak. We do second opinions and difficult medical boards. All quite interesting and, as you can see, fairly civilized. Thank you, Corporal Houseley. We may need a little time . . .'

'Sir.'

The door closed. 'So you thought we might usefully have a chat, David?'

Campbell moved well forward in his chair and was about to speak. Temple smiled. 'The main reason for asking you to come across was to make sure we could talk freely . . . You can.'

Campbell sat back. 'Thank you. One or two things around the unit since . . .'

'April first or so?'

'Yes. Quite a few things, really . . . to do with investigation for Parkinson's disease, and some things about teaching, and the way the wards are run, you know, generally, and . . . well, money really.'

Dr Temple, trim for his sixty-four years and retaining with the courtesy rank a distinctly military style, let Campbell falter then said, 'And I'm sure you're aware that the General Medical Council takes a very dim view of doctors who take it upon themselves to criticize colleagues.'

'Um . . . Yes.'

'. . . unless there are substantial grounds for doing so. And conversely, of course, we have major responsibilities via the GMC to the public in respect of colleagues who, for any reason, might be failing to conform to the standards expected by the public of our profession. I take it you wish to discuss matters where, shall we say, the latter considerations apply.'

'Well, yes . . . but I'm not sure it's actually a GMC thing.'

'What isn't?'

'Well, being a bit short with patients and students and probably overinvestigating some patients. I know that how far you investigate anything obviously varies a lot from doctor to doctor, and different people are keen on different things, but one or two of the people – patients – who've gone across to the Southern seem to have done quite badly, and I wondered . . . well, if there's anything that can be done.'

'To stop neurosurgeons doing neurosurgery?'

Put that way the question did not seem to help with what Campbell had in mind. The related matter of Swift's confession to a perfect basal ganglion biopsy under only light neurosurgical supervision was perhaps too complex to introduce this early in the discussion. There was a pause. Campbell picked up his coffee cup again.

'As you probably know, David, none of my patients seem to have needed such an . . . advanced diagnostic technique. And of course accordingly none of them have come to any harm. But I gather my colleague's have had their troubles.'

Campbell briefly related the five deaths and three instances of damaged survival arising from the procedure. Dr Temple listened intently. 'Out of a total of how many? Roughly.'

'Twelve, or fifteen at the most.'

'I can tell you, in absolute confidence, that some of my neurological consultant colleagues at the Southern have expressed great anxiety about the whole business. But like me they're not directly involved. Concerned, as I am, about what appears to be going on and how it affects . . . wider considerations. But consultants, as you know, aren't responsible for each other, except in the broadest sense I mentioned earlier. What the . . . other neurosurgeons feel can only be guessed at, of course, and it may be that they have matters in hand.'

'Really?'

'. . . but I doubt it. It's a very grey area. You mentioned money.'

The problem with talking about the funds for the European conference was that Campbell had no legitimate or freely admissible means of knowing about them. However, in the security of a military establishment a mile at least from the Institute and in the presence of a man with a reputation for absolute discretion he felt it not unreasonable to mention how he had come by his information, particularly in view of Fiona's enthusiasm for police involvement. Again Temple listened intently. When Campbell had finished there was a long pause. Muddied soldiers wrestled with the wheels of a horsedrawn ambulance crossing a stream in a battered landscape of sixty years ago. 'And you have personally examined these accounts?'

A small figure floundered waist-deep, clinging to rather than pushing at the tailboard of the ambulance. 'Well . . . No.'

'Still, you may be right. But it's a serious allegation to make about accounts that are more or less bound to be audited in due course, David.'

'I suppose so.'

'And you also mentioned teaching and ... general deportment.'

At the end of a rather lame account of two or three of the more specific atrocities Campbell had witnessed, Dr Temple, obsessionally considerate himself and visibly harrowed by some of the details, looked out of the window for a moment then said, 'Difficult ... all very difficult. It would be an awful lot more straightforward if someone, either a student or a patient, had made a complaint, and preferably one in writing. Has anyone ... so far as you are aware?'

Campbell shook his head.

'Difficult ...' said Dr Temple again. 'I can tell you, in absolute confidence, that both our ward sisters have felt it necessary to mention some of the things you've mentioned, and one of them actually has it in mind to resign unless ... things generally improve fairly soon. And a junior medical colleague who shall be nameless broadly shares their view, and yours, of some of our undoubtedly gifted senior academic colleague's rougher ways. But I tell you, David, it's no simple matter. Our friend is a forceful and persuasive character who's demonstrated his ability to survive and prosper despite or because of attributes that you and I and no doubt many others before us have found difficult if not obnoxious, and he knows that. Causing offence doesn't bother him, and anything more serious would have to be proved, beyond a peradventure, as old Shaky MacKenzie used to say.'

'So ...'

'I'm glad you've felt you could come and discuss these matters with me, and I shall respect your confidences as I trust you will respect mine, but – for the moment anyway – probably the most important thing to do is to keep a close eye on such problems as might eventually require some detailed attention from the neurosurgeons. Meantime we must, as good physicians sometimes have to, remain watch-fully inactive.' Dr Temple got up. 'But we may have to wait for some time. Who knows?'

As he was conducted by the corporal out into the civilian world again, Campbell wondered momentarily if he had understated his case, in particular if some more detailed account of the motor neurone disease study, its finances and the relationship between the two principal investigators would have influenced Dr Temple towards something other than physicianly inertia. On reflection, it did not seem so; and he had passed on quite enough to make himself feel uneasy: slightly guilty, and disloyal, and even, curiously enough, a little sorry for Sinclair.

In the second week of September, like a component of the Edinburgh International Festival that had somehow been hopelessly delayed in transit, the Thirteenth European Conference of Clinical Neurologists came to town. Amid the fading posters for plays, exhibitions, concerts, happenings, experiences and other less organized events of the Festival and its Fringe, new signs arose bearing the inscription '13 ECCN' and the conference logo, an unimaginative device in which a map of Europe was embraced by a stylized nerve cell.

Similarly labelled neurologists, many of them clutching conference folders gifted by a drug company whose generosity could have been construed only as some kind of apology for the uniform inefficacy of its products, gathered from all over Europe and drifted in groups of up to twenty or adventurously alone around the University campus and the main residential accommodation, a cheerless gulag of student halls of residence two miles away in the shadow of Arthur's Seat. It rained.

In preparation for the three-day programme of scientific meetings, poster sessions, workshops, receptions, dinners, entertainments, and outings Sinclair had assembled a hugely enlarged support staff, recruited mainly from the medical students' society and rewarded as much by proximity to the glitter of international clinical science as by the modest amounts of drug company money on offer. His junior medical staff, once more including Andrea, were to function as marshals of these lesser acolytes, and, equipped with distinguishing conference badges in dayglow green, had been charged with ensuring the smooth running of all things from slide projectors to queues for toilet facilities.

Neurology patients contributed too, whether they knew it or not, and with their co-operation the clinical service had been reduced to a minimum in order to free medical personnel for more important duties. Outpatient clinics were cancelled. All those patients in the wards with reasonable prospects of an early death were hurried on to hospices and nursing homes. Any new patients whose admission and investigation could be deferred – in practice in all new patients – were made aware that their condition would come to no harm and might even benefit from a delay of a week or so, and sent away. Of the customary twenty or so Sinclair patients in the wards there remained, stubbornly unmovable and by now rather cherished by the nurses simply because Sinclair was known to loathe her, only Mrs Robson.

The champagne reception which opened the conference was held in the Upper Library of the University Old Quad. Neurologists queued four deep on a red-carpeted stair to be greeted by the President and Vice-President of the Association and the Principal of the University. Campbell and Mhairi, who had gone for a drink with Andrea and Alastair in their New Town flat beforehand, stood patiently with them in the line as it moved upwards under a series of immense portraits of forgotten local academics.

'Hamish is tremendously optimistic about the whole

thing,' said Andrea suddenly, under someone called Professor Sir Lionel Farquharson-Forrest, KB, MD, DL. 'We had them across to dinner ten days ago and he said that he'd been fairly confident before, but going round and spending a bit of time in the places that really mattered, especially Madrid and Zürich, made it more or less a foregone conclusion. And he'd be awfully good for the Association. I mean, just look at what he's done for the department.'

Campbell nodded. Andrea smiled and said, 'Come on, David, he's simply terrific if you can stand the pace.' Campbell muttered something about Sinclair probably having enough on his plate, in a new post and with a new lab on the way. 'No, David, the whole point is that it'll give him time to sort all that out, at the same time as he's playing himself into the international scene. And when the German who's following the Irishman hands the whole thing on to him he'll really know the ropes. And he's actually pretty clued up already, even more so after going round . . . You know . . .'

'With Dolores?'

'Well, she does speak Spanish, and knows Madrid. But he's got so many ideas, and the whole thing really does need a good shake. Old Dr Begorrah, as he calls him, the last of the pick and shovel neurologists, hasn't exactly made his intellectual mark. And the German only got in because the French lot knew he couldn't speak English. So with Hamish in charge the association's in for quite an interesting couple of years quite soon. And of course it benefits the department too.'

'Really?'

'Well, he's more or less promised me an exchange fellowship, in Zürich probably. Just for a couple of months.' She hugged her husband's arm. 'Alastair's going to let me go, and come across himself for a couple of weeks at least, unless he's started a mistress.'

When they got to the top of the stair a bald man in a tail coat was announcing the guests, bawling out much simplified versions of their needlessly complicated names in a strong Aberdeen accent, to the obvious discomfort and bewilderment of the receiving line. Its three dignitaries grinned over their chains of office, nodded and shook hands mechanically with people who were already looking round for the champagne. Behind the three stood Sinclair, solid and unadorned in the manner of a detective or bodyguard, noting who was passing, nodding occasionally and always watchful. As Campbell drew closer it occurred to him that his head of department was drunk: he seemed somehow both tense and irresponsibly happy, grinding his teeth, as he did sometimes when he was unavoidably delayed, and grinning at the same time. He winked at Andrea as they passed.

'He's distinctly odder,' said Mhairi after they found a waitress. 'Acting as if it's all his show already.'

'Hmm. Odd, but probably not odder. Whatever it is, it's always his show. And the chances are he really does have it stitched up.'

'Because he's spent all their money making sure?'

'More or less . . . And . . .' Campbell lowered his voice. '. . . because no one sensible would want anything to do with it.' They looked round. An international gathering of successful medical specialists busy drinking champagne provided in abundance by the drug industry is not an edifying sight.

The election of the next vice-president of the association took place in a second closed session of its governing body on the morning of the second full day of the conference. Campbell heard about it from Andrea over lunch.

'I just happened to be having coffee in the office when they came out, and I knew right away. Obviously Hamish was busy, and everybody wanted to talk to him, but he took a moment to tell me, and I suppose I'm supposed to pass it on to everybody, since it is going to affect the department quite a bit in the not too distant future. Anyway, it all went off just as he thought it would, even better really. A no-hoper of a Frenchman got his own lot, half the Belgians and an Italian or two, and Hamish got just about everyone else. Preparation, really, I suppose, and people knowing that you're basically very good. I'm awfully pleased for him. Something for him to look forward to. And Zürich's definitely on now. I'm really pleased about that. As well.'

Campbell spent the second half of that afternoon sitting at the back of an auditorium recently vacated by a gory student production of *Coriolanus*, the venue of the plenary scientific sessions of the conference, a modern hall with seats for more than three hundred. As the weather had improved, attendance had fallen off and the current session on movement disorders had attracted no more than fifty, many of them apparently now asleep. Sinclair was in the chair, and a little Frenchman with a difficult accent and hopeless slides was wading through a piece of rather obvious drug company-financed propaganda.

'. . . and, as you weel see, the median duration of dyskinetic manifestations in the group of control, as shown in the third set of histograms in the top 'alf of the slide . . .'

'Right . . . Stop . . .'

'. . . ees always at least twice as long as the seemilar manifestations, see, here, of the group of treatment, with a significance . . .'

'I said stop . . .' Sinclair had stood up and was shouting into his microphone. The Frenchman looked round, blinking and bemused. 'Just bloody well stop . . .' Sinclair was shaking with rage. 'You've had your ten minutes. I'm not going to go through all the warning light stuff. Just stop and get off the podium. Your stuff's terrible, nobody can read your slides and nobody's interested.'

'Mais, m'sieur, ily a encore trois minutes . . . of great significance, the probability less than . . .'

'Just bloody well shut up and get off. The next chap can't be half so bad.'

This unusual, even unprecedented directness from the chair caused stirrings in the scattered and dimly lit audience. There was a grumble of disapproval from one little group near the front. Someone, perhaps still drunk from lunch, yelled, 'Yeah . . . S'right . . . Gerrimoff . . . Terrible . . .' The Frenchman grasped the lectern in a way that suggested violence might be necessary to remove him from it. Sinclair advanced on him as though violence might be offered.

Campbell, sitting at the back of the hall between the slide projector and the various black boxes of the public address system, felt sorry for the Frenchman, whose contribution had been obscure and undistinguished, it was true, but no more so than those of half a dozen of his predecessors that afternoon. It was all very difficult. At previous scientific meetings he had seen the microphone being switched off as a last resort when speakers had overrun, and that was perhaps a legitimate protection of the time of subsequent contributors, but when he checked his watch he found that the speaker had had only a little over eight and a half minutes of his scheduled ten.

Audience interest was now at the highest level it had been all afternoon, as down at the front Sinclair closed menacingly on the smaller and much slighter Frenchman. He snatched the microphone from his victim's neck and growled into it, 'Right, doctor, you can finish what you're saying. Just finish your presentation in one sentence.'

The Frenchman grabbed the microphone back and returned to his text. '. . . which shows conclusively that thees preparation, ketobenzamine fentachloride from the Compagnie Altmann, is clearly one of the most promising preparations ever to have emerged for the treatment of these difficult syndromes and conditions, being far superior to all of the benzodiazepine group so far tested and also a very considerable advance on the non-benzodiazepine central sedatives and the so-called relaxants musculaires, being virtually free from side-effects, cheap and well tolerated, being applicable in the conditions of tardive dyskinesias, les états dystoniques, the disease of Hallervorden-Spaatz and many other difficult-to-treat conditions such as . . .'

Sinclair had seized the man's forearm with one hand and the microphone with the other. 'All right, all right. Just give me that and get off the bloody platform . . . Now. Where's the girl from Utrecht who's supposed to be talking about dopamine-depletion in baboons with hemiballusmus?'

A fat blonde waddled up from the front row. The Frenchman, now outnumbered as well as outgunned, withdrew towards his group of supporters, muttering 'incroyable' and the like as he left the range of the sound system. Sinclair performed once more the little ceremony of investiture with the microphone, smiled at the audience and went back to his place on the higher tier of the stage with the air of one who had done no more than his duty but would nonetheless not be surprised by a round of applause, then sat down and introduced the next speaker. Campbell checked the time again.

'No, I don't find it particularly depressing. In fact I quite enjoy it. I was in gastro-enterology before, and for the whole of the first six months I thought to myself every morning, great, another day I don't have to take a peek into someone's bum.'

'But the patients . . . all those ghastly things they have.'

'Well, you see, Dublin's a great place for just having a touch of something. "My doctor says its cancer . . . but just a touch." Or motor neurone disease or whatever. And they do remarkably well on it. The whole of terminal care in Ireland runs on understatement. And Guinness.' Dr Begorrah's first assistant lifted his glass of claret as though in a toast. 'It's what I'd want myself.'

Dr O'Rarity, if Campbell had caught his name correctly (and it seemed as good a name as any for an Irish academic neurologist) was proving an agreeable dinner companion. 'Cheers.'

'Cheers. And how's your man Sinclair to work for?' He pronounced it with the stress on the second syllable. 'A bit of a tartar, I would have thought myself, from his perform-ance the other day there. That poor little Frenchman coming all this way to be half-strangled with a microphone cord.'

'Yes. Not very hospitable of him, I suppose. Well . . .'

'You don't have to say anything of course. But I can tell you old Dermot'll be glad to step on the plane tomorrow. The finest thing about giving it all up will be never having to talk to that man again, is how he puts it. God help Ilgenfritz, with that man, as he calls him, breathing down his neck for three years, and probably asking quite fre-quently after his health. Will you be working for him long?'

'A few more weeks.' That morning Andrea had confided in Campbell over coffee that Sinclair had heard from Bobby Watson, the lecturer at present on a sabbatical in the States and for whom Campbell had been doing the locum. For reasons as much to do with working conditions as with money, Watson had finally decided to stay abroad. Andrea had been 'strongly advised', as she put it, to apply for the permanent post thus vacated.

'Well, that's something. He can't be the easiest of men to work with. What's your next job?'

There wasn't one. From the first of November Campbell, for the first time in his life, was going to be quite seriously unemployed. 'I'm looking round just now.'

'You'll be staying in neurology, of course.'

'I hadn't intended to. It was just a locum, a study job, really, that came along at a good time. Glad to have done it. Interesting but a bit gloomy.'

'Medicine's dismal science, Dermot calls it. And we do have a terrible lot of MS, from the rain and the potatoes.'

The closing dinner of the Thirteenth Conference of European Clinical Neurologists had filled the hall of the Royal College of Physicians to the point of discomfort. Elbow to elbow, at long tables scarcely a yard apart and extending here and there into dim recesses between marble-painted pillars, diners by the hundred worked their way through a menu of expensive blandness mitigated only somewhat by wave after wave of drug company wine. Tomorrow, Campbell was pleased to reflect, it would all be over. Conference posters would fade indistinguishably among the debris of the Festival, patients would return to clinics and wards, baboons would be mangled as before and life would return, for a few weeks anyway, to normal.

At ten the retiring President got up and made a gracious little speech, referring briefly to the excellence of the conference arrangements and ending with a sentence or two of good wishes to his successor, perhaps in Gaelic but more probably in German with a Dublin accent. People began to get up. Campbell said goodbye to his Irish neighbour, and was then slightly embarrassed to find that they were to spend the next five minutes standing close together simply waiting to leave the hall.

There were queues for the loos and then a vast huddle just inside the main door of the college, as though people were not yet quite resigned to leaving. Outside a long line of tour buses waited to transport the majority of them back to their spartan student bedrooms three miles away. Campbell, who had lived in one himself for a bleak undergraduate year, recalled a hard, narrow mattress and instantly understood their reluctance. The party was over. A cold draught came in from the street.

'Campbell!'

Campbell turned round. From the edge of the huddle Sinclair was beckoning him back into the building. 'Come on, you're not finished yet.' With some foreboding Campbell moved against the slow outward tide and back in to where the association's new vice-president stood at the side of the main staircase. 'Down this way . . . Just one last thing . . . There's some stuff needs shifting across to the Caley, for a party. I should have told you . . . A drink with the council . . . Come along. For all you've done for us . . . Come on, Campbell . . . Down here.'

Sinclair led the way through a little doorway under the main staircase and down some steep steps to a service corridor leading to the back of the basement. A door led out on to the lane behind. 'Get that one, Campbell. And be bloody careful with it. It's better stuff than you've ever drunk before, I tell you.' Two sealed cardboard cases lay on the floor at the end of the corridor. Sinclair took one and headed out into the lane, where his red Porsche, a dull orange colour under sodium street lighting, waited with its nearside door open

They put the cases side by side on the diminutive back seat. Sinclair got in but Campbell hesitated. 'Come on, Campbell . . . Time's passing. We're going on to the Caley, where Diaz and the rest of them are staying. And we don't want them hanging around worrying about where the next drink's coming from.'

Once more Campbell had wondered if Sinclair were drunk, but his swift, precise manipulation of the case of champagne and his customarily clear diction were reassuring. He got in, and put on his safety belt very carefully indeed. The Caledonian Hotel was not far away, but it had been raining again and the cobbles ahead were gleaming wet.

The Porsche came deafeningly to life in the high, narrow space of the lane and snaked forward, leaving only inches to spare between a series of cars parked on either side. At the end of the lane they turned left, and then left again on to Queen Street and along the front of the College, where less fortunate neurologists were slowly beginning to fill the half dozen buses bound for Dalkeith Road.

'Poor buggers,' said Sinclair over the engine noise, 'but at least we gave them quite a good dinner . . . and as much as they could decently drink in the time.'

Campbell started to say something vaguely complimentary about the wine but Sinclair was not listening. They stopped for traffic lights, with much impatient revving, before turning south up the hill to George Street then west round a piece of Victorian statutary and past the Assembly Rooms, from which another crowd was emerging, spilling out on to the road and lingering convivially around parked cars.

The evening just finished, Campbell concluded from the appearance of the crowd now slowing Sinclair's progress, must have been an excruciatingly Scottish one. Middle-aged and older people formed a large majority, with most of the men in kilts and the women in long tartan skirts. A few carried violin cases or accordions. As they milled around his car Sinclair became suddenly furious, treading the accelerator so that the car roared menacingly, then leaning on the horn and moving steadily forward, as though the Porsche were an armoured personnel carrier and the genteel Edinburgh highlanders a mob of hostile tribesmen.

An old lady, stooped and silver-permed and wearing a short fur jacket with her long, mainly white tartan skirt, either did not see Sinclair or saw him and was unimpressed. She lingered in front as he flashed his headlights. He revved the engine again then darted forward as though to scare her. She stumbled and fell and the car lurched sickeningly over her, bumping twice. There were shouts and shrieks above the engine noise. Campbell twisted in his seat to look back, at the same time grabbing the door handle and releasing his seatbelt. Already several aged gallants in kilts were kneeling round the broken figure in the roadway, and one stood shaking a fist high above his head. Sinclair drove on.

'Hamish . . .'

'Silly cow. I gave her plenty of time.' He glanced in the rear-view mirror, grimaced and accelerated away. Campbell reached hurriedly for his seat belt and clicked it home again just in time for a sudden double swerve as Sinclair successively negotiated, at over forty miles an hour, the end of a slowly moving bus and the plinth of another piece of Victorian statuary.

On the next block of George Street they briefly touched sixty before turning right at another statue down the hill to Queen Street then off again into the cobbled maze of terraces and crescents comprising the west end of the New Town.

'Hamish . . .'

Sinclair ignored Campbell. He was driving fast but calmly, enjoying the car much as he had done on the way back from the restaurant in East Lothian, flicking it through greasy cobbled corners, changing gear a lot and hardly ever braking. There was little traffic about and a series of tall Georgian façades slid past in a kind of speeded-up parody of a tourist film. In other circumstances, it might even have been faintly enjoyable to be his passenger.

A slithering left turn and gentle, rightward-curving upward slope, taken so fast as to throw Campbell over against the door, brought them to a red traffic light on Queensferry Road, a normally busy thoroughfare leading to the centre of town from the Forth Bridge. For the first time Campbell felt really scared, as Sinclair charged on against the light and swung left, back into town. A lorry suddenly only yards behind flashed vast headlights. In seconds the gap opened and they were swinging into a long left hand turn leading into Charlotte Square. Sinclair, it appeared, was still heading for the party in the Caledonian Hotel.

Another Georgian tourist sequence flashed by at nauseating speed and they were almost on Princes Street, the castle floodlit high on the left and the hotel only a few hundred yards away to the right. Traffic lights happened to be green. With yet another howl of rubber, the Porsche hurtled towards a solid mass of around a dozen cars waiting at the last set of lights before the hotel.

Did champagne explode on impact, Campbell wondered in what might yet prove to be his last seconds. He was not to find out, or perhaps not just then. Sinclair jinked to the right into the opposite lane and wove briskly forward through thin oncoming traffic. Horns sounded and lights flashed, but there was nothing even close to an impact.

Now that they were almost there, what Sinclair had done seemed impressive but futile. Dozens of people had seen the accident, and Sinclair's car was an unusual one. Already someone would have phoned for the police, and in any case police automatically attended emergency ambulance calls. A few words with a witness, a quick call to base, and an awful lot of patrol cars would be rushing about looking for a red Porsche somewhere in central Edinburgh.

The first of them, a white Rover with its blue light already flashing, was coming in from the west just as they turned across the cars still waiting at the last and most troublesome red light. Sinclair appeared to have seen it before Campbell, for instead of heading to their right for the hotel he sat back and pushed his foot to the floor, forcing Campbell back into his seat and hitting seventy or eighty before slowing to skid left and then right and up on to the long hill behind the castle. Behind them, the bigger, slower police car was doing well.

'Hamish . . . don't you think . . .' Campbell had to shout to be heard, but was ignored anyway. The cliffs of the Castle Rock flashed by to the left, then a blur of shop-fronts. They slowed a fraction for the turn into the top of the Royal Mile and skidded momentarily on its wet cobblestones. Regaining control, Sinclair seemed to hesitate. Down the narrow canyon of jumbled tenements another blue light was flashing.

He jabbed into reverse, shot back fifteen yards or so, swung round and then slithered at great speed up the narrow street towards the Castle, stopping short of it and turning right down a steep winding alley that led back to the Mound and Princes Street. Across the Firth lights twinkled in Fife. Below them lay the New Town, with most of Princes Street easily visible. Another two blue flashing light swept along it from the west.

As they neared the Mound the white Rover that had been first in the chase appeared again behind them, its siren blaring a kind of view halloo. The two blue flashing lights on Princes Street turned uphill, their sirens joining in. Sinclair responded by speeding up and heading across the Mound even though their way was all but barred by a double decker bus beginning to draw away from a stop. They darted in front of it, missing it by a foot or so on Campbell's side. As they roared on past the Black Watch statue and down towards the station there was a mighty and reverberating metallic crash behind. The Rover, it seemed, had done less well.

Sinclair reacted to nothing but the road ahead, sweeping between derelict warehouses and the blank southern side of the station. At the end of the long straight loomed a T-junction and a blank grey wall. Sinclair sat calmly, his face impassive, as the car sped towards it. Was this his last resort in avoiding arrest, a kind of death ride with sirens and blue lights? Campbell braced himself and vomited.

A long swirling skid ended with the Porsche still upright and not in contact with anything but the road. Sirens howled and blue lights flashed behind, and slowly the car began to pick up speed again, heading downhill to where the road disappeared under the cavernous railway bridge at the end of the station. Beyond, through its darkness, there were several more blue flashing lights.

'Interesting,' said Hadden. 'All that should come to around fifteen years, with the usual stuff about a tragic aberration bringing a brilliant career to an end, and of course a good deal of sharply indrawn breath at the disciplinary committee of the General Medical Council. Not that it greatly affects your lifestyle if you're sewing mailbags in Peterhead. Are you thinking of applying for the chair, young Campbell? You really do need a steady job.'

Campbell thought of the nurse in the outpatients whose sacking Sinclair had insisted on after she had been found guilty of shoplifting, and of Sinclair's house in the Grange and his gentle, sensible psychiatrist wife. At the end of the chase there had been a scuffle in which Sinclair had punched a sergeant, breaking his nose. Three constables had seized him and thrown him to the ground, with a couple more hauling Campbell up against the wall just in case of further trouble. Sinclair was still in custody, facing an impressive list of charges including causing death by reckless driving. 'He really is finished.'

'Mais certainment,' said Hadden. He crouched forward and twirled the end of an imaginary moustache, transforming himself quite passably from a large Scottish orthopod to a small French detective. 'Ze brilliant master-criminal, 'e make one tiny mistake ... Zees Napoleon of medical crime, 'e defy detection until he make just the one simple error ... And start to kill zee old ladies *outside* ze 'ospital.'

Campbell laughed and Hadden sat up suddenly, shaking the table and spilling some of his pint. 'I tell you what's wrong with him ...'

'He's a hypomanic psychopath.'

'Fine. He's a professor. But as well ... something else. Neurological ... Progressive ... Fatal.' Hadden punched the air. 'Obvious when you think about it. Come on, Campbell, the fourth-year students know all this stuff: man in late forties, gradual onset of disinhibition, inappropriate behaviour, mood swings and all that.'

'Neurosyphilis?'

'Rubbish. Ask me his job. He's a brain surgeon, or was. And a kind of odd one, with a prolonged occupational exposure to human and baboon neural tissue. Come on, come on ...'

Campbell reflected that if there was a missed diagnosis he was in good company, since several hundred neurologists from all over Europe had missed it too. 'Sorry.'

'Jacob-Kreutzfeldt disease. Bloody obvious when you think about it. Basically a dementing illness. Odd, patchy onset, often behavioural. And you can get it from poking around in other people's brains. A slow virus, affects primates too. He's done hundreds of brain biopsies, right?

269

He only has to have stuck a needle in his finger once, with the right patient or baboon, to give himself the whole ghastly works. Incubation period anything up to two years. So he got it before he came here. Any funny twitches, tics, anything like that?'

'He's been grinding his teeth quite a lot lately.'

'That would do . . . So not the jail . . . the loony bin, and not for all that long.'

'Poor chap.'

'Less than a year, most of them. Poor bugger.' Hadden picked up his drink. 'So the baboons got him in the end.'

Sinclair appeared the following week in the sheriff court and was remanded again then declared unfit to plead. Confirmation of Hadden's diagnosis came when Dr Temple, who had been called to examine his former colleague, summoned Campbell once more across to the MRS. Over a cup of the corporal's coffee he explained, having sworn Campbell to more than ordinary secrecy: 'We have done our friend a great wrong, you and I. He was a sick man and we should have been aware of it long before he . . . reached the position he now finds himself in. I deeply regret that . . . Well, you know how we concluded our last discussion . . . but as his consultant colleague I myself am especially guilty. And the poor man, as I'm sure you're aware, has a short and terrible prognosis . . .'

Sinclair was transferred from custody to a locked psychiatric ward. The fast, accurate bush telegraph which keeps Edinburgh medicine fully informed of every detail of the mental and physical health of its senior members soon made discretion on Campbell's part unnecessary. Even before Sinclair died a few months later the case was widely known, almost mythic: that of a brilliant figure laid low by one of the more unusual hazards of the profession.